PRAISE FOR

A First Date with Death

"Loved it! Daring, funny, and unforgettable, Georgia is a protagonist you'll identify with. Dreamy men, romance, and a plot that twists to the end. I was drawn in by the memorable characters and a glimpse into the crazy world of 'reality' television."
—Nancy J. Parra, author of the Perfect Proposals Mysteries and the Baker's Treat Mysteries

"A great vicarious adventure . . . Diana has a hit with this new series! I highly recommend this novel [to readers who] enjoy well-written cozy mysteries with more than a little bit of romance, strong female characters, humor, and a challenge."
—Open Book Society

PRAISE FOR
DIANA ORGAIN'S OTHER NOVELS

"Fast-paced and fun."
—Rhys Bowen, *New York Times* bestselling author

"Stellar . . . A winning protagonist and a glorious San Francisco setting . . . Highly recommended."
—Sheldon Siegel, *New York Times* bestselling author

"A fantastically fun read . . . Not only offers humor and suspense, but also makes sure to not solve the puzzle until the last pages."
—*Suspense Magazine*

"An over-the-top good-time cozy mystery. With a feisty heroine and with lots of humor, plenty of intrigue and suspense . . . this novel is a delightful treat to read."
—*Fresh Fiction*

A Second Chance at Murder

DIANA ORGAIN

BERKLEY PRIME CRIME, NEW YORK

BERKLEY PRIME CRIME

An imprint of Penguin Random House LLC
375 Hudson Street, New York, New York 10014

A SECOND CHANCE AT MURDER

A Berkley Prime Crime Book / published by arrangement with the author

ISBN: 978-0-425-27169-8

PUBLISHING HISTORY
Berkley Prime Crime mass-market paperback edition / January 2016

PRINTED IN THE UNITED STATES OF AMERICA

10 9 8 7 6 5 4 3 2 1

Cover illustration by Bill Bruning.
Cover design by Danielle Abbiate.
Interior text design by Laura K. Corless.

Penguin
Random
House

Un beso y un abrazo fuerte para mi mamá,
que siempre me apoya en todo.
Te quiero.

¡Viva España!

Acknowledgments

....

Thank you to my wonderful editor, Michelle Vega, and the entire crew over at Berkley Prime Crime for your never-ending support. Thanks to my agent, Jill Marsal, simply the best in the business.

Special thanks to my dear friend, KJ. I always know I can count on you no matter what. Your love and support have always been an inspiration to me.

Thanks to Marina Adair, who endlessly listens to all my plot twists, both real and imagined. You always make *everything* better!

Thanks to all my early readers, especially Mariella Krause and Chrystal Carver, for keeping me and the story on track.

Shout out and hugs to my Carmen, Tommy, Bobby, and Tom Sr. You all make life worth living.

Finally, thanks to all you dear readers who have written to me. Your kind words keep me motivated to write the next adventure.

One

········

The cold snap in the Spanish Pyrenees was a surprise. My sleeping bag had only been rated for forty degrees and it was already thirty, if not lower.

I shifted in the bag, hoping to share a little body heat with my boyfriend. The space beside me was empty, so I stretched my arms and reached across the length of his sleeping bag, thinking maybe he'd shimmied over to the side of the tent in his sleep.

"Scott?" I murmured.

When no answer came, I pried an eye open and scanned the dark tent. "Scott?" I said, bolting upright. My head rubbed against the microfiber of the tent, making my hair stand on end.

Where was he?

Perhaps nature called.

I sighed, shivering as the low temperature caught up

with my brain. My back ached, too, and I realized I must have been sleeping directly on a rock. What in the world was I doing tent-camping? How had I gotten myself into this mess?

Oh, yeah. Becca.

After our stint on the breakout show *Love or Money*, where Scott and I had met, we'd agreed to appear on the reality TV show *Expedition Improbable*. The show was a series of races and competitions. Whichever team came in last in each leg would either be penalized or eliminated.

There were five teams of two people. Scott and I were up against an NFL player and his manager, two girls trying to break into the Nashville scene, a mother-son team, and a brother-sister team.

How or why I had agreed to be on the show was still a bit fuzzy—except that the prize money we'd won on *Love or Money* had seemed to evaporate into thin air.

First off, there was the issue of taxes, and then the matter of the medical bills Scott still owed for his deceased wife's care. Finally, the drought in California had made the cost of water astronomical, so much so that my dad had nearly lost his farm. Scott and I had agreed that we'd loan him the money he needed to buy water from the state. That pretty much accounted for the prize money. And being that my recent resume lacked any marketable skills, I was hard-pressed to land a job. Not that I'd ever find a job as a cop again after starring on reality TV.

I guess you could say, *When reality TV comes to an end, reality kicks in!*

Grabbing my phone from the end of my sleeping bag,

I clicked on the flashlight app. I unzipped the tent and poked my head out. The frigid air snapped through my hair, leaving me feeling cold and exposed. My vision adjusted to the darkness and I could make out the other tents scattered across the campsite.

The ten contestants were all camped out here along with a skeleton crew who looked out for us. This was our first camp. Tomorrow we would be given the first quest to locate something—like a scavenger hunt—and we were warned it would include an extreme sport. God knows what the producers would cook up for us.

The rest of the crew was staying at what was considered "base camp," a bed-and-breakfast in a nearby town. In short, they got to sleep in warm beds, drink *sangría*, and gorge on tapas, while we poor slobs froze. My best friend, Becca, the show's producer, was probably out flamenco dancing at this very moment.

I shrugged on the down jacket the crew had provided me with earlier and zipped it up, shoved my feet into cold-weather boots, and put on a knit cap. All bundled up, I'm sure I wasn't the epitome of sexy, but hey, at least I wasn't shivering out a samba beat with my teeth.

I left the tent and took the dirt trail toward the outhouse. Scott had probably just taken a quick trip and hadn't wanted to wake me. I watched my breath float out around me as I hiked toward the outhouse.

"Georgia!" A deep voice called out.

I whipped around and came face-to-face with Parker, one of the contestants who'd come on the show with his sister, Victoria.

I lowered the flashlight, so as not to blind him. "Hey, Parker. You can't sleep, either?"

He shook his head. We wore matching gear: down jacket, black boots, and knit caps. We probably looked like stalkers. "Something woke me. Did you hear it?"

"Hear what?" I asked.

I hadn't actually heard anything—but why had I awoken in the first place?

"Something like a roar. Do you have bear spray on you? We probably shouldn't be walking around unarmed."

A chill edged up my spine and the hairs on the back of my neck tingled.

I *was* unarmed, save for the pitiful cell phone I wielded in my hand. We all were unarmed and, come to think of it, it made no sense. Who camped in the mountains completely vulnerable to nature?

Goodness, I hate the reality TV show business.

Parker stepped closer to me. "Do you have a weapon?"

I shook my head before questioning the stupidity of admitting I was unarmed to a relative stranger in the dark woods miles away from civilization. "Do you?"

His eyes flickered to the left, shifty-like. "No."

I remembered earlier in the day Parker had seemed overly interested in Scott and me and I'd found it odd. My former cop instincts took over and I subtly moved away from him.

Where was Scott?

Why was Parker walking around the campground? If there had really been a roar why wasn't everyone else clamoring around to see what it was?

4

Parker took a step toward me, but I was faster. I swept his knee with my booted foot, pitching him forward. He tripped over himself and fell to the ground, letting out a wail before dropping his light in an effort to break his fall. I dove on top of him, my knee pressing on his throat. I shined my flashlight at him. His eyes were wide and there was a look of dumb confusion on his face.

Damn.

Had I just made a mistake?

No. Something was off about Parker and after my last experience with murder on the show, I needed to stay on my toes.

His hands faltered against my leg, the stupid fish look still on his face.

I suddenly felt bad. I eased up on his throat, enough to let him speak.

"Georgia," he squawked out. "What are you doing?"

"What the hell are you doing?" I hissed. "Wandering around camp in the pitch dark and asking me if I'm armed."

He swallowed, his throat constricting under my knee. "I heard the roar—"

"Liar! There was no roar."

Anger flashed across his face and he found his strength, pitching his hands against my shoulders and toppling me to the side. He slipped out from under my grasp and pinned my arms to the ground. My phone dropped, skittering away; blackness engulfed us.

The cold earth clawed at my back; the freezing ground stealing warmth from my body. That would show me. How many times did I have to learn the same lesson over again? I had to be smarter. Tougher, not lenient just because he looked pitiful. His grip on my wrist let up a bit and he said, "I couldn't sleep, okay? I woke up and wanted to take a walk."

I wiggled out from under him and he let me go.

He backed off and I got up from the ground. When he let his guard down, I shoved him hard. "Don't you ever tackle me again, you creep. Understand?"

He nodded slowly and then he sagged like a deflated balloon. "My sister's not in our tent," he confessed. "I came out to find her. She's got a bad habit of going off on her own and I want to win this stupid contest. If I don't get control of her, I can kiss this thing good-bye."

A nervous energy wiggled through my stomach.

His sister was missing and so was Scott.

Okay, maybe missing was an overstatement. But he sure as hell wasn't where he was supposed to be and according to Parker, his sister, Victoria, wasn't, either.

I picked up my phone. "Where do you think she skulked off to?"

He shrugged. "I was going to check the outhouse. She's probably not there though, because she would have come back by now, right?"

I remained silent. Silence was usually the best way to get information out of people. At least that's what they'd taught us at the police academy.

"Anyway," Parker continued. "I figured I'd walk down the trail to the restrooms, then check the path that goes to the mountain stream. It'd be just the kind of thing she'd do alone."

My stomach churned as I considered that perhaps she wasn't alone. A midnight stroll to the mountain stream would be right up Scott's alley, too. I flashed my light against the dark soil, illuminating a small circle. "Let's get a lantern," I said. "If we're going down to the river, we'll need more light than this."

Parker disappeared back into his tent. I returned to my own tent, tossed my cell phone onto my sleeping bag and grabbed my lantern. When I left my tent, Parker was already at the picnic table, igniting his gas lantern. He stretched out his arm and blue light shined across the path.

Before we left camp, I grabbed a slim log near the fire pit. Parker gave me a strange look, then picked up his own log. "If we come across a bear, we'll be prepared, eh?" he asked.

I didn't answer him and we set off in silence. It was so dark I could make out the stars. I hadn't seen the Little Dipper since I'd been home at Cottonwood. One of the things I hated about living in a city was not being able to appreciate the stars. It had to be country dark in order to see the constellations.

The dirt trail crunched under my boots as we walked. I cursed myself again for letting Becca talk me into the show. What exactly was I doing walking in the pitch dark next to a stranger I didn't trust, freezing my derriere off, and carrying a stick?

Looking for my boyfriend, that's what.

Scott.

My heart did a little flip-flop as I thought of him. He'd been excited about the trip, looking forward to seeing places he hadn't traveled to yet. Spain was only the beginning of our journey. The final locations hadn't been disclosed to us, but we knew we could expect at least five destinations.

Parker and I reached the outhouses, which were as we'd expected: dark and empty.

Earlier in the day we'd all arrived at camp by bus. It'd been hot in the afternoon and we'd gotten filthy pitching our tents. The crew had suggested a short hike to the river and even though everyone was exhausted from the day of travel, we'd enjoyed the time by the water.

Parker turned toward the stream. "Everyone thinks you and Scott are particularly tough competition."

He was making small talk to ease his nerves. I knew the feeling.

"Why's that?" I asked.

"Because you won the other show."

"The other show had been a glorified version of *The Dating Game*. If that's even the right way to describe it. I mean, we didn't have to do anything. No zip lines or rafting or whatever extreme things they have in store for us here."

"You guys rock climbed," he said.

I didn't want to tell him the rock climbing had been staged. After we'd had a disaster with the bungee jumping, the producers didn't want to risk the liability. Anyway, what good would it do to argue my limitations? That would be silly.

We walked down the steep path in the dark, the lantern barely casting light a few inches ahead of us.

"I think we should be noisy," I said. "That way any

critters drinking by the stream will know they have company and skedaddle."

Parker called out loudly, "Victoria? Vicky? Are you here?" He glanced nervously at me. "No offense, but if we find the two of them in a compromising position, you won't hold it against me, will you?"

Fear jolted through me.

What an idiot I was!

Until that moment, the thought of Scott getting to know Parker's sister in the biblical sense hadn't occurred to me. Could it be that my brand-new boyfriend, the one I'd fallen for so hard at the end of the last show, was cheating on me? I felt sick to my stomach.

"Don't say that. Why would you say that?" I asked.

"Well, don't get me wrong, I love my sister, but she plays fast and loose with social mores. Like she wouldn't think twice about getting together with someone else's boyfriend. She'll just excuse the behavior by saying she's breaking down the competition."

A howl pierced the night, stopping Parker and me in our tracks. It'd come from the direction we were headed. I tightened my grip on the log I carried.

"Was that animal or human?" Parker whispered.

"I don't know for sure," I said. "I think animal."

"Maybe we should go back and get some of the others," he said.

He was probably thinking of Cooper, ex-NFL, the guy was bigger than a jeep, with muscles on his muscles.

Another howl skirted across the night. This one definitely human.

We took off running, down the embankment. Suddenly the earth fell away from us and we flew through the air.

Oh, my God!

What the devil was going on?

Parker screamed out. My arms helicoptered through space, my life flashing before me.

Dear God! We'd just run ourselves off a cliff.

Could it really end like this?

The wind buffeted my face as I sped through air. The horror of my impending fall sent my nervous system into overdrive. My fists tightened, my jaw clenched and my heart ached for Scott. I wanted to see his face again.

Did he know how much I loved him?

The ground seemed to rush up to meet me, and abruptly my feet crashed into the earth. I landed with a jolt, dropping my lantern and the log. My boots locked onto the ground, pitching my body forward so that my hands dug into the sandy beach of the riverbank.

Air rushed into my lungs as Parker hurtled down next to me. He landed awkwardly twisted on his side, his lantern and log smashing together near a rock.

"What the . . . Owww!" Parker shrieked

"You okay?" I asked.

"My back. Awww. My ribs, too. What happened?"

We were in a clearing by the river, the light of the waning moon barely enough to make out the cliff we'd taken a tumble off of. It was only about six feet high, but in the pitch dark the fall had felt eternal. I was lucky to have landed on my feet.

There was a rustling sound approaching us. Someone

running toward us. I grabbed the lantern and called out. "Scott?"

"Parker?" A woman yelled. "Is that you?"

"Victoria!" Parker said, moving himself into a sitting position.

She rushed forward. "What happened? What are you doing out here?" She gave me a strange look.

"Looking for you," he said. "What are you doing out here?"

She was bundled up like both of us, holding a small LED flashlight. "It was so cold I couldn't sleep."

"Is Scott with you?" I asked.

A blank look crossed her face. "Who's that?"

"My boyfriend," I said, impatience building inside me.

"I figured that. I meant, what does he look like? Which one was he?" She pressed a hand to her temple. "We met so many people today."

"He's tall. Shaved head." *Sexy as hell and you better keep your hands off him.*

She smiled. "Oh, yeah. That guy. He's hot." She shined her flashlight on me, giving me a cursory evaluating glance from my head to my toes, then back again.

I'm sure I looked great sausaged in the parka I had on.

"I was hoping maybe he was your cousin or something," she said.

"Have you seen him? He's not at camp, either."

She shrugged. "The only guy I've seen is the NFL guy."

Parker struggled to his feet. "Ah, my ribs. I think I busted something."

Victoria pushed hard on Parker's shoulder. "Oh, no you don't. I know you didn't want to come here in the first place but you're not getting out of it!"

Parker grabbed his side. "Stop pushing me!"

I stepped between them. "Victoria. We heard something howling . . ."

"Howling?" Victoria looked alarmed. "I haven't seen any wildlife. Maybe we should get back to camp." She pointed upstream. "The path actually bottoms out over there. We don't have to scale this cliff."

We walked upstream, my eyes scanning the river.

"The river's so high," I noted.

"It's been a high-water year," Parker said. "I remember them telling us that on the bus ride."

They had? I didn't remember anything about the bus ride except that Scott hadn't let go of my hand. I'd been content to hold his hand and rest my head on his shoulder feeling happy and full like a cat that'd eaten a canary. Practically bursting with joy.

Now, that feeling seemed like a distant memory.

"The river's moving fast, too," Victoria said. "Someone could get swept in it, huh? Scary!"

My throat constricted.

Oh, Scott. Where are you?

Two

....

E ven though I'd wanted to search for Scott, Parker and Victoria convinced me to go back to camp. After all, it was likely Scott could have returned in the time we'd been away. When we arrived at camp, the silence was ominous.

Parker unceremoniously announced, "My ribs are killing me. I'm going to lie down."

I turned to Victoria, shining the lantern in her face. "You said you saw the NFL guy. Did you mean Cooper or his partner, Todd?"

Victoria snorted. "Todd's not NFL. He's more like a sumo wrestler, if you know what I mean."

It was true that Todd hadn't played football for the NFL, but he was still associated with it somehow, as Cooper's manager or something. I realized with a shudder how little I knew about the people I was stuck here with.

Victoria shrugged. "Anyway, I meant Cooper. He was hanging around the campsite when I got up. We chatted for a few minutes, but when I asked him if he wanted to walk to the river with me, he said no and went back to his tent." She motioned toward one of the two-man tents across the meadow.

My mind was whirling. Should I wake Cooper and ask him if he'd seen Scott? Should I call Becca or the authorities and start a search and rescue? In the States, anyone could call for search and rescue as soon as someone in his or her party was overdue. Was it the same in Spain?

Was Scott overdue, or was he just taking a midnight stroll?

Scott was a writer and I knew he liked to take long walks, but I hadn't known him to do so in the middle of the night.

Indecision bit at me, but I found myself marching over toward Cooper's tent all the same.

Victoria called after me, "What are you doing?"

I ignored her and stood outside of Cooper and his partner Todd's tent. "Cooper," I called out in a loud whisper.

I was rewarded by some rustling and rummaging sounds coming from inside the tent, then someone murmured, "Who's there?"

"It's Georgia."

A head emerged from the opening of the tent and the man shielded his eyes from my lantern. It was Todd. "What's going on Georgia?" He half smiled. "Is it reveille?"

"No. It's the middle of the night. I'm looking for Scott. He's not at camp."

Todd frowned up at me and scratched at what little hair remained on his head. "Well, he's not in here!" He sounded offended.

"I understand. Sorry for waking you, but Victoria said that Cooper was up a while ago. I'm wondering if he knows where Scott is."

Todd chewed his lip. "Oh. You want to talk to Coop?"

"Please."

Todd ducked back into the tent, mumbling. "It's always about Cooper."

I heard a thump as if Todd had socked Cooper's arm. Then some hushed exchange between the two of them. "Darling, I don't know where your beau has gone off to," a deep groggy voice called out.

A light flashed from inside a neighboring tent. I couldn't recall whose tent it was, either the girls from Nashville or the two crew members assigned to baby-sit us.

"Cooper, did you see Scott leave camp? Do you know which way he went?"

"Nah. I didn't see nothing, baby," Cooper said. "Go back to sleep. He's probably just off on a nature call."

"Or on a booty call," Todd snickered.

Anger surged through my body, heating my veins. I clenched my teeth and stalked back toward the picnic table. Victoria, I noticed, had retired back to her tent.

I added some logs to the smoldering embers that remained of the campfire and paced. I desperately wanted to search for Scott myself, but that wouldn't be prudent in the dark. I could easily fall and injure myself worse than

Parker had and not be able to make it back to camp and then the team would have to find two missing persons.

No, better to wait until daylight.

I fingered our lantern and then the thought occurred to me that Scott likely had his phone with him. While we were prohibited from using devices during the competitions, we were allowed to have personal items with us. Not like on the previous show, *Love or Money.* And since the lantern was here with me, he'd probably used the flashlight app on his phone.

I dashed to our tent and picked up my cell phone. Unfortunately, the cell phone coverage in the mountains was nonexistent, and I realized with a sinking heart that I wouldn't be able to call Scott, much less Becca to organize a search-and-rescue team.

I glanced at the dim digital display on the phone.

Four a.m.

The deadliest time of night.

The emerging sunlight woke me, the empty sleeping bag next to me jolting me back to reality. Alarm and dread mingled in my stomach as I realized Scott had not returned in the middle of the night.

Where could he be? It was still cold out, but not freezing. I zipped up my down jacket anyway and exited the tent. I tossed some firewood onto the smoldering embers of the fire I'd made the night before.

My shoulders were tight and my neck sore, and what little sleep I'd gotten had been spent tossing and turning.

There was some rustling behind me and I turned to find Juan Jose, one of the crew members, walking toward me.

"Good morning," he said, striking me as overly cheerful. Perhaps it was my sour mood. Juan Jose was a local, hired to help with the show. He was in charge of logistics. He was supposed to know the terrain like the back of his hand.

"Juan Jose, I need your help. My boyfriend, Scott, isn't at camp."

A look of surprise crossed Juan Jose's face. "What do you mean? Not at camp? Where is he?"

"I don't know. He's missing," I said, anxiety fluttering in my chest. "I woke up in the middle of the night and he wasn't in our tent. I went looking for him with Parker."

"Parker?"

"Yeah, the tall guy. The one here with his sister. He was looking for her, too, but she was down by the river—"

The look of surprise on his face changed to alarm and he whispered almost to himself, "The river?"

"Yeah. She said she was alone and hadn't seen anybody. Well, except for Cooper, but I already talked to him. He doesn't know where Scott is."

Juan Jose stroked his dark stubble, a concerned expression clouding his features. "Mmm." After a moment, he said, "The river is very high this year. Very dangerous."

"Right." Unease strangled the breath out of me as a vision of Scott's dead body floating down the river crossed my mind. "We need to organize a search party! Can you help me with that?"

Juan Jose nodded, looking slightly dumbfounded.

"He cannot have gone far. The terrain is very steep." He shrugged and stifled a yawn. "Maybe he is hurt."

"What's the situation with wildlife around here?" I asked. "We heard howling. Are there bobcats? Bears?"

Juan Jose shook his head. "Not many bears. We tried to reintroduce the brown bear to the mountains, but the program hasn't been very successful. There are a lot of wild boars, though."

The mother-and-son team emerged from their tents. The son, whose name I'd already forgotten, approached me. "What's going on?" he asked.

"My partner's missing. Scott. Do you remember him? Tall—"

"We remember him, Georgia." His mother stepped forward. She was in her late fifties, the skin on her face still smooth. "He's a doll. Where did he go off to?"

"That's what I'm trying to figure out. I don't know."

The two glanced at each other and then back at me and Juan Jose.

The son said, "Maybe he went looking for firewood or something."

"It is really cold, isn't it?" the mother asked. She crossed her arms and stepped closer to the fire. "Practically freezing!"

I glanced at the firewood piled neatly by one of the pine trees that lined the perimeter of our camp. "Well, being that we're not short on firewood, I doubt it."

"Is anyone else missing?" the mother asked.

There was a sound of boots crunching on gravel from

behind us and a deep voice called out, "Todd and I are here," Cooper said.

"Maybe he got scared of the competition." Todd said, as they joined us by the fire.

Cooper laughed and flexed his massive bicep while chuckling, "He should be!"

The action seemed so stupid and superficial it immediately irritated me.

What was wrong with these people? Couldn't they see the difference between a real emergency and some stupid TV stunt?

Todd frowned at me and suddenly became serious. "Don't worry, I'm sure he'll pop up any moment."

Juan Jose glanced at his watch. "The rest of the crew will be here in an hour."

"I'm not going to wait for another hour to pass! I'm going to look for him now."

Cooper reached out a large hand and rested it on my shoulder. "Calm down, darling. We'll go with you. We can all look for him."

"I'll wake the others," Todd said, transitioning into action mode. He strode across the meadow toward the tents.

Soon the girls from Nashville emerged; both had taken the time to do their makeup. Really? It was thirty degrees in the Pyrenees mountains, we were without showers, and the camera crew still hadn't arrived. I didn't get it.

Parker and Victoria joined us at the picnic table along with the other crew member who had overnight duty with us, Miguel. Juan Jose explained the situation to Miguel in Spanish while Cooper brought the others up to speed. Miguel fetched a trail map from his tent and laid it on the table.

We divided up the nearby trails, agreeing to work in three teams. I was to go with the local crew members, hoping they had the expert knowledge of the trails that would help us find Scott first. Cooper and Todd were to set off with the gorgeous girls from Nashville, DeeCee and Daisy, who called themselves Double D, making me question exactly how much terrain that search party would cover. Then the mother-and-son team agreed to search with Victoria. While Parker, with his ribs still sore from last night's fall, was to stay at camp in case Scott returned.

As Miguel, Juan Jose, and I headed down the main trail, I saw a familiar figure approach. I sprinted down the path nearly trampling my best friend.

Becca hugged me, her auburn curls brushing against my check. I sobbed into her shoulder.

"Georgia! What's wrong?" Becca demanded, pulling away from me so she could see my face. "What's going on?"

"Scott's missing," I cried.

A small group of people led by Kyle, one of the makeup artists I knew from the previous show, turned the corner of the trail and approached.

"What do you mean missing?" Becca asked, her delicate features crinkling.

"He's gone. I woke up in the middle of the night and he wasn't in our tent. I went looking for him with Parker."

She pinched the bridge of her nose, a look of distress

on her face as she glanced at Juan Jose and Miguel, who both looked stoic. "This is going to get complicated, isn't it?"

I choked back my tears as the other crew members approached us. "I don't know. I just know I need to go and look for him."

"We organized a small search party," Juan Jose said. "Some have gone to look for him down by the river and others took the trail north."

"What's going on?" Kyle demanded.

Becca ignored him and pulled out the walkie-talkie that was permanently affixed to her hip. "The rest of the crew is behind me. I'm going to radio down and see if anyone still has some cell reception. We've got to call the authorities."

"Authorities? Oh! Sounds exciting," Kyle said.

"Shut up," Becca admonished him, as she wrapped her arms around me. "Don't worry, G, we'll find him. I'm sure he's fine. Maybe he got lost or disoriented or something, but we'll find him."

I felt myself nod in agreement, but the thought that penetrated my consciousness was, *I just hope we're not too late.*

Three
....

After searching the woods into the afternoon and coming up empty-handed, Juan Jose, Miguel, and I headed back to base camp to check in with Becca and the others. I prayed that Scott had made it back to camp during our absence. After all, if he'd gotten lost last night, the sensible thing to do would have been to wait for daylight to find his way.

Becca was pacing by the picnic table, the other cast and crew members gathered nearby; everyone looked downtrodden. I immediately knew by the look on Becca's face that Scott hadn't returned.

When Becca saw me she looked at me hopefully, but surmised quickly that we hadn't had any luck, either. Becca's walkie-talkie chirped and she said into it, "What?" She held it away from her ear, glanced at it, then said, "Reception up here is choppy."

I sagged onto the picnic table bench. Victoria and Parker, who were standing close by, distanced themselves. Suddenly the others, who'd been roaming by the campfire, disappeared into their tents, as if my bad luck was catching.

Becca patted my shoulder. "Don't worry honey, we'll find him. I know we'll find him." Then into the walkie-talkie she said, "Our GPS coordinates are forty-two north, uh . . . Oh . . . Yeah . . . The camp that's over . . . okay, okay sure," she said, hanging up. "They're here."

I sprang to my feet and we both looked down the trail. A tall woman with honey-blond hair slicked back into a ponytail came into view. She wore black pants and a windbreaker with an official logo on it. She seemed capable and sure of herself. On a leash was a Great Pyrenees dog. Behind her was a group of people, each with dogs. There was also a man, who walked a bit apart from them. He had dark hair and wore a matching windbreaker.

The woman stuck out her hand and I shook it. She had callused palms, giving me the impression that she'd done search and rescue a thousand times over. I hoped they'd been successful. She introduced herself as Montserrat. The man who stood apart from her shook my hand as well, introducing himself as Sergio. In contrast to Montserrat, his hand was smooth and warm.

A desk cop.

We went through the necessary intake procedures for a missing person, complete with description, last time seen, and various search-and-rescue protocol.

"Do you have something of his for the dog to smell?" Montserrat asked me.

Becca squeezed my elbow. "It'll be okay, honey."

I retreated to my tent and pulled out Scott's sweatshirt, pressing my nose against the soft cotton. It smelled like him, a bit of cedar mixed with musk. I choked back a sob and quickly exited the tent. The dog seized Scott's sweatshirt and sniffed it, growling and howling in between his sniffs. Montserrat nodded and patted him. Then she took the sweatshirt around and let the pack of dogs smell it.

Montserrat tapped her walkie-talkie and waved to Sergio saying, "*Nos vemos*." The pack of dogs tore off in the direction of the river, the same path Parker and I had hiked the night before.

I started to follow Montserrat, but Sergio stopped me. "Wait! Please, I have some questions for you."

I hesitated. "But they're going to try to track my friend down."

Becca gave me a queer look, and I realized I had omitted the word *boy* in front of *friend*. What was wrong with me? Just because the cop looked like Antonio Banderas's younger brother didn't mean I could throw my boyfriend under a bus.

"Sit," Sergio said. Becca and I went to comply.

"You are free to go," he said to Becca, "if you like." She gave me another look, unsure what to do. "Or if you want to wait nearby, perhaps it is better. I'll have some questions for you, in a moment." He nodded toward the tents, implying that he wanted to speak with me alone.

"All right, I'm happy to help any way I can," Becca

said, pinching my arm. "Everything is going to be fine, Georgia. They'll find him, you'll see. He's smart. Maybe he fell and twisted an ankle and is staying put, that's all." Becca went to wait in my tent.

None of what she'd said made me feel any better. If he'd twisted an ankle, wouldn't we have found him last night or this morning? Sergio indicated the bench at the campsite table. I sat, a splinter sticking into my leg. I made no effort to remove it. The pinching and biting sensation would keep me on my toes. Let's see what Mr. Banderas the Younger had to say. He took a notebook out of his pocket.

"So the man who is missing, can you tell me more about him?"

"What do you want to know?" I asked.

He referred to his notebook. "We have a physical description: six feet, one hundred eighty pounds, shaved head, dark eyes." He glanced up from the notebook. "Correct?"

I realized that if Scott were standing next to me, he would have said, "And I'm funny, warm, and smart! Tell him that!" The thought made my heart ache and all I could do was manage a nod.

"Okay," Sergio said. "What is your relationship to him?"

"He's my boyfriend," I said.

Sergio's dark eyes held mine for a moment, something flashing through them that I couldn't read. His lips pressed together and he jotted a note.

"Were you having any problems?"

"No. We didn't fight the night he disappeared, if that's what you want to know."

Sergio gave me a strange look, but didn't say anything. He seemed unconvinced.

"He didn't run away from me," I said. "Do I look that much like an ogre, that I'd chase a man away in the middle of the night? In a foreign country, no less?"

Sergio waited, watching me as I spoke. I was getting carried away. I knew it. I shouldn't let it get to me. He was just doing his job. I stopped myself suddenly. Sergio was quiet.

"What?" I asked.

"What's an ogre?" he asked, his Spanish accent making it almost sound cute. "I do not know that word."

"A monster," I said.

He nodded his understanding, then very seriously said, "You do not look like a monster."

I sighed, tension releasing from my body. "I don't want you to start thinking I have anything to do with his disappearance," I said. "That only wastes our time and energy. Look, I used to be a cop in the United States. I understand that our best chances of recovering someone who's missing are in the first hours—"

Instead of reassuring me, he asked, "Does he take any medication?"

"What?" I asked.

"Does he have diabetes, or—?"

"No, no, he's healthy."

"Prescription medicine?" He touched his temple.

I fought the desperation surging in my chest. "Are you asking if he's crazy?"

Sergio shrugged. "Depressed or epileptic—"

"No," I answered, my impatience mounting. "Look, we won't get a second chance at this tiny window of opportunity to—"

"Who else is here?" He made another note and glanced around the camp. "Were you the last person to see him?"

I recounted the hike with Parker, and mentioned the scream we'd heard.

He nodded gravely, then asked. "What's going on here with the cameras?"

I told him about the TV show we'd been getting ready to film.

"Reality program?" Sergio asked. "It's worse than I thought. A missing American, that is one thing, but a TV celebrity?"

"We're not celebrities," I said. "Not like that. I mean, he wasn't kidnapped by the paparazzi or anything," I said.

Sergio made me walk through the events of the previous night one more time. I knew the drill. He was listening for inconsistencies in my story.

The walkie-talkie on his shoulder holster beeped, a burst of Spanish firing across the wire. I sprang off the bench.

Sergio listened, a grim look on his face.

"What is it? Did they find him?" I asked.

Sergio frowned as he listened, giving me an almost imperceptible shake of the head.

Anxiety clawed at my chest. "What then?" I asked.

Sergio stood and walked away from the table, speaking rapidly into the walkie-talkie. My heart raced and I felt like I was about to come out of my skin. Even though I couldn't understand Sergio's words, I could tell by the tone of his voice something was desperately wrong.

I rushed to the tent and called Becca's name. She popped her head out.

"What's going on?" she asked.

"How good is your Spanish?"

She glanced toward Sergio and frowned. She shook her head after a moment. "He's talking too fast."

I buried my head in my hands, the uncertainty taking a toll.

"Damn, he's hot though, huh?" Becca asked.

"I hadn't noticed," I lied.

She snorted. "Please. I know this is a tough time for you, Georgia, but anyone with a pulse can see the guy's gorgeous."

"Go for it," I said.

Becca said, "You know I'm sworn off men, at least for the time being. Plus, what kind of a jerk would it make me?"

"What do you mean?" I asked.

"He's trying to locate Scott. I don't want to be the one to distract him." She batted her eyelashes at me.

We giggled. My shoulders relaxed ever so slightly, then I immediately felt guilty. Scott was missing, what the hell was I doing, laughing and yukking it up with Becca? Sergio turned around toward us.

"We have a situation, I need to leave you two ladies. Please call me if you have any more information."

"Wait, what? What situation?" I asked.

"I need to go check in with my team," he said.

"What's going on?" Becca asked.

He ignored our questions. He handed us a card and turned without speaking. Becca and I shared a look. We'd follow him, wherever he was going. The search-and-rescue team hadn't been gone that long, they couldn't be that far away.

Sergio hiked down the dirt trail toward the river, but took a left instead of a right where Parker and I had fallen from the cliff the night before. He walked with purpose, as if he had intimate knowledge of the trails. We kept our distance and followed him in silence. The trail descended into a small canyon, the ground becoming slick and muddy. I could hear the sound of running water up ahead. Sergio ducked through some bushes, stepping over fallen branches and avoiding protruding shrubs.

Despite last night's freezing temperatures, the day was heating up and sweat dripped off my brow as I struggled to keep my footing. In the distance, the dogs were growling and barking. Montserrat's voice greeted Sergio.

"*¡Aquí!*" she called.

Sergio moved forward, his gait steady and even. The trail gave way to a small clearing that was bordered with several rocks large enough to sit on. There was something in the ground, hidden near the bushes; something large, like a heap.

Something lifeless.

My heart lurched and I took off in a mad dash. A scream echoed through the canyon that I hardly recognized as my own.

Dear God, no, no, please don't be Scott.

I ran so hard I collided into a bush and then Sergio in my attempt to get to the body. Sergio grabbed me and said "Eh, eh, it's okay, it's okay."

His hand was on my head, pressing it to his shoulder, trying to keep me from seeing the corpse that had already been burned into my retinas.

It was a woman. Her body was partially obscured by the bushes, but I could make out dark long hair and a polka-dot skirt that seemed gruesomely out of place.

Equal parts relief and distress coursed through my body. A woman.

Not Scott.

I was both elated and disappointed with myself at the same time. How could I be happy over finding a dead body? But the single thought reverberating through my head was that Scott was still alive.

Montserrat was blocking Becca from coming any further. But one glance at my friend and I knew she'd surmised the same thing as I had: The body was not Scott. Tears were streaming down my face and I pushed away from Sergio.

"It's not him," I said.

"I know," he said. "The dogs followed his scent up the road." He jutted his chin toward the hillside, where there was a narrow gravel road.

"The scent has disappeared from there," Sergio said.

The weight of what he was suggesting hit me suddenly.

"Scott didn't harm this woman!" I protested.

Montserrat came to my side. "Please, miss, we don't know the circumstances yet. Please go back to camp."

The dogs were growling miserably at the woman's body and hastily unearthed something.

"*¿Qué es?*" Sergio demanded.

"*Un reloj*," Montserrat said. Next to the woman was a watch.

Seeing it, my mouth went dry and my stomach dropped.

It was undeniably Scott's sports watch. Becca flashed me a look.

"Is that your boyfriend's watch?" Sergio asked.

I shrugged. "I don't know. Lots of people have watches like that."

"Yeah," Becca said, "they sell them everywhere in the U.S."

Montserrat and Sergio said something to each other, again in rapid-fire Spanish, their exchange ending with Montserrat turning to us and saying in short, clipped English, "Ladies, let me take you back to camp. Please."

Sergio was on his walkie-talkie to another team, presumably the crime scene team. Would they run a DNA scan on Scott's watch? Did they even do that in Spain? Or was the fact that a dog growled at a watch enough to try and convict him? God help us.

Montserrat walked Becca and me back to camp. When we got there, the cast and crew were huddled around the picnic table gossiping. They grew quiet as they watched us approach, the silence deafening.

"I'll need your passports," Montserrat said.

"Our passports? For what?" Becca asked.

"You and your friends"—she indicated the cast and crew—"will not be allowed to leave Spain until we clear up the matter of the woman."

"Oh, my goodness," Becca said, pressing a hand to her forehead. I knew what she must have been thinking, about the production schedules and the cost. Strange that it was the furthest thing from my mind.

I ran into my tent. They could have my passport because there was no way I was leaving Spain without Scott. I rummaged through my bag, immediately finding it. I dug through his gear. First through his duffel, then his sleeping bag, then finally through mine again.

Oh, God.

Where was Scott's passport? Why wasn't it in our tent? Did he have it with him? Who went for a midnight stroll in the woods and took his passport? For what? Just in case . . . of what? I battled the sinking pit in my stomach. Emerging from the tent, I handed my passport over to Montserrat. She took it from me, still engaged in conversation with Becca.

I grabbed Montserrat's arm. "Please, please keep looking for him."

"We will keep looking for him, yes," she said.

The unspoken implication hung between us; of course, they would keep looking for him.

He was now a suspect in a murder investigation.

Four
···················

Anger, fear, and despair ripped through me. Scott was missing and the police now suspected him of murder. I sat dumbly on the picnic table bench, numb to the goings-on around me. I was vaguely aware of Becca negotiating something with Montserrat, but my brain was dulled and I couldn't follow the conversation.

Please, God, let Scott be all right.

Parker approached me. A hand protectively gripping his ribs as he lowered himself onto the bench next to me. "Any word on your boyfriend?"

My mouth went dry. I looked from Parker over to the cast and crew huddled nearby. "The police haven't found him yet . . ."

I could feel the weight of everyone's eyes on me, a combination of pity, worry, and something else. I glanced at Victoria, who seemed to be hiding a smirk. She had a certain smugness about her that disturbed me. Was she glad that Scott hadn't returned?

"But they found something, right?" DeeCee asked. She gestured toward Montserrat.

Was it on me to tell the cast and crew about the woman?

As if in answer to my question, Sergio appeared on the trail hustling toward Montserrat. There was a quick exchange between them and then Becca nodded and turned toward Juan Jose.

"Can you please make arrangements for the cast to stay at the Jaca B&B, the one that the rest of the crew is in?"

Juan Jose frowned. "We're leaving camp? Why? What's happened?"

Becca bit her lip and turned to Sergio. He gave a firm shake of his head. He didn't want the news of the dead woman coming from us.

Fine.

Good.

It wasn't my business to tell anyway, right?

After all, the fact that Scott was missing could be totally unrelated to the fact that a dead woman was found.

The logical part of my mind served up the small detail that his wristwatch had been found at the scene of the crime and a sick feeling churned in my stomach.

There could be a lot of reasons for his watch to be there, I reasoned. First, we didn't even know if it indeed was his watch and if it was . . . well . . .

When had the woman died?

34

Perhaps Scott had taken a stroll and come across her. He tried to help her or resuscitate her or whatever and lost his watch in the process. He'd then run off to find help . . .

It could have happened like that.

"All of us?" Juan Jose said, interrupting my train of thought. "There are so many of us . . . and the Jaca B&B is so small."

"We'll have to double up if needed." Becca glanced at me. "Georgia can stay in my room."

Juan Jose didn't look happy, but he nodded anyway. "I'll take care of it."

She took a deep breath and clapped her hands to get everyone's attention. "Gang, it's unfortunate, but due to the turn of events we have to leave camp and head into town. We'll be staying at the Jaca B&B with the rest of the crew."

DeeCee sprang forward, suddenly happy. "Oh, goodness!" She clasped Daisy's hand and asked, "Does that mean we get a bathroom?"

"With a shower and everything?" Daisy squealed.

Juan Jose frowned.

Becca said, "I don't mean to disappoint, ladies, but it's a small B&B. It only has a few floors and the rooms don't have their own lavatories. There's a shared bathroom on each floor."

Daisy's face crumpled, and she squeezed DeeCee's hands for strength.

Watching them process the information that they'd have to share the restroom with the other ladies on the cast and crew, as if they were being given a death sentence, made my heart plummet. What would that poor woman have given for the opportunity to spend a few nights in a B&B, regardless of the shared bathroom situation, instead of cold, alone, and dead on a trail in the Pyrenees.

Dead but not forgotten.

Anger burned behind my eyes and tears spilled down my face.

I'd see that she got justice.

No matter who was responsible . . .

I felt strange leaving camp. It was as if I were leaving Scott behind. We weren't allowed to take any of our personal belongings with us to the Jaca B&B, as the crime scene team had taken over the campsite. It felt incredibly invasive knowing they would be swabbing my gear, but somehow I found comfort in the fact that maybe if they looked at everything closely it could mean finding Scott sooner.

On the ride into town, DeeCee and Daisy continued to complain about the bathroom situation.

Cooper, acting as the voice of reason, said, "Staying in a B&B, even if it is small, is better than staying in a tent. And anyway, sharing the bathroom is better than an outhouse any day."

Daisy batted her eyelashes at him and said in a tone as smooth as honey, "Oh, that's easy for you to say, you're used to sharing."

Cooper eyed her suggestively. "Not used to sharing everything, doll."

"Oh! You're so bad, Cooper." DeeCee screeched. "She meant, as in sharing a locker room!"

I turned away from them and stared out at the rolling countryside. The hills were green and lush, and flocks of sheep could be seen in the distance. Soon, we pulled into the small town of Jaca, meandering around the cramped streets, until we turned off onto a narrow dirt road.

The B&B, a three-story white building, sat atop a hillside. There were potted plants in the balconies and I was charmed immediately, wishing that the circumstances of my visit were different.

Each team would share a room, and Becca and I would bunk together. Even though I didn't have Scott next to me, I felt grateful to have my best friend by my side.

The ladies team, DeeCee and Daisy, were given a room on the second floor, while the other teams were assigned to the third floor. Because Becca had already spent the night in our room, her belongings covered every surface in the tiny room.

"Sorry," she said, as she pulled a flowered skirt off what was to be my bed.

I sank onto the twin-sized mattress and laid my head down, sighing, "No problem."

Becca tapped my foot. "Don't get all depressed. We're going to find him. Everything is going to be all right."

I nodded. "Uh-huh."

She made a disapproving sound but said nothing.

I covered my eyes with my hands and thought back to the woman. Who was she? Where had she come from? Had there been another group camping near us?

Becca touched my foot again. "Listen, G. I have to get organized here. Get clothes for the cast and stuff. Are you going to be okay if go downstairs?"

I lifted my hand off my eyes and looked at her. "Yeah. Go ahead and get your work done. I understand."

She stared at me, studying me. "I don't want you to be alone."

"Come on, Becca. I'm not going to freak out or anything."

"Still. Why don't you go take a shower and then come downstairs?"

I shrugged, then sat up on the bed. "Okay. If it'll make you feel better."

She walked me out of the room. "It will make *you* feel better. Clear your head, you know?"

The small communal bathrooms were at the end of the hall. I walked toward them and waved at Becca as she headed in the opposite direction toward the staircase. She was right, I supposed. Sulking in bed would do nothing to find Scott.

DeeCee and Daisy were already in the lavatory. The water was running in the shower, steam escaping out to the sitting room where Daisy was perched in front of the mirror, blow-drying her impossibly long, golden hair. She flicked off the dryer when she saw me.

"Any news on Scott?" she asked.

For some reason it bothered me that she'd said his name. It was silly, of course. I'd wanted her to refer to him as my boyfriend. How very possessive of me. Not to mention insecure. Would it have bothered me if she wasn't gorgeous?

I shook my head.

The water from the shower turned off, then DeeCee stepped out into the waiting area and dripped onto the rug. She had fire-red hair, was tall with long legs, a big bosom, and flat stomach. I tried not to stare at her perfect-ten body as she reached for a white towel that was neatly stacked on the counter.

Daisy turned to DeeCee. "No news."

"I'm so sorry, hon. I know it's got to be awful for you."

I nodded. "Thank you. Is the shower—"

"Yes!" Daisy said. "Absolutely. It's all yours. Are you going to the dining room later? You should eat. These kinds of situations take a toll and you have to fuel your body."

Was she nervous I was on the verge of passing out? I felt like I was. Did it show?

I glanced at my reflection and startled myself. There were dark circles under my eyes and my hair was greasy and matted against my forehead from wearing the knit cap last night.

When the girls left the small bathroom, I disrobed and entered the narrow shower stall. The hot water pelted into my shoulders, working out some of the tension. God. Where was Scott?

I tried not to focus on any bad thoughts and just simply visualized him appearing before me.

He would like the bed-and-breakfast. He would tease me about my worrying and simply say that he had gotten lost.

I finished with my shower, turned off the water and grabbed a towel. When I pulled back the shower curtain I was half expecting Scott to be standing there and when he wasn't I began to weep into the towel.

I quickly blow-dried my hair, grateful for the electricity. What a difference it made. My lips were dry and chapped from camping, so I put on a little lip gloss to try to revive them, not to mention that the color it brought into my face made me look less zombie-like.

I finished my minimal primping and then there was a rap at the bathroom door and Becca peeked in.

"Are you going down for dinner?" she asked.

"Yes. I'm starving," I said.

"Good," she said. "I'm going to shower and then head down myself. Sergio said he wants to ask me a few questions."

I looked her in the eyes. "He's going to ask you about Scott, you know that. He's going to ask you about the watch."

She nodded. "I know. I'll tell him what I said before. Lots of people have those sport watches. That's an absolute fact. But he's talking to Cooper right now and I don't know what about exactly." She hesitated. "But if they ask to see the show's promo footage, Scott's wearing the watch in there."

I cringed. "You're right."

She gave me a ferocious hug, pulling my head into her shoulder. I hadn't realized until that moment that I was crying again.

"Everything is going to be all right," she said. "I promise."

Five

....

The dining hall in the bed-and-breakfast was cheerfully decorated: a colorful mosaic covered the ceiling, yellow paint with teal trim on the walls, and a pendant chandelier. If I hadn't been so distraught, I actually might have enjoyed drinking some *sangría* at the bar with the rest of the cast and crew. As it was, I sat by myself at a booth and perused the menu.

My mouth watered as I read. The dinner special was rack of lamb. It came with homemade soup, salad, Basque beans, home-baked bread, french fries, and bread pudding! My stomach growled and I realized with a shock that except for the PowerBars I'd gnawed on, I hadn't eaten anything in over thirty-six hours. I could definitely put away a full seven-course Basque dinner.

Cooper, the NFL player, sauntered over to my table. He was African-American, his face undeniably striking, despite a scar near his left temple. "What are you doing here sitting all alone, dollface?"

I looked up into his eyes. Victoria had mentioned Cooper roaming around camp—what did he know that he wasn't telling me? He placed the glass of whiskey he was holding onto the table and slid into the booth opposite me. Leaning in on his elbows he said, "The *sangría* is too sweet for me. You might like it though."

I leaned across the table, mirroring his body language. "Cooper, did you hear anything strange last night?"

He squinted at me. "I did hear something. Just like I told you. Told the cop in there, too." He motioned to a door on the opposite end of the dining room. "I heard howling and all sorts of noise. Catlike sounds. They probably got mountain lions up there." He stared at me, presumably waiting for my reaction. When none came he added, "Anyway, I'm sure glad we're not out there."

I traced the edge of the table with my fingertip and thought for a moment. Cooper had never said anything to me about hearing howling. He'd told me he hadn't seen anything, but that wasn't the same. We'd all heard howling that night.

Could it have been the woman's screams?

Did anyone know about the woman yet? I wondered what the heck Sergio was asking everyone. I decided to press Cooper a bit further.

"What all did the cop ask you?"

Cooper sipped his whiskey. "Said they're looking real hard for your boy. Asked me if I've ever been to Spain before. Asked me who I knew here."

I rubbed at my temple suddenly wanting a glass of *sangría*. I needed something to squelch my nervousness. Instead I clapped my hands together and folded them into my lap. "And have you ever been here before?"

He shook his head. "No. Football was my life before I blew my leg out." He grimaced. "Speaking of which, the ol' leg is barking at me right now. Funny how that happens. Don't bother me none, until I talk about it." He pulled out a pill bottle from his pocket and popped a couple of tablets into his mouth. "I ain't never been outside of the U.S. except to go to Fiji. Went there for my honeymoon."

"That's nice," I said, feeling a pang in the center of my heart. As part of winning the previous game show, Scott and I had won a trip to an island of our choice. He'd wanted to go to Fiji; me, I was partial to Bora Bora. So we hadn't taken the trip yet, but had been enjoying trying to decide where we'd end up. We'd made a game out of persuading each other. Would we ever get a chance to go now?

Oh, Lord, don't think the worst, Georgia.

Focus on the present. On finding Scott. On finding out what happened to the dead woman.

"You okay?" Cooper asked. "You're a little pale." He fingered his whiskey glass. "Do you want something from the bar?"

I shook my head. "So you've never been to Spain before? Do you know anyone here?" I understood what the police might be thinking. We all had opportunity to kill the woman, but who had motive?

There were several local people on the crew. I had to get to them. Question them. My gut told me the woman was the link to finding Scott.

Cooper laughed, his large body shaking and jerking in a way that made his laughter contagious. "Girl, I don't know anybody here in Spain, 'cept for you all. How about you? You been here before?"

The woman who ran the bed-and-breakfast walked up to our table. She was middle-aged and heavyset, wearing a yellow-and-blue apron and a smile that would warm anyone's heart. "Do you want to eat dinner with your group?" she asked. "We serve family style." She motioned to the large picnic table that the staff was setting up in the middle of the room, where our group was making their way to be seated.

I squared my shoulders. It was time to get information.

The rack of lamb was out of this world but the *sangría* gave me a light-headed feeling. I'd sat between Becca and Kyle, the makeup artist, who alternated between refilling my glass and pushing me to eat.

"Girl, if you don't eat, your ribs are going to show," Kyle said. I shrugged, but he insisted. "No amount of starvation is going to bring that sexy man of yours back any faster."

Daisy, who sat on the other side of Kyle, squealed and grabbed his arms. "You are so cute when you talk all smart!"

Kyle thankfully became distracted with Daisy's attention and turned to refill her glass instead. I pushed my plate away and then polished off my remaining *sangría*, attempting to drown my sorrow with bites of liquor-soaked fruit. Becca was absorbed in conversation with some of the crew. They were discussing something about the show's timeline, which only gave me a headache.

I glanced at my watch and did a quick calculation for the time on the West Coast. It was midmorning. Now would be a good time to call Scott's mother.

What would I say?

I poked Becca. "I have to call Scott's mom."

Becca's eyes widened. "What are you going to tell her?"

"I'll just tell her what I know." I took a deep breath. "Scott's missing and I'm going to find him."

Becca's hands wrapped around her napkin. "Do you think she'll want to come here?"

I shook my head. "She agoraphobic. I don't think even Scott missing will be enough to get her on a plane."

"Get who on a plane?" Kyle interrupted. "Cheryl?"

"What? Cheryl? No, butt out, Kyle—"

Kyle raised a shoulder at Becca as if to deflect her animosity. "Geez, Miss Cat, no need to have a hissy fit. I just thought we needed some reinforcements."

Becca narrowed her eyes at him. "What are you talking about?"

He shrugged. "I called Cheryl this afternoon—"

"You called Cheryl?" Becca exclaimed. She looked as if she were about to strangle Kyle with the napkin she was clenching. I put a hand on hers, but she shrugged me off.

Kyle feigned innocence, but a smile played on his lips. "I thought we needed to tell the boss that one of our contestants had gone missing." He turned to me. "Cheryl and your dad are catching a flight."

I could feel anger coming off Becca in waves. Cheryl was the executive producer of the show. She'd put Becca in charge as the line producer, but now Becca's role could be in jeopardy if we didn't get back to the planned production schedule immediately.

Cheryl and my dad had started dating during the filming of *Love or Money,* and while I wasn't always crazy about her, I knew that having my father close by would definitely add to my moral support.

"When are they getting here?" I asked.

I heard Becca grit her teeth and felt like a traitor.

"They're already in the air," Kyle said. "Their flight arrives tomorrow morning in Madrid. The bus will bring them into Jaca by afternoon." He gave a self-satisfied little grin and then held up the pitcher of sangria. "More, anyone?"

Daisy perked up and held her glass out for Kyle. When he turned away from us Becca whispered, "He's after my job, you know."

"He is? I didn't know that," I said.

"Well, look at him, calling the boss in. Of course he's after my job."

"Don't worry Becca. It's no reflection on you that Scott's gone missing," I said.

She sighed. "It is a reflection on me if I let the whole show slide off the rails—"

"I'm sorry."

"Don't be stupid. It's not your fault." She picked at her bread pudding with a calculating look in her eye.

"Don't hold up the show," I said. "Just replace Scott and me."

She shook her head. "I can't do that."

"Yes, you can," I said, getting up before she could argue with me. I felt woozy, too much *sangría* and not enough sleep. I stumbled away from the table and staggered right into Sergio. He grabbed me before I careened back into the dinner table and knocked over a pitcher of *sangría*.

"Eh. I was coming to get you," he said.

I suddenly felt sober. "Do you have news?"

He wrapped a hand on my elbow and put another on my lower back in the way that cops do, so you go with them lockstep without even having a moment for your brain to click in to protest.

He led me outside to the patio. There were potted red geraniums along the border of the patio and the evening breeze was filled with their sweet scent. Sergio dropped my elbow and pulled out a chair for me. He waited for me to sit, but instead I wandered toward the edge of the patio and looked up at the stars. Despite the breeze, the evening was warm and clear. For a fleeting moment I felt like I could fall in love with Spain, but the thought of the dead woman shocked me back to reality.

Sergio stood his ground by the chair and said, "I have

questioned all the members of the game show." He studied me a moment. "It's a strange game, no?"

"What?"

"The show. You are all to run around Europe and what? Zip-line or scale the citadel?"

I laughed. "Scale the citadel? Is that what they told you?"

He shrugged. "I saw your, what do you call those commercials?"

I winced. He'd seen the promo. An image of Scott rappelling down the fake rock wall from the set of *Love or Money* popped into my mind. I knew Becca had planned to use some of the images from that show for the promos of *Expedition Improbable*. I knew without a doubt Scott was wearing his sports watch in those reels.

"Promos," I muttered, gazing out into the garden trying to buy time.

Sergio abandoned the chair he'd been standing next to and stepped toward me. "*Sí*, the promo. *Expedition Improbable*." He said the name of the show in a deep voice, much as I imagined they'd used in the promo reel, only with Sergio's Spanish accent I had to smile. "What an adventure for you all. Crossing deserts, river rafting, hiking the snow-covered Pyrenees . . ."

He stopped there. We both knew what had happened in the Pyrenees.

After a moment, he said, "There's a lot of competition for the prize money."

I nodded. "Fierce competition."

"Is that why you are on the show? For the money?"

"In part, yes. But mostly because Becca is my best friend and she asked me. The show Scott and I were on . . ." I suddenly felt embarrassed. Sergio was watching me intently and I knew I sounded foolish. I was about to declare my undying love for someone I'd met on a reality show.

"Go on," Sergio said. "Tell me why Scott was on the show."

"We were on another show and got a bit of a following . . . uh . . . fans?" I said. I paused to see if he understood me.

He nodded. "Yes."

"So, my friend, Becca, convinced me to come on this show, because she thought we'd get good ratings. Do you know what ratings are?"

"TV ratings? Yes, many people told me about these ratings tonight."

I laughed. "You talked to the crew."

He folded his arms. "They are obsessed, is that how you say it? Obsessed with the ratings."

"You got it. Yes. Ratings equal work. Lots of viewers, lots of pay."

He ran a hand through his thick black hair. "Ratings are important to them. It's as if they would do *anything* for these ratings . . . no?"

A chill crept up my spine. "The ratings are important, sure. But I'm not clear on what you're trying to say."

He leveled a gaze at me. "I looked at your background. You had said you used to be a police officer."

I cringed. I hadn't ever really been a cop, not the way he meant anyway. I'd been a public information officer, basically a glorified PR person for the San Francisco Police Department.

"Not exactly a cop," I said. "Rubber-gun squad."

He squinted at me. "What's that?"

"I was a talking cop. I talked to the press, the media. I didn't do investigations or homicide or anything."

He smiled, tilting his head to the side and appraising me. I felt uncomfortable under his gaze. "You have the face of a camera cop," he said.

I laughed. "Well, better than a radio face. Is that what they call it here?" I studied him for a moment. He was strikingly handsome in a chiseled sort of way and I cursed myself when I involuntarily glanced at his ring finger.

"Here they use you for what they want. Whatever is best for them. Sad to hear that in America it's the same thing. I thought people had more of an opportunity there."

Had I just misunderstood him or was he saying he thought I was more than a pretty face?

I decided to change the subject. "Do you know who the woman is? How she died?" I asked.

He shook his head. "No, *el médico forense* will have to examine her."

Emboldened, I blurted out, "I can help you with the investigation."

Six

....

slept deeper than I'd expected, a sure sign that I was more exhausted than even I realized.

When I awoke, Becca was already up and out of the room. My cell phone was on the dresser next to two plastic-handled shopping bags. I padded over and grabbed my phone to see if I had any messages. I'd called Scott's mother the evening before, but got her voice mail. Checking my phone alerts, I realized she hadn't called me back yet. I wanted to try her again, but it was past midnight in California right now. I'd have to try her again later.

Peeking into the bags, I saw they were filled with garments probably intended to replace my clothes left in the Pyrenees. I rummaged through the bags, finding a skimpy, practically see-through flowered top and a hot-pink leather miniskirt. In the other bag was a pair of matching stilettos. These items had Kyle's signature all over them.

I turned away from the bags and reached for a pair of Becca's jeans. They were a size larger than what I usually wore, but having grown up together, Becca and I were used to living in each other closets. I didn't mind that the jeans were a bit baggy on me, better that then the awful miniskirt and stilettos Kyle had selected. At the bottom of Becca's bag, I found a tan halter and put that on under the see-through flowered top. At least my modesty would be preserved.

I stepped into my hiking boots from the day before, and gathered my dirty clothes in a heap. If I could find the nice senora who ran the B&B, I could likely talk her into letting me use the washing machine.

The hallway corridor was eerily quiet and the shared lavatory was empty. I quickly brushed my teeth and washed my face, then headed downstairs. I found the senora wiping the bar counter. She gave a wide smile when she saw me.

"Give me the dirty clothes," she said taking them from me. "I'll clean them this afternoon." Before I could protest she asked, "Café con leche?"

I nodded and looked around the immaculate dining hall. "Where is everyone?"

"Most have gone to see Jaca today. Shopping and maybe to see the medieval walls and *torres*." She gave a satisfied nod, like she was proud of what her town had to offer tourists. "You don't like to go with them?"

I could safely say that sightseeing was the furthest

thing from my mind, but I didn't want to be rude. "I needed to sleep," I said. "I have a few things to figure out."

She steamed the milk for my coffee. "Ah. *Los policías?*" She indicated the room off the dining hall they used as headquarters last night.

When I turned to look I saw that the door was open and Sergio and Montserrat were in a huddle. Then as if she sensed me watching, Montserrat stiffened and turned toward me. She offered me a tight smile, then closed the door.

Damn.

I turned back to the senora.

She put the café con leche in front me and asked, "It's about the young woman, isn't it?"

"Yes," I said, not certain if I should elaborate. "Do you know who she was?"

"Annalise Rodriguez," she said, with a hardness in her eyes.

This surprised me. If the senora knew the woman, why wasn't she sad?

I sipped my café con leche, letting the hardness simmer. Experience told me that usually a story followed a look like that. She glanced at the police's makeshift office, then over her shoulder. "ETA," she whispered. *"Terrorista."*

The senora had been unwilling to elaborate on ETA, so I spent the morning wandering around the bed-and-breakfast trying to get the best Internet signal I could on my cell phone in order to do some research. I'd ended up in the gardens of the B&B under an olive tree.

ETA stood for *Euskadi Ta Askatasuna*; which meant "Basque Country and Freedom." It was a paramilitary group with the goal of gaining independence for the Basque Country in northern Spain and southwestern France. The group was responsible for almost a thousand murders, thousands of injuries, and orchestrating dozens of kidnappings. They had a logo that was prominently displayed on a Web page I'd read: a snake wrapped around an ax.

If the woman, Annalise, was a known member of ETA, then certainly there were plenty of motives for her murder. However, on the surface, I couldn't attach a motive to anyone in our cast, but what about the local crew members, Miguel and Juan Jose?

Were they part of the ETA?

I could ask Sergio, but the way he stiffened last night after I'd offered to help with the investigation told me he wouldn't likely be sharing any info with me, at least not voluntarily. Instead, I made a note to ask the senora of the B&B.

As for the cast, I began by Googling Cooper. He'd had a pretty long career with the NFL. The media loved him. Lots of articles on his generous philanthropic donations.

Why was he on the show?

Had his NFL money dried up?

I probed a bit further and read that he'd been married, but now there seemed to be a messy divorce underway.

Likely starring on a reality show, even if he didn't win the prize money, would boost his celebrity status, bringing in lots of sponsor offers.

Okay, so Cooper probably needed the money, but that wasn't enough to tie him to the woman and I certainly didn't see any obvious connections to the terrorist group ETA.

Next I researched Cooper's partner, Todd. He seemed to show up in a lot of photos next to Cooper, but wasn't mentioned in most of the articles. All I could learn from the Internet was that they'd grown up together and were good friends.

DeeCee and Daisy really didn't have an Internet presence; I found only a homemade website with a link to their country music demo, also homemade, but they had a lot of talent.

The mother-and-son team, Helen and Eric, had only Facebook pages, on which recent posts promised "juicy" reveals. I knew, according to our contracts, they weren't allowed to announce on any social-media sites that they'd been picked for *Expedition Improbable*. I found out Eric's wife was home pregnant and missing him as he was on a mysterious "business trip."

Parker and Victoria were equally muted on social media, at least in terms of current events and posts, but as I poked around Victoria's Facebook page, I saw that she'd graduated from the University of Nevada, Reno, with a degree in political science and a minor in Basque studies. She'd even participated in a study abroad program in Bilbao, Spain, at the University of the Basque Country.

Goosebumps grew on my arms as I clicked on a photo of Victoria wearing a T-shirt with a snake wrapped around an ax.

Oh, my goodness!

Could Victoria have met Annalise in her previous travels to Spain?

My heart sped up and I took a deep breath to enjoy the heady feeling of discovering an unexpected lead. "I got you, Victoria! I got you." I exclaimed to myself.

Suddenly, I heard a rustling in the garden. Startled, I looked up to find Becca waving at me as she approached.

"What are you doing out here?" she asked.

I sprang to my feet. "Becca, I have news!"

She rushed over to me. "Me, too!"

My heart pounded through my chest. "You do? Is it Scott? Is he okay?" I glanced around the garden frantically as if Scott would magically appear.

Becca shook her head. "Oh, no, nothing like that. Sorry, honey. I don't have any news about him. It's just that I wanted you to know that Cheryl and your dad will be here soon."

A feeling of warm relief flooded me and I wrapped my arms around Becca's neck. "Thank God."

Dad was on his way.

Everything would be fine now. He would help me find Scott. At the same moment that I found solace in Dad's arrival, the logical part of my brain screamed out that Dad's being here was in no way connected to Scott actually reappearing.

"When do they get here?"

Becca glanced at her watch. "About an hour, but we need to talk first."

"What it is?" I asked.

She leaned against the olive tree, raising a hand to shade her eyes from the springtime sun. "Cheryl is going to put pressure on us to get filming again."

I nodded. "Right. There's a lot of money on the line. I get it. Don't feel bad. You can replace me. No problem."

Becca pressed her lips together for a moment.

I watched her expression and waited for her speak. When she didn't I said, "I'm totally fine with it."

"Cheryl's not going to want to replace you—"

"Well, I mean, I can't do the show without Scott—"

"We can replace *him*. We'll get you another partner," she said, without missing a beat.

Anxiety rumbled through my body. "What do you mean?"

"I know. I know how you feel, G. It's just that I'm sure that's the angle she's going to push." Becca squeezed my hand. "We have to get on with production. You know what this show means to me. If I can keep the cast and crew happy for the next few days, maybe rearrange the schedule—"

I pulled my hand away from her. "No, I won't do the show without Scott. I have to look for him. Don't you understand, Becca?"

She clutched at my arm. "I'm sure Scott will show up in a few days. I can feel it in my gut. I know he's okay."

"But I can't be part of the show if he's not here," I said.

"Wherever he is, G, I know he'd want you to stay on the show."

"I need to be looking for him, Becca. I can't just stand by and let the police—"

"Georgia, there's nothing you can do that we haven't already done to find him. We trampled all over those trails. The police are investigating. They'll continue to look for him. I'm sure he's fine. I know he is."

When I'd gone through the police academy they'd stressed how unhelpful family and friends could be when they meddled in police work, but my heart wasn't listening to my brain. I knew I could help. I was trained!

I clung to the belief that I could be an asset to the ongoing search and investigation; even as a heaviness set itself against my chest, threatening my certainty.

We walked toward the B&B and Becca asked, "What was your news?"

"The dead woman was part of ETA—"

"What's that?" Becca asked.

"It's a Basque separatist group. Terrorists."

A look of alarm crossed Becca's face. "Seriously?"

I nodded gravely.

"Terrorists?"

"They're fighting for independence for the Basque Country, but they do it like a bunch of thugs. Car bombings, gunmen, kidnappings—"

"Are we in danger?" she asked.

"I hope not. Anyway according to the senora here at

the B&B the woman was a known member of the group. Maybe she did something wrong. Blew someone's cover or tried to get out."

"They'd kill her for wanting out?" Becca asked.

"It happens. In any mafia, mob, or terror group, what have you—if they think someone in the group doesn't want to be involved anymore . . . say she knew a few things about their future plans or even the fact that she could identify people . . ." I made a slicing motion across my throat.

Becca let out a low whistle. "Is anyone else on our crew in the ETA?"

"Good question. Let's find out."

Once inside the B&B, I could see the commotion starting to wear on the senora. Most of the cast and crew were back from their early-morning sightseeing romp into Jaca and now it looked like Kyle was holding court at the bar. He had the senora frantically running around trying to keep up with tapas and pitchers of *sangría*.

Kyle was flanked by DeeCee and Daisy, who were recounting in very animated and shrill voices a bargain they'd found in town. While the smell of frying garlic was heavenly enough for me to want to join them, the thought of listening to mindless chatter repelled me.

I wandered over to the front doors and peered out the stained glass windows toward the driveway. A small black minivan made its way up the road. I yanked opened the front door and bolted toward the car.

The minivan rolled to a stop, the back doors flew open, and my father leapt out toward me.

"Daddy!" I yelled, racing into his arms.

He embraced me. "Georgia. Gosh, honey, how are you holding up? Do you have any news?"

"Dad. I'm so glad you're here!" I said, burying my head into his chest, my emotions overwhelming me.

My mother had passed away when I was young and the only family I had was Dad. He was in his early fifties and more handsome than most men half his age. I cried into his flannel shirt and inhaled his fresh, woodsy, out-doors scent.

The driver's door creaked open. The driver got out of the minivan and opened the passenger-side back door. Cheryl's blond hair came into view. At six feet tall, she towered over the short Spanish driver. She said something to him in hushed tones and he swiftly began to unload their luggage.

She strode around the minivan toward me and offered me an awkward hug. I'd nicknamed her "the Dragon Lady" before she'd hooked up with my dad, but I felt the name still applied. She was nicer to me now, only because I was Gordon's daughter, but she gave off the same don't-mess-with-Cheryl vibe to everyone else.

She wore white cotton pants, a striped shirt, and strappy sandals; an outfit that on anyone else would have looked relaxed and appropriate for a trip to Spain. However, because of Cheryl's militant demeanor, the outfit seemed more like a uniform.

"We came as soon as we heard, Georgia. What an

absolute disaster. Have the police made any headway? Do they know where Scott is?" she asked.

I sighed, then in a rush of emotion told them about Annalise.

Cheryl's face looked pinched and flushed at the same time, a calculating look in her eyes. I figured she was probably tallying up how long a murder investigation would delay the show's production schedule.

Dad frowned. "What does Annalise have to do with Scott?"

I bit my lip. I didn't want to tell him about the watch in front of Cheryl. Instead, I said, "Bad timing, I suppose. Let's go inside and get you settled."

Dad linked his arms through mine as Cheryl barked orders to the driver.

Inside the B&B the party at the bar was in full force. Cheryl took immediate control of the cast and crew, clapping her hands and calling for their attention. She launched into a speech about our delay and what her plan was to get us back on track. I tuned her out as I noted that Victoria and Cooper had joined the festivities.

They seemed awful chummy. She was leaning against his shoulder and he had an arm wrapped around her waist. She was decked out all in black and wore a red beret, what they call a *boina* here in Spain.

Had she just bought the hat while shopping in Jaca? Or was it a souvenir from her semester abroad in Spain?

I itched to confront her, but Dad took my arm. "Can we get a word in private?"

I looked at him, his blue eyes were serious and I felt my stomach drop.

"Let's go out to the garden," I said. "I made a friend with an olive tree today."

My father escorted me out to the patio and we walked down the little dirt trail toward the shade tree. When we were sure we were out of earshot, Dad leaned in close to me. "I didn't want to say this in front of the others, but I wanted you to know as soon as possible."

My throat went dry.

"I've received an email message from Scott," Dad said.

I clutched at my chest not realizing I'd been holding my breath. "He's alive! Oh! Thank God!"

"I got the message when Cheryl and I landed in Madrid." Dad lowered his eyes. "I haven't told anybody, not even Cheryl."

"What? What is it?" I asked.

"You know, honey, it's tough to meet somebody the way you two met . . . on a reality show—"

"Dad!" I shook his arm. "What did he say? Is he hurt? Tell me."

Dad held my gaze. "He slipped away in the middle of the night, honey, because he didn't want to do the show."

The earth seemed to tilt a bit, like something was wrong with the gravitational pull. It took me a moment to realize that it was me who was off balance. I grabbed at the olive tree for support. "What?" I stuttered. "Why wouldn't he tell me?"

"I don't know." Anger flashed through Dad's eyes and I knew he had something else to tell me.

"Is there more, Dad?"

"He knew . . . it was complicated . . ."

"What else did he say, Dad? Why didn't he tell me he was leaving the show . . . was he leaving me, too?"

Dad embraced me. "I'm so sorry, Peaches. I'm so sorry that he wasn't man enough to tell you to your face."

Humiliation charged my system and suddenly I was flush with resentment. "He broke up with me via an email to you?"

Dad tsked. "I know this is really tough."

"Where's the email? Did you print it out? Where is it?" I demanded.

"No, I didn't print it out, honey. I told you I was in the airport." He rummaged through his pockets and pulled out his cell phone.

"I'm so glad you finally upgraded phones!" I said.

Dad scrolled through the screen, searching for the email, and looked flummoxed. Up until recently Dad had carried a flip phone with no Internet access. He said Scott and I had finally convinced him to upgrade, but I knew Cheryl was probably more behind the new phone than either of us.

"Why didn't you tell Cheryl about the email?" I asked. "Why the secrecy?"

"It's not my business to tell it, is it?" he said.

He was trying to spare me some embarrassment.

Dad showed me the email, my eyes clouded over with

tears as I read Scott's brief note. Part of me was relieved; Scott was no longer a missing person.

The other part of me, though, felt empty; as if a piece of *me* was missing.

"We have to tell Sergio right away," I said.

There was no reason for the police to be searching for him now . . . except, of course, there was the matter of the dead woman.

Seven

....

Disbelief and astonishment rolled through me, quickly followed by anger. I'd been worried sick about him, and he didn't even have the decency to break up with me in person!

I walked away from my father, staggering as I moved, the emotion overwhelming me.

"You don't have anything to prove, Georgia. It's okay to fall apart in front of me, honey," Dad said.

"I loved him, Dad." The tears stuck in my throat and I buried my head in my hands. It suddenly made sense that Scott's passport was missing. He'd taken it with him. Leaving me intentionally? I wept in my father's arms.

"He's lucky he's not here," Dad said through gritted teeth. "I'd kill him."

• • • • • • • • • • • •

D ad and I made our way back into the bar area of the
B&B, only to find that the cast and crew had cleared
out, leaving Cheryl and Becca alone to chat. Two chilled
glasses of sangria sweated in front of them, the condensa-
tion dripping down the sides and saturating the tabletop.

By the way they grew quiet when we entered, I knew
they were up to no good.

"I think we'll need a pitcher of that," I said, indicating the *sangría.*

Becca eagerly hailed down the senora who ran the
bed-and-breakfast. "*Uno más,*" she said, pointing at me.

Dad cleared his throat. "*¡Dos más!*"

The senora gave me a sympathetic nod and got busy
pouring our drinks.

"Where is everyone?" I asked.

"There are fiestas in town tonight," Becca said.
"Cheryl gave everyone a pass for the night." She sipped
her *sangría.* "Well, I mean, she gave *most everyone* a
pass for the night. They're upstairs getting ready."

Cheryl stiffened and I knew that *most everyone* obviously didn't include Becca. Becca looked away from us
and pretended she didn't care, but I knew she desperately needed a night off.

I patted Becca's shoulder. "You should go to the fiestas, too. I'm sure Cheryl won't mind," I said pointedly.

Cheryl bristled, but Dad said, "Fiestas? What are
they celebrating? A saint day or something?"

The senora leaned in. "The first Friday of the month."

Dad chuckled. "The first Friday? Heck, we should all go to the fiestas!"

"I'm not going. I have work to do." Cheryl narrowed her eyes at Dad. "You can go if you like."

Dad waved a hand. "Oh, no. I'm jet-lagged. Why don't we stay here on our own? Get comfortable. Let the others go out and enjoy themselves."

Cheryl perked up at the idea. "Yes!" She turned to Becca. "You can have the night off. Go into town with Georgia—"

"No. I'm not in the mood for fiestas," I said. "You may as well tell them, Dad."

Dad shrugged, not wanting to be the bearer of bad news. Instead, he pulled out his cell phone and slid it across the bar.

Becca shrieked when she saw the email and Cheryl gasped. "He doesn't want to do the show? He's under contract!"

Becca shook her head at Cheryl. "Don't be so insensitive."

"Insensitive?" Cheryl screeched. "The man has put us behind, costing us tens of thousands of dollars! Do you know what it cost to house the entire cast and crew here?"

At that, the senora behind the bar chuckled.

Dad put a hand on Cheryl's lower back. "Darling—"

"I'm going to sue him, that's what I'm going to do!" she howled.

I laughed bitterly. "He doesn't have any money."

Cheryl frowned at me. "Come on. He's a big-time author!"

While it was true that Scott had authored quite a few hits, financially he'd been wiped out paying for his deceased wife's medical treatments.

"It's doesn't mean that he has—"

Cheryl interrupted me. "I'm going to sue his *New York Times*–bestselling behind!" When Dad pulled his hand away from her, she continued, "Don't get upset, Gordon. It's nothing personal, just business."

"It is personal!" Becca protested.

"It's personal to Georgia!" my Dad said. "And to Becca and me, too."

Cheryl's eyes fluttered and her entire head began to tick nervously back and forth, as if she couldn't understand ordinary people. She couldn't get her mind around the fact that Becca and Dad had actually liked Scott and I had loved him.

"You all are being ridiculous!" she admonished. "The man walked off my set!" She poked Dad in the chest. "And he left your daughter in the lurch! She was worried sick about him. You were, too! We flew halfway across the world in order to straighten out this mess!"

The senora had been watching our drama unfold, and when we all quieted down, she gave a shake of her head and said, "*Ai yai yai.*"

Dad covered his face with his hands and repeated the expression.

Becca pushed her empty *sangría* glass toward the senora. "*Uno más.*"

I slumped into the bar stool next to Becca and pushed my empty glass next to hers. The senora refilled our glasses without a word. Then she disappeared into the kitchen, only to return with a tray of tapas: grilled mushroom in a wine and garlic sauce, white beans with sausage and ham, and calamari in an aioli sauce.

My mouth watered and despite my severe angst about Scott, I dug into the food. We grew quiet as we savored our meals.

Dad dipped a piece of warm crusty bread into the garlic sauce. "Oh, my word. Is all the food in Spain this good?"

The senora smiled. "*Sí.*"

"Dinner last night was pretty amazing," Becca said. She poked at me and said, "Right, G?"

I nodded, listless again.

She put her arm around me. "I'm so sorry, honey. Guys totally stink."

I grumbled but didn't answer.

"It's not really like him, is it?" Becca persisted. "I can't believe he'd break up with you via email."

"I want to go home," I whined.

"Home!" Cheryl squawked. "Not on your life!" She slammed a fist into the bar. "We have a show to film."

Oh, great.

Dread filled my belly.

She was going to make me go through with the show.

"I don't . . . I can't . . . I don't have a partner," I stuttered.

I suddenly envisioned Cheryl partnering me with

Kyle and a red itchy blotch appeared on my collarbone, as if the thought had given me hives. I glanced nervously at Becca for reassurance, but she feigned interest in the white bean tapas.

Cheryl whacked Dad in the back, causing him to choke on his piece of bread. "Whaddya mean? Gordon's right here! We have the mother-son team. Why not a father-daughter team?"

Dad's eyes grew wide in horror. "Oh, no! No, no, no, no."

"Why not?" Cheryl insisted. "You need the money. You want to save your farm, right? You and Georgia can win this thing!"

"Uh . . ." Dad looked pained. "This is *Expedition Improbable*! You all have a bunch of torturous challenges planned. Like hiking and rafting, and God knows what!"

Cheryl batted her eyes at Dad, pouring on the sweetness. "Oh, Gordon—"

"No. I'm not going to do it. I'm old—"

"You're not old, Gordon," Cheryl said.

Dad patted his flat stomach. "I'm fat, there's no way I'll make it through those challenges."

Becca snickered. "You're not fat, you're downright skinny!"

"I'm out of shape, then," Dad whined.

"No you're not, darling," Cheryl wiggled her eyebrows in a suggestive fashion. I turned away, willing my mind to redact any unwanted images she'd just implanted with that stupid look of hers.

"I don't like to get up early," Dad said.

Becca laughed. "Gordon! You're a farmer! You've been getting up early your whole life!"

"Georgia doesn't want me as a partner!" Dad insisted. "She needs someone young, someone who can—"

"Dad!" I exclaimed, a little louder than I'd intended. I couldn't risk Becca or Cheryl getting the bright idea of partnering me up with a flamboyant stylist. "You would make a good partner, I think."

Dad pressed his lips together.

"At least we can trust him not to walk off the job," Cheryl stated.

I smiled to myself. I knew the real reason Dad didn't want to be on the show was that he didn't want to look foolish on national television. And I couldn't blame him. Looking like a fool was tough. I'd been humiliated in front of all our family and friends when I'd been left at the altar by my former fiancé, Paul. Worse, now I'd look like an even bigger idiot for choosing Scott over Paul on the last show.

But there was another reason not to pack up and go home.

Annalise Rodriguez.

Had Scott known her? Who was she to him? More important, why was his watch at the scene of the crime?

If I stayed in Spain, I might be able to get some answers; some closure.

I got up and walked over to Dad. "You know, I think the only way I can do the show is with you by my side, Daddy."

Dad blinked up at me, a stoic expression on his handsome face.

He couldn't say no to me. All my life, Dad had always, always stood proud in my corner. He was my hero.

He turned away from me, plucked a toothpick out of the small holder on the bar and speared a mushroom. He waved the mushroom at Cheryl. "I'll do the show if meals are included."

Eight

· · · · · · · · · · · · · · · · ·

The narrow streets of Jaca were crowded and noisy. It seemed the entire town had come out to celebrate. There was a loud band on a makeshift stage that alternated playing Spanish folk songs and contemporary hits, but no matter what music they blared, the crowd joyously danced.

The cast and crew pressed up against me, almost in a protective manner. The heat of the day had passed, but the cement and the crowd still pulsed with fire and I felt nauseous. I regretted letting Becca talk me into the fiestas.

The crowd was dressed in the traditional white fiestas outfits with red sashes and bandanas, some wore red *boinas,* too. Kyle had pulled one of his magic tricks and had produced white outfits for the group. I'd refused to change into the transparent white dress he selected for me, so in essence he wasn't speaking to me. He occupied himself with DeeCee and Daisy, showering them with attention like it was going out of style.

They were dressed in matching outfits; white short-shorts that left little to the imagination and halter tops so clingy and revealing that no one would forget their team name, Double D.

Victoria had attached herself to Cooper, who seemed happy to let her stick to him like a second skin. Her brother, Parker, chatted amicably with the mother-and-son team, Helen and Eric. While Todd seemed to sulk by himself.

Most of the cast was drunk on red wine and when the band played the chicken dance, they went wild, jostling up against me and driving me crazy. My nerves were so on edge that each time someone bumped into me, my skin crawled.

"How long are we going to be out here?" I asked Becca.

She pinched my cheek. "Cheer up, monkey. Aren't you having a good time?"

"I have a headache. The music is too loud," I said.

Daisy shook her behind in front of me and screamed. "Shake a tail feather, Georgia!"

I moved away from her, not able to get Annalise out of my mind. Juan Jose, one of our local crew members, was near me. I asked him, "Juan Jose. Did you know Annalise? The woman who was killed in the woods."

He stiffened. "No. I did not know her. She was ETA, why would I know her? I hate ETA and their Molotov cocktails and their bombings and their killings!" His face grew red. "They are savages!"

"I'm sorry. I didn't mean to upset you. It's only that—"

DeeCee grabbed Juan Jose's arm. "I heard there's going to be fireworks!"

Miguel, our other local crew member, pointed toward a grassy mound in the distance and suddenly the cast began to peel off in different directions.

Which was entirely fine with me.

Just as I was enjoying the breathing space, a raucous Spaniard danced right into me, spilling his wine on my shirt. He assailed me with a fast string of Spanish, which I assumed was an apology. I held up my arms and tried to wave him off, indicating I didn't speak Spanish and I hadn't been hurt when he boogied into me. He grabbed my wrist and spun me around, undeterred.

"¡Olé guapa!" he yelled.

The music kicked into another folk song and soon everyone was bouncing around in a dance I didn't know.

The man was my age and had such a disarming smile that I felt guilty disentangling myself from him. I glanced over to grab Becca, only to realize she'd been swooped up by another overly eager gentleman.

Under different circumstances, I would have loved these fiestas; these beautiful friendly Spaniards in their bright white outfits, everyone offering each other a "hail fellow well met," but as it was, the sadness that had rooted itself into my heart since Scott left now throbbed. I stepped away from the crowd and rounded the corner, looking for a little quiet space to catch my breath.

On the first street, there was still a throng of people dancing and heading toward the music in the plaza.

I walked further down the narrow cobblestone path and noticed there were less people now. In a doorway, I spotted a couple locked in an embrace and then another couple passed me on their way toward the square to dance. I turned the next corner, hoping to get a bit further away from the crowd, when I saw a familiar pair.

Todd and Parker were in a huddle, heads bowed together, obviously discussing something serious.

Goosebumps grew on my arm.

What were they discussing so urgently?

I approached them. "Hey guys."

They bristled, suddenly growing quiet.

"Oh, hi, Georgia," Parker said.

"What are you guys doing here, off by yourselves?" I asked. Hey, I'd once been on the police force, being direct had never been a problem for me.

Todd leveled his eyes at me. "We're discussing strategy."

Apparently, Todd didn't have a problem being direct, either.

Parker made a face, as if he didn't agree with Todd sharing their secret. Out of the corner of my eye, I saw Parker press a finger to his lips to silence Todd.

"What kind of strategy?" I asked.

Todd glared at me. "How to win the show, obviously."

An uncomfortable sensation snaked around my belly. There was a lot of money at stake on the show.

How far would someone go to make sure he or she won?

"You're not even on the same team," I said. "Are you guys colluding?"

"You're one to talk," Todd said.

Before I could respond, Parker asked, "You're in tight with the producers, huh? Is that why you're still here?"

I squinted at him. "What do you mean?"

Parker shrugged. "Your boyfriend's gone missing. I figured a thing like that might make you quit the show."

A chill rushed up my spine.

"How are you going to do the show without a partner?" Todd asked.

Oh, no!

Just wait until they realized that my new partner, my dad, was dating the executive producer. Sparks were going to fly.

Before I could reply, Parker asked, "Do you know what the challenge is going to be tomorrow?"

"I'm not privy to that information," I said. "It's against the rules for them to share what the challenges are with anyone."

"Pfft, yeah right," Todd said. "You're bunking with one of the producers and I heard you two go way back." The look on his face turned angry and trepidation filled my chest.

"Becca won't tell me anything. It would cost her her job," I said.

Parker leaned in close to me. "It could cost you something worse." His jaw tightened and his hand balled into a fist.

My pulse quickened.

"What exactly are you saying?" I demanded.

Even as the words tumbled out of my mouth, I regretted confronting him. We were alone now. It was me against these two large men. If things got ugly, I didn't stand a chance.

Todd laughed in my face, his breath reeked of stale wine. "I think you do know what the challenge is," Todd said. "And I think you better tell us right now."

Parker shifted, almost imperceptibly, but I feared he was about to block my exit.

My heart raced as I dove to my left knee and executed a right thrust kick into Todd's thigh. He buckled over and collided into Parker, as I sidestepped him.

"Georgia!" someone called. I looked in the direction of the voice and was glad to see Sergio approaching.

Parker and Todd froze against each other, awkwardly caught in a man hug.

Sergio neared our strange little group. "Hello! I got your message, you wanted to talk to me?"

Parker and Todd disentangled themselves, swearing under their breath.

I gave them an over-the-top smile. "Excuse me, gentlemen. I'll leave you to each other." I jogged toward Sergio. "Is there somewhere private we can talk?"

Sergio glanced in Parker and Todd's direction, but he said nothing, only offered me his arm. The gesture wasn't very coplike, but I linked my arm through his and found comfort in his steady gait.

He was dressed like most of the Spaniards out tonight, in all white with a red sash around his waist and a red bandana around his neck. I suddenly felt bad, he was supposed to be off duty, having fun with friends or a girlfriend at the fiestas, and instead he was escorting me away from drama.

"Have you been to the plaza yet?" he asked.

"Where the band and dancing is?" I asked.

He smiled. "Yes."

"I was there earlier, but I'm not in the mood for dancing right now."

"I'll take you someplace a little more quiet," he said. "My favorite place, actually."

We strolled up the narrow windy street, my heels clicking on the cobblestones. The street bottomed out into a square flanked with small shops. In the center was a large fountain. The square was busy, with groups of people drinking red wine and singing. A teenage couple was passionately making out by the center fountain.

I envied the couple for a moment. Not only did they have each other, but it also seemed like they didn't have a care in the world.

"Is that a wishing fountain?" I asked.

"Any fountain is a wishing fountain, no?" he asked.

I shrugged. "I don't know."

He reached into his pocket and pulled out a coin. He handed it to me, but I pushed it back at him.

"At this point, I'm so confused I wouldn't know what to wish for," I said.

He cocked his head to the side and shrugged, tossing the coin into the fountain. "No problem. I do."

Ahead there was a mass of people moving toward the grassy mound, presumably to watch the fireworks. I hesitated. Sergio noticed and tightened his grip. "It's okay, trust me."

I clung to his arm as he pulled me through the sea of people. As we jostled our way through the crowd, red wine stains peppered my shirt and pants. Sergio's clothes on the other hand were pristine.

"How do you do that?" I demanded.

"Pull you through a crowd?" he asked.

"No, keep your white clothes clean."

He looked down at himself and shrugged. "Practice."

We turned down another block, this one deserted, and in the distance a small church with an octagonal tower was visible. It was illuminated by outdoor lighting and it seemed to glow.

I gasped. "Oh, my! It's beautiful."

Sergio smiled. "Eleventh century. Romanesque church. It's quiet here, too. Look, no one. And we'll have a nice view of the fireworks."

We sat on the stone steps, in time for a first burst of red light into the night sky. Little squiggles of multicolored light zagged away from the main ball and for the first time in a long while I felt my shoulders relax.

Another burst of fire lit up the sky, this one green, accompanied by classical music. I clapped a hand over my heart. The music boomed from nearby speakers and I looked up toward the octagonal tower.

Sergio laughed. "It's marvelous, no? This is one of my favorite music pieces, *Nights in the Gardens of Spain*."

The fireworks seemed to accompany the music perfectly, filling the night sky in time with every swell in the music.

We listened and watched the show in silence. After a while, Sergio touched my cheek. I turned toward him surprised by the feeling of intimacy between us.

Sergio asked, "What did you want to tell me, Georgia?"

My mouth went dry. I'd wanted to tell him about Scott's email, but instead I said, "Annalise. Did you know she was part of ETA?"

He quirked an eyebrow at me. "You know about ETA?"

"A little, only what I got off the Internet."

He shrugged. "We're looking into her background."

"Do you know that one of the ladies on the show, Victoria, studied in Bilbao? I saw photos of her wearing a shirt with the ETA logo." Even as I said it, it sounded like a flimsy distraction.

Oh, please, look into that girl and charge her with murder, because I saw a picture on Facebook. Don't worry about the guy whose watch was found at the scene of the crime!

"Hmmm." Sergio stroked his chin. "Victoria told me about that. I didn't find anything unusual in her travels to Spain."

"But—"

"In America do you arrest someone for what shirt they wear?"

"No, of course not. It's just that—"

"What happened with you and those two men before you came with me?" he asked.

"Todd and Parker?" I shrugged. "It was nothing really. They think I have an inside track on the show because my friend is one of the producers. They're angry about that."

Sergio leaned back to rest on his elbows. "Did you know Todd has a criminal record?"

My breath caught.

I tried not to show my excitement—it would come across as crass—but if someone had a criminal record, a cop always thought they were good for the crime. So, if Sergio liked Todd for the murder, he might loosen the chokehold on Scott. Especially, since he'd barely blinked at Victoria's ETA ties.

"What was he convicted for?" I asked.

"Drugs."

"Drugs? What kind? Marijuana? Coke? Heroine?" Although Todd hadn't struck me as an addict, it didn't mean he hadn't been busted for possession, maybe on his way to negotiate something nefarious.

"Marijuana and hashish possession, cultivation with intent to sell."

I mulled the information over. Just because Todd had been arrested for growing pot, it didn't mean he was a murderer. On the other hand, I knew what Sergio would think—a criminal was usually guilty in a cop's mind until proven innocent. I could steer him into looking at Todd more closely, based on cops' biases, but that didn't make it right.

"Do you have anything else? Anything on Cooper or the girls, DeeCee and Daisy?"

Sergio nodded. "I'm not supposed to tell you these things, you know."

I leaned back on my elbows, suddenly our faces were dangerously close. The flash from the fireworks illuminated Sergio's dark eyes, and nerves shot through my stomach. He touched my cheek and we were suspended in time.

Heat surged between us, transferring only from his finger on my check, but igniting my entire body.

For a brief second, I let myself imagine that I wasn't discussing a murder case with another cop, but that I was someone else entirely.

A girl in a movie, maybe, about to kiss the leading man.

I sat up. Jolting myself out of whatever romantic reverie I'd just been in. Sergio let out a slow exhale, accompanied by a little sigh, presumably of disappointment.

After a moment, he said, "Cooper got caught with a prostitute, but charges were dropped."

"That type of thing isn't uncommon for an NFL star," I said.

He shrugged. "Love can make men do crazy things."

The weight I'd been carrying all day seemed too heavy now. I sighed. "My father arrived in Spain today. He had news from Scott."

Sergio sat up straight. "Where is he? We must interview him as soon as possible."

"Dad? He's staying at the B&B—"

"No, no. Scott. Where is he? Do you know? Did he tell your father?"

I shook my head. "I don't know where he is. Only . . . that . . ."

Sergio waited for me to continue. The fireworks show was nearly at a crescendo—the finale. And my mind somehow associated it with the finality of Scott's email.

"He broke up with me, Sergio. Said he walked off the set, because he didn't really want to do the show and he didn't want to continue a relationship with me."

He frowned. "Is it typical for Americans to break up by sending an email?"

"It's not typical, no, not if you have any class," I said. But then what was typical? Leaving your bride at the altar?

Maybe it's me. Guys can't face me when they've lost the loving feeling.

"Do you believe the email was from him, Georgia?" he asked.

I shook my shoulders. "I suppose so. How would I know?"

Sergio laid a warm hand on my shoulder. "Our technical team may be able to track him from it. Can you get me a copy of the email?"

I nodded.

"You still love him?" Sergio asked.

What had prompted the question, I wondered.

I swallowed, the emotion building in my throat. "Yes."

He turned his face toward the repeated spherical blasts of colored balls that filled the night sky. The music drifted off as the last burst of fireworks left a visible trail of red sparks.

Then nothing.

The sky was dark again and the only sound was my breathing.

"Some men don't know how lucky they are," Sergio said.

Nine

....

When I arrived at the B&B, most of the rooms were dark. I entered mine to find Becca asleep in bed wearing her pink-leopard eye mask and snoring lightly. The first thing I did was check my cell phone. Reception in the town of Jaca had been spotty, but at the B&B it was pretty consistent. I saw that I'd missed a call from Scott's mom, Bernice.

I dialed her back but got voice mail.

I decided to leave a message for her, instructing her to call the B&B instead of my cell phone. No use risking missing another call due to bad reception.

Slipping off my clothes, I went to settle into bed, but saw a note card on my pillow. It was a cream-colored envelope with my name on it. My pulse raced as I ripped open the envelope.

I was hoping this was some secret communication

from Scott, instead it was a note from Cheryl, presumably the entire cast had gotten a "love note" from her.

Dear contestant,

You are to report to the lobby at eight a.m. sharp to receive instructions for your first challenge. Hope you get enough rest tonight. It's going to be a long haul . . .

Sincerely yours,
The executive producer of Expedition Improbable

I lay back in bed and pondered the "long haul" part of the note. Were they going to make us move something? Haul something somewhere?

I remembered Todd and Parker and how furious they'd been tonight. Had they formed an alliance? Certainly Cooper and Victoria seemed hot for each other, so it didn't seem that drastic of a leap to imagine the teams had agreed to pair up.

How far would they go to win?

Surely murder was out of the question, but could they have scared Scott off somehow?

I had mixed feelings about the entire email. It was hard to believe he would break up with me in that fashion. Even though we'd met on a reality TV show, I'd still thought we'd had something. How could he walk away from me so easily? And without even a good-bye.

Maybe I was just a fool.

But, instinct told me there was something wrong with his email. Something about the tone. It didn't seem like Scott.

Was he afraid?

What would scare him? I closed my eyes and imagined his face. He had strong, handsome features, and he wasn't someone that scared easily. Or at least he hadn't struck me that way. Had Cooper or Todd threatened him or someone he loved?

His mother, maybe . . . or . . . could Scott have been defending me somehow?

My heart ached. Did he love me?

Not if he'd run off like that, he didn't.

Morning came quickly, and when I woke up I saw that Becca had already left the room. This time I slipped on exactly what Kyle had selected for me. A violet top and cargo pants. If I knew him at all, the women would be decked out in jewel tones and the men in neutrals. So I needed to comply or I'd get read the riot act. At least the pants were roomy enough for me to stick a few essentials in the pockets: a Swiss army knife, ChapStick, and matches. I latched my paracord survival bracelet onto my wrist and made a quick restroom stop.

The halls were deserted and I worried that I was late. I rushed downstairs and found the cast nervously milling around the bar. The senora had left out a tray of pastries and fruit for us and was busy whipping up café con leches.

Dad waved me over, he looked fresh and rested and I instantly regretted staying out so late with Sergio.

"Hiya, pumpkin!" Dad said.

Next to Dad was Harris Carlson, the host of the show. Harris was busy chatting with the mother-and-son team, while Kyle primped DeeCee, applying some powder to her nose. He'd styled her fire-red hair so that it puffed out around her face and she looked like a lioness.

He nearly screamed when he saw me. "Ack! Did you even brush your hair?"

I turned away from him and snagged a pastry off the bar. "Don't be so obnoxious. My hair's fine." I wore a ball cap and had neatly pinned my hair underneath.

"I wouldn't know," he hissed.

Cheryl flew into the room with Becca trailing behind her.

"All right, listen up, folks," Cheryl said. "As you may know, one of the contestant teams has had to have a substitution, but, like they say in Tinseltown—the show must go on!"

There was a general mumbling from the cast as Cheryl introduced my dad. "So this morning," Cheryl continued, "we're going to take you in buses over to a hiking trail. Each team will have to hike to the top of the trail, where you'll find El Monasterio de San Juan de la Peña."

Cheryl butchered the Spanish so bad that the senora giggled from behind the bar.

Cheryl flashed her a look, then continued. "At the monastery, you'll find hidden clues for your next adventure. The crew is going to follow you with cameras: Each two-person team will be assigned one camera. They won't be able to assist you if you have questions. But, if you get injured and you need help, we'll medevac you out. I want you all to remember that if that happens, your time will be deducted or you'll be immediately disqualified. Any questions?"

"Yeah!" Todd puffed up his chest. "Why isn't she disqualified then?" He pointed an angry finger in my direction.

Cheryl shook her head. "Scott left the show before filming began—"

"We filmed!" Parker complained. "We did all that stuff in the studio in Hollywood for the promos."

Cheryl waved a hand at Todd and Parker, completely dismissing them. "Doesn't count. The competition hadn't begun. Today's hike counts," she said.

Cooper, the NFL player, stared at her. "A hike? You know hiking's a little bit harder for us big guys," he joked.

"Are we allowed to help each other?" Todd asked.

Cheryl studied him. "You mean alliances?"

Todd shrugged. "Maybe."

Cheryl smiled. "Darling, this is reality TV. You can help anyone you like *and* you can refuse to help, too. The meaner you all are, the better. We live on ratings!"

I shuddered. Cheryl was actually encouraging them to be nasty. I groaned into Dad's shoulder.

Suddenly, Cheryl put on her headset and retreated from view. The cameramen shouldered their equipment and the lights from the cameras blinded us. We were live.

We made our way out of the B&B toward the same small bus that had brought us into Jaca. The sun was already out, heating up the ground. The day was going to be a scorcher. I was glad for my hat and pulled it down on my forehead as we piled into the buses.

"I'm so glad I'm an avid hiker," Dad teased.

Although Dad was very active on the farm, he wasn't exactly a mountain man. I knew he was tough and he'd be able to deal readily with the heat.

"I'm glad you're with me, Dad."

He patted my knee. "I'm always with you, honey."

The bus dropped us off at the base of the mountain. We were instructed to get into a large circle while Harris explained the rules to us.

"Welcome everyone to *Expedition Improbable*!" Harris boomed in his made-for-TV voice. "Where nothing can stop you but yourself!" He launched into a brief introduction of the teams, then said, "At the top of this hike, you will find a medieval monastery, one that is rumored to have protected the Holy Grail. At the monastery, you will find a clue that will lead you to something special. Only one team will be able to obtain the artifact. If you do, you will be granted a two-hour head start in tomorrow's expedition."

The teams all responded favorably, oohing and aahing at Harris's announcement.

"The other teams will need to obtain a key in order to continue. Remember! Tomorrow you'll begin the next challenge with whatever time advantage you secure today, so if you end up in third place, say fifteen minutes behind the second-place team, then tomorrow you'll start fifteen minutes *after* the second-place team."

Everyone groaned.

Harris smiled wickedly at our reaction, then clapped his hands and said, "I'm sorry to say, this is an elimination round. The last team to cross the finish line will be eliminated."

We were each given a knapsack with some food and water. Dad and I fussed over which pack was heavier. He took the dark one, which had the water bottles in it, and handed me the lighter pack. Before we even got the packs on our backs, we realized that we were suddenly alone and in last place.

"Holy night, Dad! Did everyone just take off?" I asked.

We watched the backside of the mother-and-son team as they climbed up a switchback and disappeared from view.

Our cameraman was Miguel. He'd been camping with us in the Pyrenees on the night Scott had left. Miguel hoisted the camera on his shoulder and turned on the microphone. He winked at me to indicate that he'd be capturing our every word from now on.

We headed toward the trail and began our trek, Dad giving me encouraging little tidbits along the way. "Don't worry, Georgia. It's not a sprint, it's a marathon," he said.

"Thanks for the cliché, Dad," I said.

Dad laughed. "That one is straight from the *Farmer's Almanac*."

I snorted.

We grew quiet as we ascended through the switchback. The trail was beautiful as it wound its way up quickly enough that my ears popped. We had vistas of the Spanish countryside. It was dry in northern Spain at this time of the year and I longed to take a water break, but since we hadn't even caught up with the mother-and-son team, we continued steadily on.

Finally after what seemed like an hour, I asked, "How long is this trail?"

"I don't know." Dad chuckled. "Judging by that team of producers, they probably gave us a day hike!"

"Right," I mumbled. Cheryl would do anything to make sure the show succeeded.

In the quiet of the hike my thoughts returned to Scott and the murdered woman. Who was she and what had she been doing so near to our campsite? It felt as if she should in some way be connected with either the cast or crew, otherwise it seemed too big of a coincidence.

What had I learned so far about the cast?

Todd and Parker were ultracompetitive. Cooper and Todd both had criminal records, and Victoria had a connection to ETA.

Did any of the facts add up to murder?

Miguel stopped for a moment to adjust his camera, but quickly sprinted up ahead of us, to get a shot of us climbing up the trail.

What about the crew?

Miguel had been there that night. I knew nothing about him. Could he be part of ETA?

Sweat dripped down my forehead and in desperation I called out to Miguel, "How long is this hike?"

Dad admonished me. "He's not going to tell you. They're not supposed to talk to us or offer any support."

"Well, he's not supposed to anyway but sometimes people break the rules," I said.

Dad chuckled. "Don't count on it. He'd have to deal with Cheryl if he broke the rules and even if he doesn't know her like we do, he's probably seen enough to know that he doesn't want to get on her bad side."

After another hour of hiking we decided to take a break and sat on some boulders near a small creek. From his knapsack, Dad pulled out our water bottles. I rustled through my pack and found granola bars and apples. We ate in silence for a moment. I took off my cap and dipped it in the cool creek water.

"Do you think anybody has reached the top yet?" Dad asked.

"I don't know," I said. "Honestly, I thought that mother-and-son team would trail behind us but she's as spry as a chicken." I chuckled.

"I hope that's not a crack at me," Dad said, a serious look on his face.

I laughed. "No, Dad, you're in great shape. It's a marathon not a sprint."

He laughed.

After our snack we proceeded up the hill. We crossed a waterfall and two streams and still no sign of the monastery. Two hours later we stopped at a lookout point to take another break.

"I can't believe we're not at the top yet," Dad said. "I had no idea what the heck I was signing up for!"

Miguel, the cameraman, mumbled something.

I looked at him, hopefully.

He held up a solitary figure.

"One more hour?" Dad whined.

I laughed. "I thought you weren't supposed to help us."

Miguel put the finger to his lips.

"We promise we won't tell," I said.

Dad took a swig from his water bottle and said, "You better not tell Cheryl. She would break his legs."

Miguel took the camera off his shoulder and gave us a briefing on the trail ahead.

"It's not so steep now. Soon you will see El Monasterio de San Juan de la Peña. It's fantastic. Part of the church is carved in the stone of the great cliff! *San Juan de la Peña* means 'Saint John of the Cliff.'"

"Wow," Dad said, as he overlooked the vista. "We sure ain't in Cottonwood anymore, Georgia."

I poked his back. "Not funny, now let's get going, old man."

After about another mile, we finally arrived at the monastery. The monastery itself was breathtaking, built beneath a huge rock and hanging off the cliff. But even more amazing was that the other teams, which we thought were so far ahead of us, were all standing at the entrance looking hot and bewildered.

Cooper, who seemed to be the only one happy to see us, bounded over to me. "Georgia, I'm so glad you're here."

"Why?" I asked.

"Because you'll be able to figure out where the clue is hidden."

They all looked at me.

"You mean you've all been up here and haven't found the clue yet?" I asked.

"That's right," he said.

"How long have you been up here?" Dad asked.

"A long time," DeeCee complained. Her lioness hair was now flat against her face and dripping in sweat. I was suddenly glad for my ball cap.

Dad leaned in to me. "Uh, isn't there a tortoise-and-hare story in that almanac of mine?" he teased. "Now might be a fine time to talk about alliances!"

Cooper overhead Dad and laughed, his body shaking and jerking in that way he had that made it impossible to keep a straight face.

I ignored everyone and sat down on the cool stone and thought. Where would Becca hide a clue? Because it was certain that she had hidden it or had arranged to have it hidden. We all entered the monastery and toured around. The cloister contained a series of biblical scenes that were arranged in chronological sequence. The stone halls and passageways were filled with marble and stucco medallions recalling historic battles. The second floor had a royal pantheon of the kings of Aragon and Navarre.

The other teams began to get bored with me and realized I didn't have the inside info they thought I had. Everyone started to head in different directions, fatigue and exacerbation between the pairs mounting.

Dad and I continued to meander down one of the stone corridors.

Dad pressed me. "Well? What do you think? Where's the clue?"

I leaned against the cool wall rock, pressing my forehead against it. "I can't think, Dad. I have no idea."

He patted my back, "Don't worry, honey. We'll find it. Not even Cheryl or Becca is smarter than us."

Exhaustion bore down on my shoulders, but I smiled despite myself. "That's right, Daddy."

In one of the other rooms, voices were carrying and sounded like the beginnings of an argument. Dad stepped away from me and peered into the room.

"What it is?" I asked him.

He retreated from the doorway as if stung. "Let's not get involved in other people's business."

"Who's in there, Dad?"

He shrugged. "It's Todd and Parker. I just thought . . . I heard something strange . . . they mentioned Scott."

A chill crept down my spine.

Why would they be discussing Scott?

I crossed over to the other room, but it was now empty. They'd left through a different exit.

When I returned to where Dad was he asked, "Is there a rule we can't split up?"

"No," I said. "Only that we both need to cross the finish line together."

"Right, right," he said. "So why don't I start down the trail now?"

"What do you mean?"

"I'll hike on ahead of you. It takes me longer. You find the clue, then hike down and catch up with me."

"No, Dad, it's a bad idea. What if the clue tells us to go in a different direction?"

He clucked at me. "Georgia there's no other way down the mountain but the way we came."

"Are you sure?" I asked.

He nodded.

We looked at Miguel for confirmation. He touched his nose and lowered his eyes in agreement with us.

Dad and Miguel tore off down the mountain. Meanwhile, I paced the monastery, fidgeting with my paracord bracelet. I unraveled it as I paced and reviewed the note from the night before in my head.

Long haul.

Or long hall . . .

Suddenly, I recalled one long hallway with the stucco medallions, each one depicting a historic battle. I raced toward the hallway. That was it! I was sure of it.

I found the hallway and looked at each stone; on the fourth one I saw it. A picture of the Last Supper, Jesus holding up a chalice.

The Holy Grail!

In the painting Jesus was standing on the edge of a cliff, under a huge rock. He was standing in the same location as the huge rock of the monastery south wall.

I raced outside toward the rock.

Footsteps pounded behind me. "You know where it is, don't you?" a voice screamed.

It was Victoria.

She was in hot pursuit, but there was no way she was beating me to the chalice. We raced over to the wall.

"Tell me what you know!" she shouted.

I ignored her, my eyes raking the wall. I saw it then. A small box made of stone, cleverly hidden from view, camouflaged between the rock and the edge of the cliff. I dove for the box and pried it open.

Inside was a replica of the chalice along with four golden keys. Victoria lunged at me. I grabbed the chalice and threw the box at her.

"Give it to me!" she yelled.

"No," I shouted, turning away from her.

She tugged on my arm while I batted her away. She grabbed at the paracord rope bracelet I held in my hand and it unraveled between us. She clutched at the cord and used it to whip at my face.

"Stop it!" I yelled, backing away from her.

"Give me the chalice!" she screamed.

"You're acting crazy!" I shouted.

She lunged for the chalice and I leapt backward, losing my footing on the dirt trail. Suddenly the rock wall fell away from me and I had the sickening sensation of falling through the air.

Ten
·················

EXT. WOODS DAY

Helen is looking into the camera, her sandy-colored hair is pulled back away from her face and her skin is radiant. She is dressed in a bright azure top that accentuates her blue eyes. She is standing in front of one of the tall trees that lines the perimeter of the Monastery.

HELEN
(*smiles*) Hello! I'm Helen Burke, one of the contestants on *Expedition Improbable*. I'm competing with my son, Eric. (*She motions at someone to join her.*) I'm so excited because we were the first team to make it up to the monastery, but that's only the

first leg of the competition. We still have
to figure out the clue. *(Eric walks into
the shot and she puts her arm around him.)*
My son, Eric!

ERIC
(waving at the camera) Hello, America!

HELEN
Do you have any clue about the clue?

ERIC
No. But we better figure it out or I'm
afraid we're going to end up in last place.
And, I know that Georgia already sent her
dad back down the trial. I'm wondering if
you want to do the same.

HELEN
(standing straighter at attention) Gordon,
that hunk of a man, has started down
already? This might be my chance! *(She
smoothes her hair with one hand.)* I better
hurry!
*(Shouts and screams are heard from off
camera.)*

ERIC (O.S.)
(turning in the direction of the noise) What
was that?

(Helen and Eric run in the direction of the commotion, the camera follows them, the frame shaking and jostling intensely.)

screamed out, clutching the paracord in my hand for dear life. The cord tightened and I smashed against the side of the cliff, the granite rocky edges of the surface cutting my face and knocking the wind out of me.

My hand clamped onto the cord fiercely, my heart hammering out of my chest.

Oh, my God! I was suspended above a free fall of over four hundred meters.

Victoria screamed. "Georgia, don't let go!"

I craned my neck upward only to see Victoria's face over the edge of the cliff and a huge dark Panavision Primo camera pointing at me.

Dear Lord!

I was going to fall to my death and Cheryl would end up in ratings heaven.

Cooper appeared next to Victoria. "Girl, don't let go!"

I was paralyzed with fear and couldn't even squeak out a response. Was one even necessary? I mean, of course, I wasn't going to let go!

Cooper grabbed hold of the paracord, thrusting my body against the face of the cliff again.

I screamed.

"Hold on, baby girl!" he yelled. "I'm going to haul you up. Lord! Give me strength!"

"Can you grab a toehold?" Victoria screamed out.

Diana Orgain

I tried to press my foot against the cliff, but granite and gravel slid under my shoe.

Oh, no, I was going to cause my own avalanche.

"Don't! Don't do that," Cooper warned.

"Pass me up the chalice," Victoria said.

I suddenly realized that the chalice was locked in the grip of my right hand. More faces appeared over the side of the cliff: the mother-and-son team, Double D, Parker, Todd, and a whole slew of cameras. There were loud screams and gasps from the ladies, while the men generally shouted out commands, like "Get away from the cliff!"

"Don't worry. I got you," Cooper said, his voice calm. "I ain't never dropped the ball, girl. You know that? Once these hands have the ball, ol' Coop goes right into the end zone. That's a fact!"

I stared up at his huge hands. They were the size of frying pans; callused and strong. I don't think I'd ever seen anything more beautiful in my life.

"Pass me up the chalice," Victoria said again.

"Vicky!" Parker said.

She shrugged. "I'm only trying to help!"

Cooper hauled me up, inch by inch, until I was in reach of Parker and Todd, both of whom grabbed my wrists and pulled me over the edge. I landed in a clump on top of Cooper, who wrapped his arms around me and laughed in his hearty jiggling way.

"Lord Almighty, in Heaven above!" Cooper said. "I ain't never dropped the ball and I ain't never dropped a girl!" He planted a sloppy wet kiss on my forehead and whooped out. "I saved your life!"

Trembling, I rolled off of Cooper. "Thank you, Cooper! Thank you. I owe you."

"Well, great! You owe us! You can give us the chalice then," Todd said.

"What?" Victoria screamed. "If anything, I want it! Parker helped pull her up, too!"

"Don't be crazy, girl," Cooper said to Victoria. "Georgia got the chalice fair and square. How can you all be fighting over it, when she almost died!"

DeeCee and Daisy suddenly scampered over to the box and grabbed a golden key. They screeched out in delight and tore off toward the dirt trail. Their cameraman lurched into action behind them.

Helen from the mother-and-son team screamed out, "Come on, Eric!" She rushed to the box, pulled out another key and then they tore off after Double D, their cameraman in tow.

Victoria looked around frantically. "Hey! Where's your dad? Did you send him down ahead? That's cheating!"

"It's not cheating," Cooper said. "That's smart!"

"Is it alliance-with-Georgia time?" Parker asked Victoria.

Victoria gave me the fiercest dirty look imaginable. "Hell no," she spat.

Parker sighed, then took a key from the box and waved Victoria toward the dirt trail that led to the finish line.

"Come on, come on!" Todd yelled, as he picked up the last key from the box. "Let's go," he said to Cooper.

Cooper helped me to my feet. When I stood my ankle throbbed.

Oh, no!

I must have twisted my ankle when I lost my footing off the cliff moments ago.

Todd started down the trail. Their cameraman was stuck in the middle, filming Todd as he left, then panning over to capture Cooper and me.

Todd yelled back at us, over his shoulder, "Hurry up, Cooper!"

Cooper noticed my limp. "What is it? Are you hurt? Hold up, Todd."

"You got to be kidding me!" Todd complained. "What? You're going to want to stick around for a medevac for her now? Leave her behind or we're gonna be in dead-last place and you know what that means!" With that, Todd spun on his heels and disappeared out of sight.

Cooper put an arm on my shoulder. "Lean on me, girl. If I have to, I'll carry you down the hill."

"You can't do that Cooper. You're already in last place. Let me give you the chalice. I'll have them call for medev—"

"Wha'?" Cooper screeched. "What you gonna call for a medevac for, when you got ol' Coop! Come on, girl. You know how many training runs I did in the NFL with three-hundred-pound men on my back? Why, a little nothing waif of a girl like you, ain't gonna slow down ol' Coop."

He swooped me over a shoulder and started jogging down the trail.

Oh, my goodness!

There was no way we'd make it down the six-hour hike like this, I thought. But when Cooper showed no signs of stopping, I revised my initial thought. There was no way *I'd* make it down the six-hour hike like this.

"You've got to put me down," I said, finally.

"Nah. I'm good," he said.

We were closing in on Todd.

"Put me down!" I insisted.

"No," Cooper said. "Not until we get in front of the others."

Silently and without Cooper noticing, I lifted the flap on his knapsack and dropped the chalice into it.

Todd looked over his shoulder as we approached. "I should have known," he said, snidely. He pointed ahead. "The rest of the gang isn't that far ahead of us. I can hear them every time I hit a switchback.

On the next turn, we caught up with Parker and Victoria. They were silent when we joined them, although Victoria gave off a serious hate vibe.

We stopped to rest and Cooper finally put me down.

"I'm feeling better now," I lied. "Thank you for helping me."

Cooper gave me a warm smile and winked.

We all started off together down the trial and finally caught sight of Double D, Helen and Eric, and my Dad. They were trotting along slowly, looking worse for the wear.

DeeCee grumbled when she saw us. "I'm so sorry, Daisy, but I have to rest!"

Double D stopped by a creek to wet their hair and cool down. Helen and Eric continued walking slowly, but Dad ran toward me.

"Georgia! Oh, my goodness!" He embraced me. "I heard about your near miss."

I filled Dad in as we walked. We were all in a clump now, except for the mother-son team and Double D, who were lagging behind. As we proceeded down the trail, they dropped out of site.

The heat of the day had receded and we hurried to make it down to the end of the trail before dark. Since we were with the others I hadn't had a chance to tell Dad that I had given the chalice to Cooper, but I was sure he wouldn't mind.

In the distance we saw the crew bus and a blue tarp laid out. Painted on the tarp was a bull's-eye and standing on top of the tarp was Harris.

Cooper and Todd took off in a full sprint. Victoria and Parker followed suit, but weren't as quick. Dad eyed me. "Are you in pain, honey?"

I nodded. "I need an ice pack and pain relievers in a big way, but I'll live."

"Well, we certainly don't have to run," Dad said. "We'll have a two-hour advantage tomorrow, and Lord knows, I need it—"

"Dad, I gave the chalice to Cooper. I'm sorry."

Up ahead we saw Cooper and Todd reach the finish

line first. Moments later Parker entered the bull's-eye circle and Victoria trailed.

Dad smiled and grabbed my hand. "You don't have be sorry, honey. I'm so proud of you."

We walked the rest of the way in silence and stepped into the bull's eye.

Harris, the host, clapped his hands. "Georgia! Gordon! Welcome to the finish line. I'm happy to say you are the third team to arrive and are therefore safe from elimination. However, I understand you have the chalice, so you'll enjoy a two-hour head start tomorrow!"

"I don't have the chalice," I said.

The others, who were standing off to the side, suddenly came to attention.

"Did you drop it?" Harris asked. He attempted to look concerned, but with all the Botox he'd had, his face didn't quite cooperate. "I understand you had a little excitement after finding the chalice."

"I didn't drop it," I said. "I gave it to Cooper."

Victoria shrieked and looked ready to cry.

"What are you talking about, girl?" Cooper asked, surprised.

"Without your help, I wouldn't be standing here, Coop. Check your bag."

Cooper shrugged off his knapsack and peeked inside. "Well, I'll be!"

Harris clapped his hands again, this time repeatedly in unrestrained host delight. "Why, how *very* generous!"

Out of the corner of my eye, I noticed Cheryl preening. She'd be happy about today. She'd use the clip of me hanging off the cliff to garner new audiences far and wide. My giving Cooper the chalice was icing on the cake to her.

Dad and I moved to join the others by the side of the tarp and waited to see who would emerge from the dirt trail next. The sun began to set as we waited. On the side of the crew bus was a red clock that kept track of the time. So far the other groups were seventy-two minutes behind us and counting.

Finally, we heard voices and footsteps. From the trail emerged the mother-and-son team and Double D. All were struggling. DeeCee and Daisy had their arms linked and were running together as if in a sack race. Helen hobbled along, looking like she had blisters on her blisters. Eric trotted along the quickest, but still looked exhausted. Both teams moved forward neck and neck, screaming at each other.

Eric grabbed hold of his mom to try to usher her along, but he tripped her up and she fell.

There was a loud gasp from the cast. We knew all too well how exhausted Helen was.

Eric scooped her up, but DeeCee and Daisy crossed to the finish line.

They collapsed onto the tarp with Harris clapping his hands in childish delight. "DeeCee and Daisy, welcome to the finish line. I'm happy to say you are the fourth team to arrive and are therefore safe from elimination. You will begin tomorrow's challenge exactly"—he glanced at his watch for dramatic effect, although we were all keenly aware of the red clock that hung on the crew bus—"one hour, seventeen minutes, and ten seconds after team three begins."

DeeCee squeezed Daisy's hand. "One hour! See, we're not all that far behind!"

"Which will be exactly three hours, twenty-one minutes and twenty-seven seconds after team one begins," Harris clarified.

DeeCee's shoulders dropped and Daisy buried her head in her hands.

Helen and Eric lumbered into the circle.

Harris put on his serious host face. "Helen, Eric, We're so happy you made it down the trail safely. But I'm sorry to say, you are the fifth team to arrive and are therefore eliminated."

Helen and Eric embraced each other. Helen was in tears and kept apologizing to Eric.

My heart sunk. Even though I hadn't really had time to get to know them, I knew losing was tough. And likely Eric would have enjoyed winning the prize money to help welcome his new baby that was on the way.

"You can take a moment and say you're good-byes," Harris said.

Eric said, "Thank you, everyone. We've really enjoyed the experience. Don't feel bad for us, please. My wife's at home and she's expecting our first baby.

It's really a blessing to be able to go home and be with my family."

Helen looked at Eric and squeezed his hand. "You're right, honey. You're so right. We have to get out of here while we can. What with all we've seen in the short time we've been here, we're lucky to be alive!"

Eleven

....

I fell into an exhausted heap on the bus and tried to tune out Cooper's over-the-top reenactment of our adventure. As far I was concerned, he was my MVP and was entitled to any and all hero worship.

When we arrived at the bed-and-breakfast, everyone piled out of the bus and into the bar. I wanted to make a beeline for my room, but ran into Sergio waiting for me at the bar. "Georgia, do you have a minute? I'd like to talk to you."

Apprehension jolted through me, the exhaustion I'd been feeling only moments ago, evaporated. "Yes! What is it? Have you located Scott?"

Sergio shook his head.

Suddenly the senora who owned the B&B scurried out from the kitchen, a cordless phone in her hand. "¡Ay! ¡Señorita Georgia, teléfono!"

My heart raced. The only person calling me here would be Scott's mother. Could she have had news from him?

I turned to Sergio. "Excuse me. I have to take that call. It's probably Scott's mother."

He waved and nodded, indicating I should take the call. The senora handed me the phone and pointed in the direction of the small room that Sergio and Montserrat had set up as a makeshift office. I crossed the dining hall and entered the quiet room, but when Sergio followed me, I regretted telling him it was Scott's mother on the phone.

I covered the phone's mouthpiece with my palm. "Uh . . . can you give me a minute?" I asked Sergio.

He frowned. "I have some questions for her, too."

I hesitated. I wanted to speak with Bernice in private, but I knew it was probably important for Sergio to speak with her, too. I nodded, then put the receiver to my ear.

"Hi, Bernice."

"Georgia!" The older woman said, "So good to hear your voice. I got your message. How's the show going? Is Scott giving you problems? You know, sometimes he's just like his father was—"

"Bernice, have you heard from Scott?"

"Heard from him? No, what do you mean? That boy doesn't call me. I'm just glad that you two hooked up, otherwise I'd never have news from him," she said.

I knew that wasn't true, Scott called his mother several times a week. But I also understood she would have liked to talk to him every hour. Sergio quirked an eyebrow at me, as if hoping I'd report Bernice's every word to him.

Instead, I turned my back to him, in an effort to get some privacy.

"Bernice, Scott left the show. He walked off the set the other night. He didn't say anything to me, but then he sent an email to my dad saying it was over between us."

Bernice clucked. "Over between you? Why, that no-good . . . He's just like his father—" Her voice broke off and she choked back a sob.

"Do you have any idea where he could have gone? I'm worried sick about him."

"No," she whispered.

"No," I repeated, more or less for Sergio's benefit.

"You could ask that girl," Bernice said suddenly. "Maybe he went to visit her."

My stomach dropped.

What girl?

I bit my lip and waited for Bernice to continue.

After a moment, Bernice said, "There was a girl in Spain he was interested in, way back when. It was nothing serious. Not really. But I know they were still in touch and he got pretty close to her when he was writing that book."

The room seemed to spin and I grabbed for the office chair that was near me.

Sergio made a face, unhappy with my silence. "*Que?*" he asked.

I held up a hand to wave him away and sat in the chair.

"It was nothing serious," Bernice insisted, but her voice got high-pitched and I doubted her sincerity. "He visited her a few times, that's all. Maybe he needed to see her one last time."

"I understand," I said, although I didn't.

Why wouldn't Scott have told me he'd been to Spain before?

Why had he been secretive about a past relationship?

"Do you remember her name?" I asked, fearful of the answer.

Please, God, don't say Annalise Rodriguez.

I pressed a hand against my temple. If Bernice spit out the name of the dead woman, I thought my head might split open.

"Uh . . ." She hesitated. "Oh, my memory fails me sometimes. I used to have the best memory for details and things. I could recite all of Shakespeare's sonnets, but now. Pfft, I'm lucky I remember to take out the trash, you know, honey? Anyway, even if I did know her name what good would that do? You can chase the boy down, honey, but if he's not ready to commit . . . well, some men aren't meant for—"

"Was it *Annalise Rodriguez?*"

At the mention of the dead woman's name, Sergio stiffened.

"Annalise? Now, let's see. Let me think. An-na-li-se Rod-ri-guez," she said slowly to herself.

My breath caught.

"I don't think so," Bernice said. There was so much hesitation in her voice, it was little consolation. After a moment she said, "I'm sure I can find her name somewhere, if I look around a little."

"Could you?" I asked. "It's important." A thought struck me. "Bernice, what book was he working on when he was in Spain?"

Sergio said, "The one he published under a pen name."

"What?" I felt stunned for a moment. The headache that had been threatening suddenly burst through and my temples were on fire. "Scott doesn't use a pen name," I muttered.

"What's that, honey?" Bernice asked.

"Did Scott use a pen name?" I asked.

"Oh, yeah, of course," Bernice said. "Didn't you know? Scott writes under the name Matthew Barrett . . ."

Matthew Barrett?

Matthew Barrett was one of the top thriller writers in the U.S. He sold millions of books each year, yet Scott was broke. Or that's what he'd told me. I felt like my world was crumbling in on itself.

Bernice continued chatting along, ". . . he published an entire thriller series under that name. In fact, the book he was working on when he went to Spain was *Spanish Moon*, the first one in that series about that separatist group they have up there. What's their name?"

ETA.

Oh, no.

Scott had been researching ETA on a trip to Spain!

Sergio watched me. He frowned. "You didn't know Scott had a pen name?"

"Anyway, honey," Bernice said. "Don't let that boy get you too upset. He'll figure out soon enough what a jewel he's lost and then he'll come crawling back. Although, his father never did figure out—"

"Bernice," I interrupted. There was only so much I could take. I couldn't listen to her recount tales about her failed marriage.

Why did I ever think love would work out for me?

"Thank you so much for all the information. Please call me back if you remember the girl's name."

"Oh, I will, honey. Don't you worry! Chin up! And if Scott does come begging for forgiveness, tell him to call his old ma!"

I hung up before Sergio could ask her any questions. My head was buzzing and I felt nauseous. I needed time to regroup before Sergio started grilling me. I buried my head between my knees and took a few deep breaths.

Sergio remained quiet and watched me sympathetically for a moment, then asked, "What did she tell you about Scott's time in Spain. Do you know who he visited here?"

"She couldn't recall the woman's name. She's going to search for it and call me back."

Sergio looked at me, an unreadable expression on his face. "You'll give me her name as soon as you have it," he said.

"Of course," I lied.

Nothing made sense anymore, but I knew I needed time to sort through things before handing the Spanish police any information that could damage Scott. Whether Scott was a liar or not, he wasn't a killer. Of that I was sure . . .

Wasn't I?

Ugh! I was always one step behind.

"What do you know about Scott's politics?" Sergio asked.

"I suppose I didn't really know Scott one way or the other," I said, standing. "We didn't talk politics."

Sergio laughed. "That's difficult to believe."

"Really? Why?"

"In Spain everyone talks politics. What else is there to talk about?"

I reached for the door, but Sergio blocked my path.

"Did he know anybody in Spain who would take him across the French border?"

"Not that I know of."

But that wasn't saying much.

"We've checked the airport, bus stations, and hotels in the area. He hasn't used his passport. So if he left the country, he didn't do it legally." Sergio clapped his hands together. "Enough business talk. Are you going to the fiestas tonight?"

"Fiestas? There's still more fiestas?" I asked.

He laughed. "Oh, the fiestas in Spain last a week. We can't get anything done in a day."

"I thought the fiestas were yesterday because it was the first Friday of the month."

He smiled. "Yes! Exactly! And today is the first Saturday."

I chuckled despite myself. A few minutes ago, I'd been ready to collapse into bed after that tortuous hike, but now that my world had been turned upside down yet again, going to see a few fireworks and drinking a couple of *sangrías* sounded like a better option.

Sergio reached for the door and swung it open. Montserrat was in the doorway and peeked her head in, startling us both.

"Sergio, I need to speak to you immediately," she said.

Sergio put a hand on my lower back and ushered me out the door. "Excuse me, Georgia. *Nos vemos*," he said.

On my way out of the office, Montserrat passed me with a smug little smile on her face.

Hmm. What had that been about?

I crossed the dining hall to the bar, which was empty except for Dad.

"Who was that?" Dad asked about Montserrat.

"She's on the search-and-rescue team," I replied.

"Maybe she has news," he asked.

"Maybe so." Although I hoped it wasn't a ploy to get Sergio away. Did Montserrat have the hots for him? Did she think that I posed a threat?

Well, I certainly wasn't ready to date anybody until I knew for sure what was happening with Scott and even then I needed time to heal. I tried to push the thought of Sergio out of my mind.

Becca and Cheryl appeared next to us, both were dressed in white and red, ready for the evening's festivities.

"What did Scott's mom say to you?" Dad asked.

"Has she heard from Scott?" Becca asked.

I held up my hands before they could bombard me with questions.

"I'll catch you all up on everything later. Right now I need to shower." I turned on my heel, but Cheryl stopped me.

"When do you think we'll be able to leave?" she asked. "I have a show to run, you know."

"What do you mean?" I asked.

"We're being held here in Jaca," Becca said.

"Held?" Dad asked.

"We've been detained," Cheryl said. "Sure, we're not in jail. But the police aren't allowing us to leave the country."

Dad frowned. "Why's that?"

"Because we were camping near where the woman was found," I said. "The police suspect one of us."

I cringed as I recalled how irate Victoria had become over the chalice earlier in the afternoon. With a temper like that, certainly she was capable of bashing in someone's skull. Had she known Annalise from her previous travels to Spain?

And what about Parker and Todd, they'd been ready to attack me last night at the fiestas.

"Don't you have an influence with that cop?" Cheryl pressed.

"No—"

"I mean, he has the complete hots for you, Georgia, use those feminine wiles," Cheryl said.

Geez, did nothing get past Miss Barracuda?

I shrugged. "I'm not really itching to leave Jaca."

Cheryl smirked. "Of course you're not."

My reasons weren't what Cheryl imagined. If I stayed

in Jaca, it would be easier to find Scott, because as Sergio said, Scott hadn't left the area. He was likely hiding out somewhere, but where and from what?

Also, the thought of leaving the area without Scott was unbearable. There was no way I could leave until I got to the bottom of it all.

Cheryl clapped her hands at Dad and me. "Come on. Come on! Let's get out to those fiestas. I didn't get a chance to dance last night, but tonight's my night!"

My second wind died a swift death. The idea of dancing all night was really out of the question for me. My feet ached and I was exhausted.

"I'm too tired," I said. "I think I'll pass—"

Cheryl pulled on my arm. "Nonsense! I heard there's a medieval jousting festival. And an archery competition and everything."

I moaned. "Oh, no."

"Is that supposed to give you ideas for tomorrow?" Dad asked.

Cheryl laughed. "Actually no, but I am a great shot. I wanted to show off for you."

Becca put an arm around me and squeezed. "Come on, G. Go get ready. It'll be fun!"

The door to the makeshift office creaked open and Sergio and Montserrat approached.

Cheryl snapped her fingers at Sergio. "Excuse me. When do you think we'll be able to leave? I have to schedule the next contest for the show and that was supposed to be in France."

"France?" Sergio asked, a look of disdain crossed his face. "Why do you want to go to France?"

Cheryl frowned. "Well, the gist of the show is to feature a variety of locations. You know get the armchair traveler excited about visiting each place."

"Armchair travelers don't actually travel," I countered.

Cheryl whisked away my comment with a sweep of her hand. "You know what I mean. We need to showcase a variety of cultures."

"You can always make it look like we're somewhere else," I said. "If we can get out to the beach and film the Mediterranean, you can use a little Hollywood magic and we can all pretend we're in France or Italy."

Dad and Becca laughed, but Sergio looked downright horrified.

"Why?" Sergio asked. "There is plenty of culture right here in Jaca." He turned to Becca, seemingly finding her a little more sympathetic than Cheryl. "You know, there is a citadel." He began to enumerate each site on his fingers: "The Romanesque cathedral San Juan, the monastery of the Benedictines, the hermitage of Sarsa, the Bridge of San Miguel, the fifteenth-century Torre del Reloj." He paused. "In fact, there is a medieval painting in town, a mural, that was recently vandalized. The town is trying to raise money to restore it. It's a very significant painting . . . Your show could bring awareness to this issue. Help us raise funds to restore—"

"Sounds fascinating," Cheryl interrupted. "But when can we go to France?"

Sergio wrinkled his nose and Montserrat shook her head.

Now it was Cheryl's turn to count on her fingers. "They've got the Eiffel Tower, Arc de Triomphe, Notre Dame cathedral, the Louvre—"

Sergio, obviously not one to be bullied by Cheryl, held up a hand to stop her midsentence. "They also have the French!"

Montserrat threw her head back and filled the room with a hearty laugh. "*Sí, sí. ¡Los francés!*"

Cheryl took umbrage at their affront. "What do you have against the French? I like the French!"

Sergio and Montserrat only laughed and turned to leave. Montserrat walked a pace ahead of Sergio and he looked over his shoulder at me. "*Nos vemos*, Georgia." Then with a wink, he said, "Maybe I'll see you at the church later tonight."

Twelve

....

Despite the evening hour, the ground still held an insufferable heat and even though I was exhausted, I'd agreed to go to the fiestas with my Dad, Cheryl, and Becca. I felt as though Dad and Becca had taken it as their personal mission to keep me distracted from thoughts about Scott. Cheryl, I'm fairly certain, just wanted to dance and drink the night away.

We'd joined most of the cast and crew in the area by the square. If possible, it seemed like there were even more people out tonight that there'd been the previous evening. I spotted Victoria dancing with Cooper. Her face became angry when she saw me, and she turned away.

Kyle was dancing with Becca, but she freed herself from him and shimmed closer to me. "Kyle and a bunch of us are going up to the grassy mound to watch the fireworks. Are you going to come or are you more interested in meeting up with Sergio and making your own fireworks?" She wiggled her eyebrows at me.

I hadn't really had an opportunity to brief her about Scott's pen name, but I knew she sensed my broken heart anyway.

"Nothing's going to happen between me and Sergio," I insisted.

She gave me a knowing smile and giggled anyway.

Cooper appeared by my side. "Are you going to dance? Or just pout?"

"I hadn't realized I was pouting," I said.

"Well you were, darling, and it's not becoming on such a pretty girl. When you're not smiling, it's practically a crime."

I fought the urge to grin. "I think your charms might be better served on Victoria or one of the Double D ladies."

Cooper made a face. "I like challenges."

A group of Spanish men, clearly ready to party until the sun appeared again, surrounded us. A bota bag was thrust into Cooper's hand while someone thumped him on the back screaming, "*¡Hombre, hombre!*"

Cooper didn't need much encouragement. He tossed his head back and raised his hand. A steady stream of red fluid flowed into his mouth. He passed the bag to me and I obliged the crowd, figuring it was the path of least resistance as I couldn't see them leaving me alone until I drank. I took a small sip and passed the bag to the bearded man standing next to me. I realized with a jolt it was Miguel, the local cameraman who had helped Dad and me during the day's competition.

He smiled warmly at me. "Are you having a good time, Georgia?"

I didn't see the need to be truthful, so I lied. "Yes."

What good would it do to tell him I was miserable? I wanted nothing more than to find Scott and try to figure out what had happened. Why had he lied to me about so much?

Could we start again?

A small woman with dark curly hair came up to Miguel. She snaked an arm around his waist and said, "*¿Vas a venir esta noche?*"

Miguel's smile fell away from his face and he straightened as if stung.

What had she just said to him?

At that moment I'd have given anything to understand Spanish. I searched my memories of my high school Spanish class. The only word I recognized was *noche.* "Night." Not very helpful.

"*Sí, nos vemos,*" Miguel said.

Nos vemos?

That meant "I'll see you later," so were they meeting somewhere tonight?

The woman seemed to take Miguel's words as dismissal and a scowl overtook her face. She turned as she dropped her arm from his waist and quickly got swept up in the crowd.

Miguel passed the bota bag back to Cooper, who was now talking to Todd.

I leaned into Miguel. "I didn't get a chance to thank you for helping me today."

He nodded at me, but he seemed antsy and turned to say something in a hushed tone to the man next to him. The man nodded aggressively in return.

Miguel patted my shoulder. "*Nos vemos mañana*, Georgia. I hope you enjoy yourself tonight."

Something about the way he was sneaking off put my senses on high alert. A moment ago, he'd been content to pass the bota bag around and now it seemed he couldn't get away from us fast enough.

A chill crept up my spine as I realized he was one of the only two Spaniards on the camping trip with us on the night that Annalise had been murdered.

Had he known Annalise?

Could he know where Scott was?

I followed him at a distance to the edge of the square, where I saw him meet up with another group of men. Nearby, my Dad and Cheryl were dancing to a folk song. Dad grabbed my arm as I approached.

"Dance with Cheryl. I need a break," he pleaded. "Do you think any of these bars serve anything stronger than wine?"

"Ack. Be careful what you wish for. We have to compete tomorrow and you need a clear head," I said. "You can't be drinking whiskey all night."

Dad looked wistful.

"Listen. I want to track someone but I don't want to be followed, if anyone asks about me, especially Sergio, can you distract him?"

"Wait a minute. Where are you going?" Dad said. "I don't want you to get into trouble."

I gripped his arm. "I can take care of myself, Dad. Please, if you don't help me, I'll have to create my own distraction by setting fire to one of these garbage bins."

Dad tsked at me, but he also knew I was usually good at following through on my threats. After a moment, he said, "I'll help you, but it doesn't mean I'm happy about it."

In the distance, I saw Miguel and the group of men he'd been chatting with peel away.

"He's getting ready to move. I gotta go." I slipped away from Dad and into the shadows of the dark alley.

I turned to glance behind me and saw a familiar figure approaching.

Sergio.

Dad intercepted him at the same time that Miguel and his gang left the alley. Excitement flooded my belly. The chase was on.

I followed Miguel at a safe distance. Luckily, tracking a suspect is "Police Work 101"—even the rubber-gun squads are trained to do it.

I actually was pretty good at tracking suspects. I remember surprising my professor at the academy. He'd told me that I'd stick out anywhere like a sore thumb, but the truth was I knew how to melt into the woodwork. You had to, growing up in the country. Animals don't take to sudden movements and it turns out neither do people you're tracking.

A breeze started to pick up and the noise from the fiesta was diminishing. Every other block, there was a small tavern where folks had spilled out on the sidewalk, enjoying the cool evening air. They'd call out to Miguel's group as they passed, but no one seemed to notice me.

Finally the group made a beeline into what looked like an abandoned building.

The group stopped in the doorway briefly, but then proceeded inside. Could I dare follow them?

I waited, and while I mulled it over, several more groups followed, all men. It didn't seem that anyone was stationed at the door. I decided to take my chances. If there was a doorman inside, I could pretend that I was a lost tourist.

It was dark inside and there was a long corridor illuminated by antique torchlights hanging from the walls. It was eerily quiet. I tiptoed through the corridor toward a winding staircase. There were lights at the bottom of the stairs and noise floated upward. As I approached the bottom, I could see a large heavy wooden door.

Oh goodness. What kind of clandestine gathering had I followed Miguel to?

Surely there would be a doorman on the other side of the door. Would they be angry that I'd followed them here? What was going on behind this door?

Common sense told me to retreat.

As soon as I turned to go, I heard voices coming from above. Footsteps echoed down the staircase.

Oh, Lord!

I was stuck, about to be found out.

Suddenly a group of people were upon me. Smiling Spanish faces gave me the "hail fellow well met" pat on the shoulder as they pushed past me through the wooden door into a crowded amphitheater.

A fiesta away from the fiesta?

Breathing a sigh of relief, I scanned the crowd, mostly men. Although there were a few women and I spotted the girl with dark wiry hair immediately. She approached Miguel and he kissed both her checks.

My heart dropped as I realized this was just another party. Nothing sinister going on here. No lead to Scott's whereabouts and Scott certainly was not in the crowd. Not that I'd expected to see him here, but I suppose I'd been hoping that Miguel could lead me to him.

I retreated to the exit and then saw the sign. On the wall, hanging in plain sight, was a banner of a snake wrapped around an ax on a black background.

The ETA logo.

The fiestas were still in full force when I rejoined our group, although I'd missed the fireworks and Sergio at the church. Instead, I found Dad and Sergio bellied up to a bar with three empty cocktail glasses in front of each of them. Dad's face lit up when he saw me.

"What do we have here?" I asked, thumping Dad on the back as way of greeting.

Sergio jumped up to his feet. "Georgia. Where have you been?"

Shrugging I said, "I took a little walk around town. Where's Cheryl?"

"Kyle loves to dance," Dad said. "Thank God. He's entertaining her. One more dance and I thought my feet were going to explode." He grinned at me. "And you know, I need to stay fresh for the next competition tomorrow."

I snorted. "You're not going to be any good to me if you're hungover," I said, indicating the row of empty cocktail glasses.

Dad looked shocked. "Those are his," he said, pointing at Sergio.

Sergio only laughed, his dark eyes twinkling. He looked much more sober than Dad, but he probably just held his liquor better.

"Where are the other teams?" I asked, looking around the dark bar. "Are they all heading to bed like good little competitors?"

As if in answer to my question, Double D appeared sandwiching Montserrat. Laughter erupted from them as they entered the dark bar, Daisy had red wine stains down the front of her previously pristine white blouse and DeeCee looked ready to make a dash toward the ladies' room and vomit.

In contrast, Montserrat looked as immaculate as she had earlier. She spotted Sergio at the bar and unglued herself from the girls.

"*¿Qué pasa?*" she asked.

DeeCee tore off to the restroom, but Daisy tailed Montserrat over to our group.

"Where is everyone else?" I asked.

"Todd and Parker have gone off to bed," Daisy said. She was flushed from dancing and wine, and was slurring her words a bit. "They're fierce competitors and I think we're in for a load of hurt."

"What about the others?" I asked.

"Victoria is off flirting with Cooper, I think. Or they've gone to bed, too, but probably not getting any rest, if you know what I mean." She wiggled her eyebrows at me.

DeeCee emerged from the bathroom and found her way over to a small bandstand. She found a microphone and tapped on it. When she discovered it was live, she squealed and called out to Daisy.

The girls broke out into an a cappella rendition of "Take This Job and Shove It," that brought the crowd in the bar to its feet.

Hmmm. Likely Double D was on *Expedition Improbable* only for exposure. Probably looking for someone to discover them. I hoped that happened. Maybe something good could come out of this entire mess, like launching a couple sweet girls into country-western singing mega-careers.

Sergio offered me his bar stool. "If you're not going to dance, you may as well sit down." He hailed the bartender and bought me a drink.

"A Coke," I said.

"With Coke?" the bartender asked.

I nodded. I was so thirsty from running around all day and night that as soon as he put the beverage in front of me, I drank heartily. I gagged and nearly choked.

Sergio thumped me on the back.

"Eh! Are you okay?"

I spit out the drink. "What is that?"

The bartender looked insulted. "*¡Calimocho!*"

133

I turned to Sergio, who laughed. "You asked for wine with Coke."

"What? No! I asked for Coke! Who drinks wine with Coke?"

Dad grabbed my drink from in front of me. "This is a very popular cocktail here, honey."

"Gross!" I said.

Dad shrugged. "It grows on you." He took a sip of the drink and headed off to join Double D in singing "Boot Scootin' Boogie."

While the others were distracted I took the opportunity to talk to Sergio. "How strong was Annalise's connection to Basque separatists?"

He frowned. "What do you know about that?"

"The senora at the B&B told me she was a known terrorist."

"Ah! *La señora* Antonia should keep her mouth shut," he said.

"Don't be mad at her. I would have figured it out eventually. Besides, I followed Miguel, the cameraman, to a meeting."

Sergio looked surprised. "What? When?"

"Just now. A while ago."

He smirked. "You are tricky. I thought you were out dancing and drinking. I thought, maybe, you were afraid to meet me alone at the church."

I ignored his remark, mostly because I didn't know how to respond. "The meeting was at an abandoned building. Sort of like a clandestine meeting. There were a lot people. Of course, I couldn't understand anything

134

they said but, you know, there was an ETA banner hanging on the wall."

He ran a hand through his dark hair. "An ETA meeting? Here in Jaca? No. Not possible. Miguel is not part of ETA. That I know."

"Well, I'm not making it up!" I said.

He stiffened. "Is this a way to get me to look into other suspects, rather than your boyfriend? The secret Mr. Matthew Barrett?"

Part of me wanted to scream. Scott wasn't technically my boyfriend anymore, but it didn't matter, I was still in love with him. And yes, perhaps it was a desperate, apparently futile, attempt to get Sergio to look into someone else. Although my pride would never let me admit it.

"An investigator has to follow all leads," I said.

"All *reasonable* leads," he agreed.

Anger surged in my belly and I fought the urge to stand up and scream, "Find Scott! He's not a killer!" but instead I balled my fists. "It's a reasonable lead," I said.

He nodded thoughtfully. "I'll ask around about Miguel."

"Thank you," I said.

He glanced at the others singing and dancing, then asked, "Have you received any more messages from Scott?"

"No."

"Would you tell me if you had?"

I suddenly felt chewed up and spit out. "Yes."

He stepped away from me, a sad expression on his face. "I have work in the morning. I hope you enjoy the fiestas."

Thirteen

························

The following morning the crew's bus was waiting for us outside of the B&B. The bus billowed smoke into the hot air, creating a thick layer of smog in front of the otherwise pristine driveway. Dad gripped my arm as we boarded the bus.

"You don't think it's another hike, do you? I don't think my head can take it," he said.

"I told you not to go overboard on the whiskey!"

"I had whiskey?"

Laughing, I said, "Look, I can only carry you so far."

Double D was already seated on the bus. Each girl was holding her head and looking miserable. They turned around and eyed us as we took the seats behind them.

"How y'all feeling this morning?" DeeCee asked.

Dad groaned. "Worse for the wear, but I wouldn't

136

trade it for anything. I had such a great time singing with you girls. You are amazing!"

Daisy perked up and rooted around the purse on her lap, which seemed to double as a suitcase, she pulled out a can of hairspray and then a small vile. "Gordon, did you have too much to drink last night? I have some aspirin."

Dad was happy to accept the pills and eagerly popped them into his mouth.

I leaned in toward him. "There's no shame in losing."

Dad quirked a brow at me. "What are you saying?"

"If we lose, I can search for Scott."

Dad squinted at me. "You don't believe that email, do you?"

"I don't know what to believe."

Dad pressed his hand against mine. "The authorities aren't going to let us leave Spain until they figure this thing out. Don't worry, Georgia, Scott is going to turn up. He better have a pretty good explanation or I'm going to wring his neck."

I looked out the window of the small bus. The Pyrenees hovered over the town like two soldiers guarding the night. I wanted so desperately to return to the mountains. To return to the scene of the crime.

What was there that I hadn't been able to see?

There were answers there, I knew it.

Victoria and Parker clomped onto the bus. They didn't speak to us and definitely had their game face on. The driver fired up the bus.

"What about Cooper and Todd?" Daisy asked.

DeeCee rubbed her temples. "I think they must have already started, right? Cooper told me he had to get up at four in the morning, because their leg of the race started at six a.m."

Dad moaned. "Now I'm happy you gave him that chalice," he joked. "Nothing gets me out of bed at four a.m." He turned to me and we said together, "Except fishing."

The bus turned onto a narrow street in the center of town. We drove slightly past a bakery and parked. A heavenly scent wafted through the air and there was a line of people waiting in front.

DeeCee poked Daisy in the ribs. "We have an hour to kill before we get to start, let's grab some coffee, and I need me a hangover donut!"

Dad's stomach growled and I had to pull on him by the collar to keep him with me, as Double D stalked off toward the bakery. Around the corner we saw our crew positioned around the familiar blue tarp. Harris was standing at the top of the tarp chatting with Becca. Behind them was a colorful mural, which would have been lovely, save for the black paint scrawled across the faces of the people in the painting. Cheryl was standing off to the side of the mural talking to another crew. I realized it was a Spanish media team. This must be the mural the town was trying to raise money to restore.

"Bless her heart, Cheryl actually listened to Sergio and is trying to help!" I said.

Dad snorted, a wicked smile on his face. "Let's not

get carried away. Probably she's helping because she thinks it'll get her what she wants a bit faster."

I laughed. "I think you're getting to know Cheryl pretty well."

Harris perked up when he saw us approach, and Kyle stepped out to adjust Harris's makeup.

Victoria and Parker jogged over to the tarp, but Dad and I lagged behind.

"No matter what. We're not separating today, okay, Georgia? I don't trust Victoria. I'd rather lose the contest than you, and that's not a joke."

I squeezed his hand. "Got it, Daddy. Don't worry!"

We lined up in front of Harris, who exploded to life with his over-the-top TV voice. "Welcome to round two of *Expedition Improbable*! Where nothing can stop you but yourself!" He launched into a brief recap of yesterday's events for the benefit of the audience, then said, "Cooper and Todd have already begun their journey, but don't lose hope. There's plenty of time for everyone to catch them, because in this game you never know what can happen." He made his fingers into pistols and shot air at us. "Expect the unexpected!"

"For this leg of the race," Harris continued, "you will have to tour the old town of Jaca, the *casco histórico*, in search of a clue that will take you on a wild, er, dare I say, wet ride. Like yesterday, you'll begin the next challenge with whatever time advantage you secure today."

Harris glanced at his gold wristwatch. "And with that, the team in second place, Victoria and Parker, get ready to begin in five, four, three, two, one." Harris held his arms up in a dramatic gesture.

Victoria and Parker exchanged confused looks and tore off running down the street, their cameraman following them.

Miguel panned his camera over toward us and filmed us standing on the tarp as Harris said, "Georgia, Gordon, you'll have to wait exactly four minutes and seven seconds before you can start. So please, let me take the time to direct your attention to this historic mural."

Dad and I stood in front of the vandalized painting as Harris prattled on, giving attention to the historic value of the painting and also the efforts the town was making in order to restore it. He even cited a website where viewers could donate to the cause.

Sergio would be happy indeed.

Harris turned his attention back to the camera. "Georgia, Gordon, get ready to begin in five, four, three, two, one." Harris shot his arms up in the same dramatic gesture as he'd given just a few minutes earlier.

Dad shrugged and grabbed my arm. "Let's go."

We strolled down the cobblestone streets toward the old shopping district. Miguel filming us looking into the store windows. The displays boasted handmade leather purses and shoes, along with elaborate dresses and the latest fashions.

"I like Spain," I said, surprising myself. "I wish we had time to shop."

Dad smiled. "I wish we had time to eat! Do you want to go back to that bakery we saw?"

"Focus! You can't be thinking about your stomach right now. You should be thinking about the clue!"

On the corner was a tavern where *jamón serrano*, the dry-cured Spanish hams, hung in the window. Dad put a hand to the glass and let out a soft puppy dog moan.

Miguel chuckled despite himself.

"They're not open yet, Dad. Let's keep moving."

As Dad and I continued down the street, I spotted an abrupt movement from one of the doorways up ahead. Victoria and Parker were huddling, trying to hide from us. Suddenly they burst down the street in a mad hustle.

I ran after them. "What doorway did they come from?" I yelled to Dad.

He jogged behind me. "The third one on the right, I think."

"Check inside! See what's there," I said, over my shoulder. I chased Victoria and Parker into a square, where they hailed a cab.

Darn it!

They had the clue!

I ran back to find Dad and Miguel, but intersected them in the alley. Dad was out of breath, but handed me a note. "We have to catch a cab! Here are the directions."

"Come on," I said. "Let's get to the square."

Dad and I hurried to the spot Victoria and Parker had just vacated and waited for another taxi to pick us up. I reviewed the slip of paper, *Grab a cab. Give the driver these directions to the Río Aragón.*

"Ah! A cab," Dad said. "Becca is so nice not to make me run a marathon today!"

I laughed. "Well, we don't know what we'll have to do when we get to the river," I warned.

"Hopefully not swim," Dad said.

A cab turned the corner and we hailed it, madly jumping up and down. The cab pulled to a stop in front of us.

"I'm sure glad this isn't New York," Dad said, "where they just ignore you."

I laughed as I piled into the car. Miguel and Dad followed suit. I handed the driver the directions and he tore off. The cab driver was talkative, but spoke only Spanish. Miguel put down his camera and chatted amicably with him, seemingly about the race and the show.

When there was a lull in their conversation, I touched Miguel's shoulder and he glanced back at me. "I saw you last night going to that meeting."

He smiled. "Oh? Did you? I didn't know."

"I would have called out to you, but I was shy. It was a pretty big meeting," I said, gently fishing for information.

He nodded, not taking the bait. "Did you enjoy the fiestas? Will you go out again tonight?"

"Not me," Dad burst out. "I think I'll stuff my face with paella and then go to bed with a hot-water bottle."

"What about Cheryl?" I joked, poking Dad in the ribs. "She'll want to dance."

Dad waved a hand around. "She can go. You, too. Have fun. I really don't mind being left alone. My ego can take it."

We could see Victoria and Parker's cab ahead of us. "Can you overtake that taxi?" I asked the driver.

He didn't respond, so I was about to ask Miguel to translate, when the cab in front of us suddenly swerved dangerously into our lane. Our driver slammed the brakes and yanked the car to the right, directly into a mailbox. The right front tire popped in a dramatic flourish. The driver let out a stream of what I could only imagine were Spanish expletives.

"I really don't like that Victoria girl," Dad said.

"Is everyone all right?" I asked.

Dad and Miguel nodded as we all tumbled out of the cab. Miguel filmed the damage on the car while he soothed the driver, who looked like he was about to have a stroke. I surveyed the area. We were now in a more modern part of Jaca. Bigger buildings surrounded us and people dressed in business suits rushed past. Almost immediately a motorcycle cop pulled over to take the driver's statement.

"Now what?" Dad asked. "Do we catch another cab? It doesn't look like there are many in this area."

We both looked at Miguel for help. He was filming us and couldn't speak, so instead he indicated for us to walk up the street. When we crested the hill, I saw what looked like a five-star hotel with a fleet of cabs waiting in a turnstile. Dad and I picked up the pace, ready to get in the next cab.

We pulled open the door to the first cab in the waiting line and piled into the back. As Miguel loaded his camera into the front seat, I turned to check out the hotel.

There was a doorman dressed in a red uniform, he held the door open for a couple exiting the building. I realized I recognized the couple.

Sergio and Montserrat stood in the doorway of the hotel. What were they doing here? Were they investigating a new clue? One that could possibly lead to finding Scott?

The cab driver pulled away from the curb and as we merged into traffic I saw the name of the hotel in neon lights.

My breath caught.

Spanish Moon . . .

Fourteen

··

I said nothing on the ride out of town. We followed the
mighty *Río Aragón* north, meandering through some
off-roads for about thirty minutes. As we drove toward
the Pyrenees, the roads turned to dirt and the ride became
more bumpy. The bumpier the road, the quieter I got.

Spanish Moon.

That was the title of the book Scott's mom said he'd
been working on when he visited Spain. What were
Sergio and Montserrat doing at the hotel? Could Scott
be staying there?

When we arrived at a grassy clearing, the cab pulled
over and dropped us off. A makeshift pole with a clear
plastic box mounted to it was visible from where we
stood. On the pole was a flag with the show's bull's-eye
emblem. Dad and I hiked over to the box and pulled out
the next note.

The note read: *Find your swimsuit and brave the rapids to the finish line. Be nice, you might have to share!*

Dad and I frantically looked around and found a trail that led toward the river. Along the way, there were several swimsuits hanging on the trees. Some of the suits were revealing bikinis, which I'd just as soon leave for Double D. I selected the most conservative offering, a one-piece suit in marine blue. Dad opted out of the Speedos and luckily found a pair of flowered boarder shorts.

"They are so you," I said, laughing.

Dad grinned. "I know those evil producers probably were hoping I'd select the Speedos, but hey, maybe Parker wants them."

"Victoria and Parker have to be ahead of us, right?"

Dad shrugged. "With any luck, maybe their taxi blew a flat."

"Maybe their raft will blow a flat," I said.

Dad and I hiked along the narrow trail, with Miguel documenting our every move. It wasn't long before Dad broke out in a sweat.

"When do we hit the water?" Dad asked. "It's going to feel good today. What a scorcher!"

Soon, the trail bottomed out to a sandy riverbank. Victoria was on the bank already in her swimsuit and life jacket. Parker was seated on a boulder with his back to the river, the cameraman taping him alone, presumably for his confessional. At some point, we were supposed to pour our hearts out privately to the camera.

Well, as privately as you could when you knew your message would be broadcast in front of millions of viewers.

Victoria scampered to her feet when she saw us. "You finally got here, huh?"

"No thanks to you," Dad said. "What kind of stunt was that you pulled in the cab?"

Victoria batted her eyelashes at Dad. "I don't know what you mean, those cabbies here in Spain can't drive worth a hill of beans! Anyway, you haven't missed much. Parker and I got here a few minutes ago. One raft floated down and we couldn't reach it in time. So here we are."

I gritted my teeth, recalling the note: *Be nice, you might have to share!*

That was Cheryl's way of making sure we all got onto the same raft together. That would definitely make for more drama, ergo more ratings.

Miguel pointed to a grassy area off to the left that was carpeted with wildflowers. "That would make a nice background, Gordon. Let's get your confessional."

Dad and Miguel tromped off, leaving me alone with Victoria. She scooped a handful of pebbles from the bank and began to throw them in the river, one by one, doing her best to avoid me.

"Do you know how to raft?" I asked over the roar of the river.

"Sure. I've been down the Gallatin a few times, always with a guide though," Victoria said. "You?"

"One time down the Sacramento. I don't think I

remember anything and I'm sure Dad's never been. He's liable to topple the raft on us."

Victoria snorted. "Well, if you hadn't said that, I'd suggest an alliance."

Right!

"I thought you already had one," I answered.

Her eyebrows shot up and she feigned innocence. "Really, no. Who would we have an alliance with?"

"Cooper. You guys are always together—"

She lowered her eyes and I could see she was hiding something, calculating how much I might know. "He's come onto me a few times, but I don't think it's wise to get all caught up in a romance here. Do you?"

I wasn't going to touch that with a ten-foot pole. Who was I to give dating advice? The woman who found her love match on reality TV only to be subsequently dumped on the next show. Ridiculous!

"Cooper would make a great alliance, he's tough competition. Whoever aligns with him will likely land in the final two."

Victoria shook her head. "Todd's not tough competition though. He's the weak link."

I shrugged. "Parker and Todd basically told me they were forming an alliance."

"No!" Victoria said, protesting a bit too much. She gestured toward her brother down the way a bit. "Parker wants to get on board with you and your dad."

"Really?" I said, unable to keep the sarcasm out of my voice. "Is that why you ran us off the road?"

She laughed and put a hand over her heart. "Well, *I* didn't run you off the road. The cabbie just sort of misunderstood me. Anyway, you did great on that monastery hike. I'm sorry. I kind of lost my mind up there. I had no idea you were so close to the edge."

I didn't mention that I didn't believe a word of what she was dishing out. A confession like that might kill her forthrightness.

"So Parker wants to form an alliance with us, but what about you?" I probed.

She rolled her shoulders almost coquettishly, a gesture I figured she refined at many a late-night party. "I don't know what to think. I want to win. I need the money. And honestly you seem like you have an inside advantage—you've been on a show before and you're friends with the producer. But your heart doesn't seem into the competition since your boyfriend killed that girl."

EXT. RIVERBANK DAY

Parker is looking into the camera. He is unshaven with several days' beard growth on his face. He wears yellow swim trunks and a life jacket. He is seated on a boulder with a rushing river behind him.

PARKER
(*smiles*) Hello! I'm Parker Wilson. One of the contestants on *Expedition Improbable*.

I'm competing with my sister, Victoria.
Truthfully, she can be a bit of a handful
and I'm nervous she's going to mess up this
opportunity for us. Because winning right
now would be amazing. I have a couple
bills . . . well, let's just say, I need to
take care of those. And Vicky, she's got
her student loans hanging over her neck.
But I'm not worried about winning. We're
making alliances with the right folks and
keeping the other competition at bay. Our
plan is to be in the final two, then we'll
have to knock out the other team. Right
now, Cooper and Todd think we're in an
alliance with them. *(shrugs)* It's
unfortunate, but, you know, we'll have to
stab those guys in the back. Cooper's
gonna be too tough to beat. So, I'm
thinking that maybe it's better to make an
alliance with Gordon and Georgia. They'll
be easy to beat in the end. Heck, I would
have made an alliance with Double D,
but Vicky wouldn't let me. She says
they'll be out next, and they'd only bog
us down, but—
*(Shouts and screams are heard from off
camera. The camera pans to reveal Georgia
and Victoria in close proximity, screaming
at each other.)*

PARKER (O.S.)
Oh, no! Gotta go keep Vicky out of trouble!

"He didn't kill that woman," I roared, unable to hold myself back any longer. "In fact, I'm thinking maybe you did!"

Victoria recoiled as if I'd slapped her. "What are you talking about? I didn't even know that woman. Why would I kill her?"

Parker turned in our direction when he heard the outburst. He scurried down the bank toward us, their cameraman in tow, now filming us, too.

"I know you have an ETA connection," I said, jamming a finger in her face. "You studied here in Spain."

"You don't know anything!" Victoria screamed.

"I'm gonna prove it. I'm gonna get you! I swear, if it's the last thing I do!" I threatened.

"You better watch your back," Victoria sneered.

"What's going on?" Parker demanded.

"Look!" Dad shouted from a distance. He pointed upstream, a yellow raft came into view, bobbing its way down the river.

Miguel and Dad rushed toward the bank, away from the wildflower area where they'd been filming Dad's confessional. The raft approached. "Let's make a daisy chain," Dad yelled out.

We all quickly linked hands, Dad anchored himself by sitting on the rocks, Parker linked to Dad, Victoria to Parker, and I somehow got the tail end of the stick by having to run out into the icy mountain water.

Ordinarily, the frigid water would have bothered me, but I was so fired up from my confrontation with Victoria that I barely noticed.

I stretched to reach the yellow raft, gripping one of the black nylon straps that wrapped around the small craft. "I got it!"

Pulling on the raft against the swift current felt hopelessly futile. I yanked on it with all my strength, jarring the raft out of the water and hitting myself in the face. Obviously, the current had its own agenda.

Finally, it seemed Miguel couldn't help himself and despite the rules against giving us advice yelled out, "Jump in Georgia, paddle over to the next eddy." He gesticulated wildly toward the north bank. "We can all get in safely over there."

I dove headfirst into the raft, water trailing me in. I grabbed an oar and padded madly toward the eddy. Dad, Parker, Victoria, and Miguel scurried over to meet me. Once on the calmer water of the eddy they were all able to climb aboard easily, even Miguel and the other cameraman with their heavy waterproof cameras.

Victoria screamed out as the icy water splashed her belly. She and Dad looked as miserable as I felt. Parker, on the other hand, looked completely in his element. He let out a loud war whoop that jolted Miguel.

"Everyone, grab your oars. I'm steering," he called out. "When I call left, Vicky, you and Georgia row, when I call right, that's you Gordon. When I say all, we all dig. Got it?"

We all agreed and within moments we were hurtling into the rougher waters of the *Río Aragón*. A large boulder loomed to our left.

"Rock on the left!" Victoria called out.

"Left row, row, dig, give it all you got!" Parker commanded.

The small raft swerved right, missing the boulder. Adrenaline shot through our crew as we all let out a whoop of delight. Parker expertly navigated us through three more rocks, when suddenly a fork in the river appeared around a bend.

"Oh, geez!" Parker screamed out. "Which way do we go?"

We were silent, an uninformed ignorant crew.

"Miguel! What do we do?" Parker yelled.

The sound of the water changed, intensifying somehow—like a loud roar that was ready to swallow us whole.

"Sounds like a freakin' waterfall," Parker said. "What the—what the heck is going on?"

"Whitewater up ahead," Vicky screamed.

"Try the right side," Miguel said.

We navigated toward the right fork of the river. The water became more choppy and came over the front of the raft in waves.

"We're taking in a lot of water," Dad said.

Abruptly, the front of the raft dipped as a rapid hit

us, knocking me out of the raft. The impact of the icy water against my chest took my breath away. I was suddenly bobbing up and down the river, a small spec in the current of life, an insignificant nothing against the mighty river's force. A large granite boulder loomed ahead of me in my direct line of sight, and my life flashed before my eyes.

"Georgia!" Dad screamed.

"Put your feet toward downstream," Parker yelled.

"Swim toward the bank," Victoria said.

Right. As if I could swim. My hands and arms flung about wildly in an awful duck-flapping imitation, but I was able to swing my feet out in front of me.

"We'll pick you up at the next eddy," Parker shouted.

My feet crashed into the huge boulder with such force, I feared I broke my leg. Then a silly thought popped into my head: *I'm out of the game now.*

Followed by relief.

Out of the game.

I can find Scott and go home.

Suddenly, I was thrust under the murky water. Thank goodness for the life jacket. I floated to the surface, only to have more water pour over me, relentlessly rushing around me, roaring in my ears. It was as if I'd been thrown inside a washing machine stuck on the spin cycle. The river continued to toss me around back and forth.

Which way was up?

I was dizzy and disoriented.

I glimpsed something yellow. The raft! I flailed an arm toward it, reaching, straining, stretching.

Then a hand grabbed me, someone pulling on my life jacket, pushing me under the water, keeping me under. My lungs burned.

Dear God!

I was going to drown right here in the *Río Aragón*.

Fifteen

....

Light penetrated my eyelids and the hands that had held me under suddenly pulled me up only to dunk me back in the water. The action was repeated again, I realized it was Dad holding on to me. He was getting leverage to pull me into the raft. On the third time, he hoisted me up over the ridge and I flopped into the bottom of the raft, like a dead fish.

The crew navigated the raft over to an eddy where we lodged it against the sandbank and climbed out. My legs were shaking uncontrollably and I had to lean on Dad just to get to shore. Before I could collapse onto the beach, Dad embraced me.

"Georgia, are you all right?"

I hugged Dad while I caught my breath. "Got the wind knocked out of me. Thank goodness I had on the life vest."

Miguel scratched his head. "I guess we should have gone left."

Parker threw the oar he'd white-knuckled through the entire ordeal and broke it against a rock, spewing out a string of obscenities. "What the heck do you mean, I guess we should have gone left!"

Miguel jumped away from Parker.

A rush of compassion flooded me. Poor Miguel. How could he have known we'd get tossed out of the raft. He was just a hired cameraman. Then a horrible thought struck me. Miguel hadn't intentionally told us to go in the wrong direction, had he?

Miguel's face flushed red with anger and he let out his own string of obscenities, from what I gathered, but in Spanish. He finished with, "Next time, do not ask me anything!" and made a gesture with his hands as if zipping his lips.

Dad, the consummate peacemaker, clapped Miguel on the back. "It wasn't your fault. We don't know that the other path is any better. We could have done worse."

Miguel looked momentarily pacified and said, "¡Sí! ¡Sí! That is true!" He flung his hand out toward Parker in a "take that" gesture.

Parker gave Miguel a dirty look but said nothing.

In the distance, we heard high-pitched screams. Floating down the river was another raft, this one carrying two beautiful girls, one with fire-red hair and the other with long blond hair. Both were wearing string bikinis sans life vests. They waved wildly when they saw us.

"Woo-hoo!" DeeCee screamed.

"Howdy!" Daisy yelled.

They looked like they were having the time of their lives, not a care in the world. DeeCee was reclining and had her feet up on the side of the raft.

Dad cupped his hands around his mouth and yelled. "Get your life vests on!"

Their cameraman had the camera in one hand and an oar in the other, leisurely guiding the raft away from any boulders or whitewater. He seemed smitten with Double D, and I guess I didn't blame him. I only regretted not waiting for them and joining them on their raft instead.

Victoria stomped around the bank. "Well, now we know, for sure. We're last!"

"We're probably going to miss lunch now, too, and I'm starving," Parker whined.

"Oh, shut up about food, will you?" Victoria said. She picked up a rock and smashed it against another one. The rocks cracked in her hand and she abruptly turned toward me. "It's all your fault! What? Do you want to lose?"

Dad held up a hand. "Now—"

But Victoria continued to scream. "I mean, it's totally obvious that you want us to lose when you jump out of the boat!"

Dad tsked at her. "How can you say that? Those were real rapids! Georgia didn't make those up!"

I lay back on the sand, shaded my eyes with my hand and tried to tune her out. My ankle throbbed from when

I'd slammed into the rock. It was the same ankle that I'd twisted the day before. If I wasn't careful, I'd end up leaving the show on a stretcher.

As Dad was scolding Victoria, I heard Parker say, "Come on Vicky. I really don't want to miss lunch."

I sat up. Parker had pulled the raft to the edge of the eddy and suddenly he and Victoria jumped into the raft. Their cameraman struggled to climb onboard.

"Hey! Wait," Dad screamed, lunging for the raft.

Victoria and Parker pushed away from the bank. Dad jumped into the river after them.

"Wait! What are you doing?" I yelled.

Victoria flashed me a dirty look, one that told me exactly what she thought of me and where I could go straight to.

"Hey!" Miguel shouted, as he realized what was going on. "Get back here!"

Dad and Miguel raced out into the icy water after them, but it was too late. With one bold stroke of their oars, the raft zipped into the current and was whisked away. Victoria laughed a shrill "in your face" laugh.

Dad and Miguel were too angry to stop running.

"Let them go, guys! We can't afford to challenge the current without a raft."

Dad and Miguel stopped short of the section where the river would carry them out. We watched the raft bob up and down with the current as Parker and Victoria sped away.

A feeling of desperation overwhelmed me. I only

wanted to lie on the beach and feel the sun warm me, but instead I was tortured by my fractured thoughts. What was Victoria so angry about? This was only a game. Why did she have such animosity toward me? The image of her smashing the rocks in her hands swirled around in my brain. Could that have been how she'd killed Annalise? By bashing her on the head with a large rock?

Dad returned to the shore, his face flushed with anger. "What nerve! I can't believe they left us stranded!"

Miguel let out a string of rapid-fire Spanish. I know Dad didn't understand the words, but he heartily agreed with the sentiment of frustration.

I stood and limped toward them. "What do we do now? Do you think Cheryl and Becca will send us another raft? Or what? Are we out of the competition?"

"We're not out!" Dad said. "Anything can happen. They can take a wrong fork, get completely lost." He held up a finger as if inspiration had suddenly struck him. "Remember! Expect the unexpected!"

I sat back down on the beach and propped my swollen ankle up on a nearby rock. "In the meantime, I'm going to enjoy the sun. How's your hangover, Dad?"

Dad ignored me. "Do you have a phone on you, Miguel?"

He sighed. "Yes, but the cell service is bad in the mountains." He trudged out of the water and over to a mound of grass. He put the camera down and pulled a mobile from an interior pocket under his life vest.

He double-checked the display and grunted.

"Is that waterproof?" Dad asked, looking over Miguel's shoulder.

"The case is waterproof, yes," he said, "but look, no coverage." He handed the phone to Dad, who handed it directly back.

"How do we get out of here? Is there a trail we can hike?" Dad asked. He looked over at me, a concerned expression on his face.

"There is a back-roads trail." Miguel sighed. "It's very long though."

"Can we make it to the finish?" Dad asked. "I mean, do we have a chance of staying in this thing? Or is it over?"

"I'm sure it's over," I said. I clapped Dad on the back. "Don't worry, it's okay."

He hugged me. "I'm sorry, Peaches."

"Oh, Dad, it's not your fault."

He pressed his hands against my shoulders and gently pushed me away from him, so he could study my face. "Maybe there's still a chance."

I shrugged. "We did our best. I . . ."

"There is a trail ahead," Miguel said, indicating a break in the foliage off to the right. "But there is also a road down this way . . ." He pointed to the left in the direction we'd come on the raft. "What if we find a ride?"

Dad and I glanced at each other. "Is there a rule that we have to arrive at the finish line by raft?"

"I don't think so," I said.

We rushed toward Miguel, who was hoisting the camera on his shoulder. "Let's go."

The trail to the road was covered with blackberry bushes and poison oak. It was a good thing that Dad was a walking *Farmer's Almanac*, because he identified every single plant along the way, guiding us away from all the dangers.

As we hiked along with Miguel, horrible thoughts about him plagued me. How smart was it to hike out into the wilderness with him? He couldn't have been sweeter to Dad or me, but what did we really know about him? He was likely a Basque separatist.

He could be planning to lead us deep in the woods right now and kill us.

And yet, he'd helped Dad and me out of a jam twice.

"Miguel, did you know Annalise?" I asked finally.

He frowned and pointed to the camera. Cheryl probably wouldn't like us discussing anything about the murder, but I couldn't help myself.

I waved a hand around nonchalantly. "Don't worry, they'll edit it out."

Even still, Miguel whipped the camera off his shoulder and turned it off. "We shouldn't discuss it. Don't talk about her," he whispered urgently.

"Why?" I asked.

Dad was marching in front of us and he suddenly turned around. "What's going on?"

Miguel shrugged. "No good can come from it."

"So you did know her," I pressed. "How well did you know her? Are you part of ETA, too? I know you went to the meeting last night."

He shook his head. "I'm not part of ETA, don't be crazy. I'm Aragonese!"

"What?" I asked.

"I'm from Jaca. We are Aragonese, here. Not Basque. ETA is Basque. There is no one here in Jaca friendly with ETA. They put a bomb near our Plaza de Toros last summer and killed three people." His face was angry now and I regretted causing him distress.

"I'm sorry," I said. "*Señora* Antonia at the B&B told me Annalise was ETA and I saw you go to that meeting—"

"It wasn't an ETA meeting," he said. "We are anti-ETA. You didn't stay for the end of the meeting."

"No," I admitted.

"That building had been taken over by ETA last summer. When they planned the Plaza de Toros bombing. We found it last week and took it back. Last night we burned their banner."

Miguel put the camera back on his shoulder and turned it on, indicating that our conversation was over.

The trail we were on had high grass and it scratched my legs. My ankle felt numb and I ached to be at the finish line.

I mulled over what Miguel had said. So he and the others at the meeting were anti-ETA. Actually in terms of a motive for murder, it didn't matter. Someone against the ETA could be just as likely to kill Annalise as someone who was in support of ETA. In fact, a case could be made that someone who was anti-ETA might have a stronger motive.

As I hiked behind Dad I noted his tan shoulders were getting red. If Dad was getting burned, what about me? My skin was fairer than Snow White's. I touched my shoulder and already felt the sting of the burn.

"Isn't there any shade around here?" I complained.

"Look," Dad said, pointing up ahead.

The trail cleared into an orange grove and at the end of the grove was a small white cottage. I don't think I've ever been so happy to see a cottage in my life!

Miguel plucked an orange off a tree and broke it open, it was bright red on the inside. He handed half to me and half to Dad. "*Sanguinello*, 'blood orange.' The best of Spain."

The orange was the sweetest fruit I'd tasted in my life.

Dad said, "Forget almonds. I should grow these."

We approached the cottage and noticed several goats and chickens in the backyard. Miguel called out and a tiny woman wearing an apron emerged. She greeted Miguel warmly and then turned to us and fired away in Spanish. Her face friendly and animated as she spoke.

Dad peppered her with a slew of questions. Which Miguel kindly translated. The woman wanted to feed us, insisting we eat some chorizo sandwiches she'd recently made. Her husband joined us on the porch and seemed only too eager to talk to Dad through Miguel about current farming practices in Spain.

"We have to go," I said to Dad.

Miguel explained that we were in a race and needed a ride, but Dad waved an impatient hand at us and continued chatting with the farmer, Augustine.

The woman, Josefa, tsked over my red shoulders and retreated into the cottage. She returned with Nivea and slathered some on. Part of me wanted to move in with Josefa and Augustine. I could live here, eat oranges and chorizo all summer long. But I knew we had to get going.

Miguel seemed to echo my sentiments, because he said in a loud voice, "*¡Bueno!*" and clapped his hands authoritatively.

Augustine sprang to his feet and disappeared into the cottage. He returned, jiggling a pair of keys in his hands and gestured to the beat-up pickup at the end of the lane. He laughed heartily and motioned for us to follow him.

Miguel filmed us jumping into the back of the pickup. When he got a shot he was happy with, he climbed into the front with Augustine.

"Do you think we have a chance?" Dad asked.

I shrugged. "I don't know. We probably should have passed on those chorizo sandwiches if we really wanted to stay in the race."

Dad looked horrified. "Pass on the sandwiches? Those were the highlight of my trip!"

I laughed. "I know." After a moment, I asked, "What do you make of Victoria? She has a fierce side to her, doesn't she?"

Dad nodded.

"Did you see her bang those rocks together?" I asked.

"She's an angry young girl," Dad said. "And didn't you say the victim had a head wound?"

"Yeah, it's disturbing. The night Scott disappeared, Victoria was out roaming around. Parker was looking for her for a while."

"I can't believe they left us like that," Dad said. "Do you think they preplanned it?"

The hair on the back of my neck stood to attention. Could she be hoping we'd not make it back?

"How could they have planned it, though? They didn't know I would fall out of the raft."

Dad shrugged. "Do you think Parker deliberately steered us into those rocks?

I sighed. "I don't know. I hate to think that. It must have been an accident."

The trunk meandered along the road until we crested up a hill. Ahead there was a rickety bridge. "We're not crossing that! Are we?" Dad asked, a look of alarm on his face.

I giggled. "This trip is full of surprises!"

Once over the bridge, we took a left turn onto an old dirt road, rugged with grooves and dips. I hung on to Dad, thinking we'd be bounced right out of the truck. Branches swept against the sides of the truck dangerously close to our faces.

I tucked my face into Dad's shoulder. "We've got to be there soon, right? And if we're not last, I'm quitting."

Dad said, "Aren't you having fun? If I hadn't been

scared out of my mind about losing you, I think I would have actually enjoyed the rapids."

I snorted. "I think I prefer the Storybook Land boat ride at Disneyland."

Dad chortled. "Tell it to Becca and Cheryl, maybe they can arrange the next episode there."

Augustine honked the horn and I looked up to see the familiar crew bus along with the blue tarp. Dad let out a whoop and jumped out of the back of the truck.

"We're here!" Dad screamed.

In the circle, I spotted Cooper and his partner, Todd. They were clearly safe and next to them was Double D, seemingly in second place. I hobbled out of the pickup truck and ran behind Dad toward the circle.

"Where's Victoria and Parker?" Dad asked, as we ran.

I looked down the hill toward the river, a sinking feeling overtaking my stomach, only two rafts were docked.

We entered the circle and Harris, the host, clapped his hands. "Georgia! Gordon! Welcome. I'm happy to say you are the third team to arrive and are therefore safe. You will be able to start the race tomorrow one hour and nine minutes after Double D."

Double D beamed bright white smiles at us.

Cooper wiggled his eyebrows. "Took you long enough. Nice ride. How'd you manage it?"

Dad grimaced. "Long story."

We both glanced nervously at Becca and Cheryl wondering if they would allow us our third-place finish, or disqualify us for hitching a ride. Before anyone could complain, another raft came into view. We'd just beat Victoria and Parker's arrival by minutes.

The raft struggled to dock, overshooting the distance and almost catching another current. Victoria and Parker scrambled out of the boat and ran up the hill. Their jaws were agape as they took in the scenery. Augustine standing by his pickup truck, Dad and I standing in the circle. It took a moment for them to process everything. In the meantime, they continued their frantic run to the circle.

Harris's expression was solemn as he said, "Victoria, Parker, we're so happy you made it through this challenge safely. But I'm sorry to say, you are the fourth and final team to arrive and are therefore eliminated."

Parker had a slack expression, his shoulder hunched, a posture of pure exhaustion and defeat.

"No!" Victoria roared.

Harris pressed his hands together and frowned sympathetically. "I'm sorry."

Parker cleared his throat. "Uh . . . thank you for the experience—"

"No!" Victoria screamed again. "No, no, no!" Her face turned beet red and she pointed her finger at me. "You cheated! You cheated!" Suddenly she rushed at me and wrapped her hands around my neck, screeching, "You cheeeeeeaaaaaaateeeeeed!"

Sixteen

....

EXT. RIVERBANK DAY

*Victoria is looking down away from the camera. She is
dressed in a yellow life jacket, her face is sunburned,
her hair matted and tangled, eyes red and swollen.*

VICTORIA
(*sniffles and wipes her nose with the back
of her hand*) Um . . . I'm Victoria Wilson,
one of the contestants on *Expedition
Improbable*. (*lets out a muffled cry*) Well,
I *was* one of the contestants on *Expedition
Improbable*! I've just been eliminated, but
I don't think it's very fair. (*She bites her
knuckle and searches the sky in an overly*

dramatic way.) I really wanted to win.
Winning would be everything. There's
this thing I want to do back home and
now . . . (*She shrugs.*) I guess it doesn't
matter. Nobody would vote for me after the
way I behaved here. (*She shakes her head
and cries violently.*) I don't know what
came over me. (*wailing*) I'm so ashamed.
(*A dejected Parker joins her.*)

PARKER
Vicky, you gotta suck it up.

VICTORIA
(*leans her head on Parker's shoulder*) I'm
sorry I ruined this for us, Parker.

PARKER
(*shrugs*) You were just being yourself.

VICTORIA
(*gasps*) No. Really? Come on, the
competition brought out the worst
in me, that's all. That woman,
Georgia, brought out the worst
in me!

PARKER
You say that about everyone.

VICTORIA
(slugs him in the shoulder) Parker!

PARKER
See what I mean?

That evening I could barely stand to shower, my skin was lobster red and I had to borrow buckets full of aloe vera from Double D. It had taken several crew members along with Dad to pull Victoria off of me. It was little consolation when Cheryl had congratulated me on a fine dramatic moment and credited me with being irritating enough to get choked on camera.

Victoria wasn't talking to me and she and Parker were getting ready to be taken to the bus stop to leave the country via the Madrid airport. I couldn't believe Sergio would give them clearance to leave, but right now I had bigger fish to fry.

Becca had gone off with Kyle and one of the local crew people, Juan Jose, to scout out the next location for the contest. Cheryl had somehow talked Dad into watching the jousting tournament they'd missed last night. Miraculously, Dad, being the trooper he was, had agreed to accompany her despite his hangover.

I really wanted to win the contest now. Dad needed the money and he deserved it.

As I hurried to get dressed, a knock on my door interrupted me. "Just a minute," I called out, as I shrugged into my clean jeans. "Who is it?" I asked, walking over to the door. I hesitated when no answer came and cautiously cracked the door open an inch.

Cooper was standing in the doorway waiting patiently, his million-dollar grin on his face.

I pulled open the door. "Yeah?"

Cooper pointed at my bare feet. "What are you doing, girl? We're all downstairs having some dinner. Then we're going into the town square for more dancing."

"Not me. Thank you. I . . ."

"What are you talking about, 'not me'? Come on!"

"No, no, no. I'm sunburned. I . . ."

"Sunburned? Shoot, don't you know you need fluids for a sunburn," he said.

I laughed. "*Sangría* will not help a sunburn."

"The hell, you say."

I laughed again in spite of myself. "Well, I am hungry. You may convince me to go down with you. On one condition."

He cocked a brow at me. "I like conditions."

"Get your mind out of the gutter. Is Victoria still down there or have they left for the bus station?" I asked.

Cooper was so big he took up the entire doorway. "Ha! That little scruff of a girl sure does talk a lot of trash. She got you scared? Is that what's on your mind?"

"I'm not scared!" I said.

He glanced up and down the hallway.

"What are you looking at? Is someone in the hallway?" After filming all day it was hard to shake the idea of someone always listening.

"No," he said, but he looked unconvinced. "I thought I heard something."

"Come in," I said, doubting my own sanity. For all I knew, Cooper could have killed Annalise, but it wouldn't have been the first time I was alone with a murderer. I was after all, a trained police officer, albeit unemployed.

Cooper smiled slowly. "Okay, sweetheart. Have it your way." He came in and glanced around the room. My side was clean and tidy; Becca's looked as if her suitcase had thrown up and strewn articles of clothing throughout. "Wow," Cooper said. He hesitated, then lumbered over to the small writing desk in the corner.

"Have a seat," I said, gesturing to the white wooden chair in front of the desk. He had to remove three tops and two skirts before he could sit down. I seated myself on my bed across the room from him.

"So, why don't you want to come downstairs?" he asked. "It can't be because of Victoria? Is it Todd?"

I laughed. "I'm tired. That's all. But since you mention it, what's up with him?"

He shrugged. "Dude's a strange duck. I know he rubs a lot of people the wrong way. But he's had my back a long time. He'd do anything for me."

I squinted at him. "He'd do anything for you, huh?" *Even kill?*

There were plenty of cases where friends took the fall for high-profile athletes. I knew of a few who'd done jail time and a few who'd gotten off, even when we were convinced they were guilty.

Cooper gave me his signature deep chuckle, the kind that sounded like an approaching locomotive. "Now, don't get all distracted with Todd. You know how good friends are." He leaned back in the chair and looked around the room. "So, where's *your* friend?"

Aha! He'd come to check on Becca.

I smiled at his cockiness. "You want to know about my friend? What, now that Victoria's gone, you're looking for another girl to take her place?"

He pretended to be offended. "What do you mean?"

Finally I had something I could use to leverage against him. Loosen his tongue. "I'll tell you where Becca is if you tell me about that night at the campground."

He swallowed, clearly uncomfortable. "I don't have anything to tell, or I would have told you already. I just took a walk. I knew Victoria wanted to hook up with me. You know, I talk a good game, but I'm here to win the contest. I can't really get messed up with chicks right now. There's a lot of cash at stake."

I studied him for a moment. "Oh? You need the cash, Cooper?"

He looked back at me blankly. "Well, yeah. Of course. Why else would I be doing this?"

I laughed. "Some people want to do it for the fun of it."

He shook his head. "Maybe that mother-and-son. They don't know what it feels like to have cameras follow you around all day. Or the Double Ds, they want the limelight so they can get discovered. Have you heard them sing? They're pretty good."

I nodded. "Yeah. But you've got money, right Cooper? Big NFL star like you?"

He leaned forward. "Well, you have money, too, right? You won the last show."

I shrugged. "No tax planning . . . old medical bills . . ."

"Me and you are in the same boat, sister. So where's your cute friend?"

I understood now. He wanted to know about Becca because he wanted to get information out of her about the next contest.

"She won't tell you anything."

He quirked an eyebrow at me, giving his most irresistible and practiced smile. "How do you know?"

"She doesn't tell me anything and I'm a lot cuter than you are."

He laughed. "Don't underestimate me."

"You don't need to cheat. You're going to win. No one can compete with you."

He drummed his fingers on his legs. "Yeah, well, don't forget about Todd."

"What about him?"

Cooper got up and headed toward the door, mumbling, "Weak link."

As soon as Cooper left, I knew it was time for action. I put on my sneakers and slipped out of the back door of the B&B.

Seventeen

The doorman held the heavy glass door open for me as I entered the Spanish Moon. Inside, the lobby resembled a historic mansion. Framed in the center of the far wall was a fresco and off to the left was a wrought-iron elevator. I followed the fancy red carpeting over to the mahogany front desk.

I felt grossly underdressed in jeans and sneakers, but the woman working the reception desk made no note of it. Her black hair was secured in a bun and she wore dark red lipstick.

She smiled when she saw me. *"Buenas noches, señorita."*

"Sí, buenas noches," I said, taxing my limited knowledge of Spanish. "I'm looking for someone. Can you tell me if a *Señor* Scott—"

She made a sharp motion with her hand. "No, no, no," she said. "Hotel guest lists are confidential."

My heart sunk. I didn't have a plan B.

What was I thinking?

This was a world-class hotel, they weren't about to give out a guest's information to someone who walked in from the street, in sneakers no less!

"*Señor* Matthew Barrett," I said. "He wrote a book. *Spanish Moon.*"

She shrugged her shoulders as if she didn't know it and could care less.

"Please," I begged. "My boyfriend's gone missing and I thought . . . I think he could be here." I pressed a hand to my heart hoping to appeal to hers.

She smiled sadly, tilting her head to the side as she said, "Yes, many men who don't want to be found are here. I'm sorry, *señorita*, I cannot help you, except to say that if your man is *missing*, forget him." She flicked her hand as if dismissing me.

"He's not that kind of missing," I said. Although I really didn't know, but it seemed worth a shot. "He's in danger kind of missing."

She leveled a gaze at me. "In danger? Then you should call the police." With that she picked up a pen and began to look over her paperwork. Our conversation was over.

I'd struck out, but you don't get fired from San Francisco's police department for following the rules. I'd stake the hotel out. I could wait with the best of them.

"Is there a bar here?" I asked.

The woman put down her pen and drummed her red lacquered nails on the desk. Her eyes were slits as she studied me, then when I thought she would kick me out she said, "Take the elevator to the top floor. You will have a lovely view of the fireworks."

I crossed over to the wrought-iron elevator and pressed the button. Humiliation swelled inside me. What was I doing here? What did I hope to find? Scott/Matthew in bed with some Spanish beauty?

I'd felt certain that Sergio and Montserrat being here meant they had a lead on Scott, but perhaps they were only at the hotel because of the name.

On the fifth floor, I stepped out of the elevator and into the bar. It was brightly lit and decorated with teal and yellow. There were groups of people at various tables. None of them Scott.

The far wall of the bar was entirely made of glass. There was a breathtaking view of the Plaza de Toros which was illuminated in bright lights.

I sat alone at one of the tables and had a good view of the door. If Scott was staying at this hotel, sooner or later he'd hit the bar. Wouldn't he?

I perused the tapas menu while I waited, carefully keeping an eye on the entrance. A familiar figure appeared in the doorway. My heart pounded out of my chest and I hid behind my menu. But by the sound of the approaching footsteps, I could tell he'd spotted me.

Had he followed me to the hotel?

"Do you like the view here better than at my little church?" Sergio asked.

It wouldn't do any good to confess to him my suspicions about Scott, so instead I gave him my best smile and said, "I heard they serve a mean *sangría* at the Spanish Moon."

"Not better than *Señora* Antonia's at the Jaca B&B. Those are the best in town."

I shrugged. "I needed to get away from the cast and stuff."

He rested a hand on the back of a chair. I noted he wasn't dressed in the traditional white garb of the fiestas. Instead he wore dark pants and a blue button-down shirt. He was working tonight. He asked, "May I sit down?"

I glanced in a very obvious way toward the door of the bar. "Oh, I'm meeting my father here," I lied.

He frowned. "I saw your father back at the jousting tournament. He was with his lady friend, Cheryl."

"Right," I said. "They're going to meet me here later," I lied.

He studied me with his dark eyes. He knew I was lying. "It is not typical in Spain for a woman to go have a drink alone." He pulled back the chair he held and seated himself at my table. "I can accompany you for a *sangría*."

"I don't need a chaperone," I protested.

"It is not safe for women to drink alone," he insisted. "Not during the fiestas, when everyone gets out of hand."

"Come on. I used to be a cop. I can take care of myself."

He smiled mischievously. "No, no. I insist. I'll sit with you."

Now I'd have to make up conversation and try to figure out how I could get him off Scott's tail. I imagined Scott walking into the bar. Did Sergio know what he looked like? He must. He had a record of his passport.

"So, you've cleared Victoria and Parker to leave town, huh?" I asked.

He nodded. "I can't hold them. I don't have the evidence."

"Are you going to release the rest of the cast?"

He shook his head. "I can't, no. Not yet."

A passing waiter came by and placed coasters in front of us as Sergio said, *"Dos sangrías."* When the waiter retreated, Sergio asked. "You look very sad, Georgia. Did you find Scott here?"

"No, did you?" I asked.

He cocked his head to the side and studied me. "No, Monse and I were here earlier. He is not registered here."

"I know. I saw you two this afternoon. Dad and I caught a cab out in front and I saw you leaving."

Sergio fiddled with the coaster that was in front of him.

"How did you know I was here now?" I asked. "Did you follow me?"

He shook his head. "No, I figured you think like I do. As soon I realized Matthew Barrett's book title was the same as the hotel, I came to investigate."

The waiter approached with our sangrias and placed a glass in front of each of us. Sergio took a sip and asked. "If he left you, why are you looking for him?"

I laughed bitterly.

It was a good question. Why couldn't I accept the fact that Scott had broken up with me?

"There was something strange about that email." I shrugged. "I can't explain it. Gut feeling."

"Monse has a gut feeling, too."

I quirked an eyebrow at him. "Oh, yeah? What's her gut feeling?"

Running a hand through his hair, he lowered his eyes, giving me a glimpse of his dark thick eyelashes. "Annalise was with a man the night she was killed. Monse thinks maybe you came upon Scott and Annalise together. She thinks you lost your temper and killed the girl. Scared off Scott."

"What? That's absurd!"

The weight of what he was saying suddenly hit me. It was me. They weren't letting the show move on from Jaca because of *me*!

I slammed my fist into the table, nearly toppling over my *sangría*. "I'm your top suspect!" I shouted.

Several people from a nearby table glanced in our direction but said nothing.

Sergio remained calm in the face of my hysterics. He said, "She thinks you sent the email to yourself to fool us."

"I didn't send the email! And anyway if I did, I would have sent the email to myself, not my father."

That was it.

Why had Scott sent the note to Dad?

My head began to throb and I found it hard to concentrate.

"She thinks you are pretending to still be in love with him," Sergio continued. "Because you think that will throw us off."

"She's wrong!" I said.

"I know." He suddenly had a wistful expression on his face. "I know you aren't pretending."

"What?"

He took a sip of his *sangría*. "You still love him. It makes no sense."

I pressed my fingers to my temples. He was right. Scott had abandoned me, lied to me. Completely humiliated me. I didn't even know who he really was.

Scott or Matthew?

And here I was camped out hoping to find him!

What was wrong with me? I was pathetic.

I stood to go, as if the hotel was on fire. I couldn't wait to get out of here and get back to the B&B to be alone with my shame.

Sergio stood with me. "Don't do that."

"Do what?" I asked.

He came to stand next to me, pulling a handkerchief from his pocket. He pressed the silken cloth to my face, wiping the tears I hadn't even realized I was shedding. He cupped my head and pulled me into his shoulders. "Don't cry, Georgia."

"I'm so stupid," I sobbed.

"No," he said. "Scott is the stupid one. But don't worry. People can't stay hidden forever. I will find him. You can be sure of that."

Eighteen

....

The following morning, I pried open my red and swollen eyes and saw that Becca, even though she'd gotten in late, was already up and had left. The only evidence that she'd been in the room at all were a few new articles of clothing strewn across her bed. She'd obviously decided against wearing them.

We were supposed to meet outside the B&B to load onto the bus at eight A.M. One glance at the clock told me I was running late. After leaving Sergio, I returned to the B&B and had been grateful to find it deserted. I'd sat in the garden and cried my eyes out, until finally stumbling to bed.

I slipped into jeans and gently pulled a cotton top over my sunburned shoulders. Downstairs the smell of café con leche wafted through the dining hall along with the scent of freshly baked madeleines.

Dad and Cheryl were seated at a small table, huddled together and deep in conversation. A plate of warm buttery pastries sat untouched between them.

"Good morning," I said, slipping into their booth and snagging a madeleine. I broke it in half and watched the steam escape before I realized that Dad and Cheryl had gone silent.

Both Dad and Cheryl glanced nervously at each other, seemingly uncomfortable at leaving their previous conversation behind.

What had I interrupted?

Dad patted my sunburned shoulder and I winced. "Morning, Peaches," he said.

"What's going on?" I asked.

Cheryl waved a hand and picked up her coffee mug. "Nothing, Georgia. I was just boring your dad with schedule and logistics stuff."

I frowned. Dad wasn't supposed to be privy to any of the logistics.

Cheryl seemed to realize this at the same time I did because she pursed her lips then shrugged.

"Is it top secret?" I asked.

Dad smiled. "Nothing between us is top secret, honey."

I couldn't shake the feeling that I had interrupted something but clearly they weren't going to be straight with me. "Were you talking about me, or what?"

Cheryl grabbed a madeleine off the plate. "Guilty as charged. We heard you were crying in the garden last night and I'm wondering when you're going to get over him."

"You heard I was crying in the garden from who? No one was here."

"That's beside the point really, isn't it?" Cheryl said.

"Well, I'm over him. Okay? I needed to get it out of my system, but last night I realized that I didn't even know who he was really. Scott, Matthew, whatever."

Dad frowned. "Matthew? What are you talking about?"

"Scott was Matthew Barrett. I suppose he has millions of dollars, hidden away somewhere—"

Cheryl nearly spit out her coffee. "Wait a minute! What are you talking about? The thriller writer? Scott's not Matthew Barrett, I know Matthew Barrett."

"You know him?" I asked.

"Yeah. All of Hollywood knows him. I've been after him for a few years now to get the rights to produce some of his titles."

"But Scott's mom told me Scott wrote *Spanish Moon*."

"*Spanish Moon*? I love that book," Dad said.

Cheryl shrugged. "Well, maybe he did, but if he wrote it, then he did it as a ghostwriter, and it's probably highly confidential. I can't see Matthew Barrett being very happy about that leaking out, so you probably shouldn't blab it around."

"I'm not blabbing it around."

Cheryl made a dismissive gesture with her hand and finished her coffee. "Let's go. We need to get on that bus."

"Where are we going? Pamplona for the running of the bulls?" Dad joked, winking at me.

"It's not the right time. That's in July," Cheryl said,

standing. "And I know you're joking, but I would have booked it if I could have."

Dad stood and put his arm around Cheryl. "I know. That's why I'm glad it's only May." They walked toward the exit.

So Scott wasn't Matthew Barrett. I felt relieved. Ghostwriting a book was common in the publishing industry. At least Scott didn't have some secret identity he hadn't told me about. I grabbed the last madeleine off the plate even though my stomach turned at the thought of another competition. I shoved the rest of the pastry in my mouth and got up. Was there a way I could convince Becca to let me stay back?

I left the bed-and-breakfast and walked down the narrow tile patio toward the front of the building. The air smelled fresh and clean and I longed to feel the same way.

Why did disaster follow me around?

The white crew bus was parked in the alley, and Becca and Juan Jose were talking to each other. Montserrat stood near them with her arms folded across her chest. She seemed to watch me carefully, or maybe it just felt that way after what Sergio told me last night.

Becca smiled when she saw me approach. "Sorry to get you out of bed so early, Sleeping Beauty. Did you have breakfast? You're going need some energy for today."

I shrugged. "Can I talk to you?"

Becca glanced from Juan Jose to Montserrat. "Of course." She stepped away from them and moved down the alley a bit.

I filled Becca in on what Cheryl had said about Matthew Barrett. "So Scott didn't lie to me about that," I said.

Becca sighed. "Come on, G. You can't still be hung up on him. Even if he didn't lie to you about that, he still took a hike. I know you don't want to face things. But he sent you an email breaking up with you and the police—"

"The police think I killed Annalise," I said.

Becca frowned. "What?"

"That's why they're not letting us leave town, Becca." I indicated Montserrat who stood at a discreet distance, watching us talk. "It's all because of me."

"That's ridiculous," Becca said. "Anyway, we all know Scott's the prime suspect—"

"He's not a murderer!"

"I know that. I didn't mean that. I only mean . . . you know . . ." She waved her hand, clearly not wanting to say it straight out.

"You mean he doesn't love me."

Becca lowered her eyes. "I'm sorry, G." She raised them to meet mine. "I just know you deserve better. You deserve someone to be by your side. Not abandon you. He's as bad as Paul."

That stung. Paul, my former fiancé, had left me at the altar, alone in front of God, my family, and all of my friends.

"It's not the same," I insisted. "What if something's happened to him? I . . ." I let my words trail off as a uniformed bus driver approached Becca.

The driver told Becca that we needed to board the bus in the next few minutes in order to miss commuter traffic. Becca nodded her understanding, then turned to wave over Juan Jose. "We need to gather everyone up. Can you help with that?"

He nodded. "We're all here except Miguel."

"Miguel?" Becca asked.

Juan Jose shrugged. "He likes to sleep in."

"Can you go get him?" Becca asked.

Juan Jose nodded, but I said, "I'll go. I want to grab some more aloe vera for my sunburn. I can swing by Miguel's room on the way."

"Hurry up," Becca said.

I checked the bar and breakfast area on my way in, still sulking over having to compete on the show today. But I knew Dad needed me now and ultimately Becca was right, technically speaking, Scott had broken up with me and I'd have to get over him.

The bar area was quiet except for the senora who ran the inn. She glanced up at me as I walked in. "I'm looking for Miguel," I said.

She nodded. "I haven't seen him this morning, but last night he was up late at the fiestas."

"Right. Thank you," I said.

I took the back staircase up to the second level, where I knew the crew's rooms were. I actually didn't know which one was Miguel's, but figured it couldn't be that hard to find him. I called his name as I knocked on the first door on the right. No answer. I jiggled the door handle. Locked.

Moving on to the next door, I gave a sharp rap and called out, "Miguel, we have to get on the bus."

He'd probably partied late into the night and was hungover, trying to rouse him would be akin to waking the dead. When I didn't get an answer from the second door, I tried the knob. Again locked.

I moved to the third, thinking I probably should have asked the senora which room was Miguel's.

At the third door, my patience was wearing thin. "Hey, Miguel. Time to rise and shine!" I twisted the knob and the door opened to reveal a small room with a single bed. Miguel was face down, dead asleep.

"Wakey, wakey," I said, from the doorway.

I heard footsteps ascending the staircase and turned to see Becca coming down the hall. "What's taking so long?" she asked.

"He's totally out," I said.

She frowned and peered into the room. "Miguel, our bus is getting ready to leave! Get up."

He was motionless. A bad feeling snaked around my heart and my breath caught. Becca and I glanced at each other.

"Let me get Montserrat, she's downstairs," Becca said.

I took two strides and reached the bed. Placing my hand in the middle of his back, I shook him. He felt rigid, lifeless. "Uh-oh."

"What is it?" Becca squeaked. "Is he okay?"

"I don't think so."

Because death seems to have a magnetic pull, Becca joined me in the room. "Is he . . ."

"Overdose, maybe," I said, pointing to an empty bottle by the nightstand. Becca made a move to pick up the bottle. "No don't. We shouldn't touch anything. We need to call Sergio right away. Get Montserrat up here."

Becca nodded. "Right. Right." Her eyes filled with tears. "I can't believe it!"

"I know. What a waste. He was so nice to me and Dad. It's awful."

"Do you think . . . do you think his death is related to the woman?" she asked.

I shrugged. "It's hard to say. They may be connected. But I don't know."

The thought occurred to me that if the deaths were connected, then Scott was totally off the hook. He'd been nowhere near here last night. A modicum of relief breathed through my body.

"It could have been an accident," Becca said. "He partied too hard and . . ."

I shrugged. "Yeah. It's possible."

Becca and I turned to leave the room and an object in the nook behind the door, caught my attention.

My stomach sank, and the madeleines that I scarfed down for breakfast burned.

Becca saw the object and gasped.

In the corner of the room, a mobile phone was on the floor. An iPhone with a cover so familiar neither of us could feign ignorance.

She squeezed my arm. "Georgia! It's Scott's phone."

We were frozen in place. Every fiber in my being

desperate to pick up the phone, to hide it, to erase whatever meaning the police would attach to it.

What was Scott's phone doing here?

Where was Scott? How was he connected to all this?

I swallowed the dread building in my throat. "I'm going to grab it," I whispered.

"You can't," Becca whispered back. "It's evidence, right? You said so yourself that we shouldn't touch anything—"

"I have to! The police are going to confiscate it. They won't tell me anything about where he is or why—"

"No. It's wrong!" Becca said.

I choked back my tears. "It's not wrong. Scott didn't kill Miguel! They're going to pin everything on him!"

"But it's illegal!" Becca insisted. "Tampering with evidence! We could—"

A pair of footsteps echoed down the hallway and a voice called out, "Becca?"

It was Montserrat. In moments she would be upon us. My window of opportunity narrowing.

Becca gripped my arm. "You can't interfere. You have to let justice take its course! You taught me that."

Another voice called out, "Georgia?" It was Sergio.

"Not in a foreign country! What kind of justice system do they have here?" I didn't know and some part of me rejected everything I'd ever been trained to do, and I dove for the phone.

"No!" Becca said.

Sergio and Montserrat burst into the room, just as

my hand wrapped around the phone. Montserrat rushed to Miguel's bedside, but Sergio was upon me. "What's going on?" he asked.

My vision tunneled and I pushed him back away from me, adrenaline firing my limbs and body with unnatural strength. Sergio stood his ground, his eyes locked on mine.

"We found him like this," Becca said.

Sergio looked over at Becca, who pointed to Miguel, giving me the necessary time to slip Scott's phone into my pocket.

"We were about to call you," I said. There was no way Sergio could know the phone I'd just held wasn't mine, although he might question my strange reaction to him. But hey, people got strange around dead bodies, it didn't have to mean I was tampering with the scene.

Guilt gripped at my heart and I found myself trying to figure out a way to undo what I'd just done. Scott wasn't a killer. Why couldn't I let the police do their job?

Montserrat was already on a mobile, directing someone into action. Sergio paced the room and stopped short by the dresser. Becca was pale as she backed herself out of the room. She stood in the doorway looking ready to vomit. We watched Sergio, both of us seeing for the first time what he found so interesting on the dresser.

A blue American passport.

Nineteen

·························

Sergio slipped a pair of tweezers from his pocket and flipped the passport open. My lovely, sexy-as-hell ex-boyfriend's mug smiled up at him.

Sergio released the cover and turned to me, silent. He looked from me to Becca without saying a word.

Becca, for her part, had wiped the sick expression from her features and had her game face on.

I feared I looked as bad as I felt, guilt emanating from every pore of my being.

"*Sobredosis,*" Montserrat declared. "Overdose." Her hands were on her hips and her eyes fixed on the empty pill bottle on the nightstand.

"Hmmm," Sergio said, his eyes still on me.

"I think I should tell the bus driver we're not going to be leaving before the morning commute, right?" Becca asked.

Sergio nodded. "I'll want to speak with everyone again before you all leave the hotel for the day." Becca nodded and turned, but before she could go, Sergio said, "One moment. Can you tell me why you think your friend's passport is here?"

Becca swallowed. "I have no idea." She glanced at me. "G? Do you know what Scott's passport is doing here?"

"Perhaps he thought he was leaving you a love note?" Montserrat said.

"It's a setup," I said, ignoring her snideness. "The killer must have planted it to point you in the wrong direction."

"Or maybe Miguel took it," Becca said. "American passports are valuable. Maybe he needed money. Maybe he had a contact he was going to sell the passport to."

Sergio stroked his chin, ruminated over what she'd said. "Aha. That makes sense. But how would he have gotten it?"

I shrugged. "He stole it."

Sergio nodded. "When? At the camp in the Pyrenees? Or perhaps last night when Scott came to Miguel's room?"

Pressure bumped up against my temples, threatening to explode inside my skull.

Becca cleared her throat. "At the camp, of course! Don't be ridiculous! Scott wasn't in Miguel's room last night. We haven't seen him since that night at the camp. And we all know Miguel was at the fiestas until late last night and stumbled back to the room. I'm sorry, we didn't know how grave it was. We could have saved his life."

Sergio's attention was on Becca and for that I was grateful. The room seemed to lack the sufficient oxygen to keep me from passing out, either that or the culpability of lifting the phone was going to bring me to my knees. I wrestled with remorse and the burning desire to leave the room and search the phone for clues.

"Who was with Miguel at the fiestas?" Montserrat asked.

Becca shrugged. "Everyone, even you, Monse."

"Not everyone," Montserrat corrected. She glared directly at me. "Not Georgia."

Oh, no.

Sergio looked from me to Montserrat. "She was with me."

Resentment flashed through Montserrat's face, then she asked. "What time did you return to the B&B?" She kept her eyes on me when she added, "I assume you returned last night, but everyone knows about American woman, so maybe not."

Crap. According to her, I was either a tramp or a murderer.

"I need to the use the restroom," I lied, pushing my way past Becca and into the hallway.

Sergio grunted something as I left the room. I thought he might have been defending my honor, but that hardly mattered at the moment. Sirens sounded down the street, and I guessed that was the result of Montserrat's phone call.

Safely inside the restroom, I retreated into one of

the toilet stalls and pulled Scott's phone from my pocket. My chest constricted and I suddenly found myself sobbing.

Oh, Scott! What's going on with you?
Where are you? What are you doing?

I scrolled his recent call log. There was nothing more current then the call he'd made to the States, to his mother, when we'd arrived in Spain. I searched his text log, also nothing current, and then his email data. The last communication was the email to Dad.

I stared at the screen. Something was there that I wasn't seeing. What was it?

I realized that Dad's contact information was saved as only his initials, G.T. Dad and I had the same initials. I was saved as "Peaches," which had always been Dad's nickname for me and Scott took to it immediately.

Scott would have never sent a good-bye email to me at Dad's address. It had to come from someone else. Whoever had stolen Scott's phone. I desperately wished I had access to a fingerprint kit. Sergio probably did, but it wasn't the sort of thing I could ask him without raising all sorts of red flags.

There was a loud commotion down the hall and I figured the crime scene team had arrived. If Scott had been in Miguel's room, they'd find evidence of him. Hair, prints, sloughed-off skin cells, something. I could rest assured that Sergio would let me know that at the very least. If Scott hadn't been here, the killer had likely stolen his phone and passport.

Who among us was the most likely suspect now?

Downstairs, the cast and crew mulled around the bar gossiping about Miguel.

Juan Jose's eyes were glassy. "I have to call his folks. I don't know if the police . . . Did the police call them?"

Dad stood and grabbed Juan Jose's shoulder. "I'm sure they did, son, but if you are close to his parents, they'll certainly appreciate hearing it from you, too."

Juan Jose took a deep breath. "Of course, of course. You are right. Please excuse me. I'll let Becca know that I need to pay them a visit now."

Cheryl stood up. "Don't worry about Becca. I'll let her know. We'll be giving everyone the day off today at least. We'll see if we can get the bus for tomorrow."

Juan Jose frowned, a deep crease lining his handsome face. "Will the police let us leave the hotel tomorrow?"

"We're going to try," Cheryl said.

Juan Jose turned to leave and Cheryl sat back down. "Anyone hungry?" she asked.

"Food? How can we think about food!" I asked.

Dad looked chagrined. "I'm hungry."

"I'm hungry, too," Cheryl said unapologetically. "I'm going to look for the senora and see if she can serve us lunch."

My stomach churned. Food was the last thing on my mind. "Eat then. I'm going out for some air."

I left the dining room and entered the hallway on my way to the gardens. I wracked my brain to review the night before. How long had I been in the garden? When I'd arrived back at the B&B it had been quiet. When had Miguel returned?

Angry voices wafted down the passageway. I could make out Cooper and Todd arguing. On instinct, I froze, then pressed against the wall out of anyone's line of vision. I slowly inched toward the voices.

"Why didn't you tell me?" Cooper asked.

"Because I knew how you'd react," Todd said.

"Man, you are an idiot. Just plain stupid! A stupid idiot," Cooper said.

"I'm not a stupid idiot! Stop calling me that."

"You're going to get caught!" Cooper said. "There ain't no two ways about it."

From behind me the dining room doors swung open into the hallway and DeeCee said, "Georgia! How are you doing? I heard you found poor Miguel!"

Cooper and Todd rounded the corner. Todd's eyes blazing with fury. Cooper looked frustrated and tired.

"What are you doing? Eavesdropping on us?" Todd demanded.

Cooper put a hand on Todd's shoulder. "Chill out, man."

"No! I won't chill out," Parker said. "I want to know what the hell she's doing sneaking up on us?"

DeeCee looked alarmed. "I'm not sneaking up on you. I only just left the dining room!"

"Not you," Todd said. He pointed a finger right at my face. "Her!"

I batted away his hand. "Don't point at me. I'm not eavesdropping. I only left the dining room a moment before DeeCee. But anyway, what are you hiding that you're so nervous we may have overheard?"

Todd turned beet red. "You're not going to trap me in with any of your ol' stupid cop tricks!"

Cooper feigned a laugh, only instead of his charming contagious laugh, this one was more of an "aw shucks, folks, nothing to see here" laugh. He patted Todd on the back, trying to steer him toward the dining room. "Let's see about some food."

Todd shrugged him off. "Why do people keep dying around you, Georgia? Are we in danger? I heard you were the only one at the B&B when Miguel got back here."

DeeCee gasped.

"Todd, stop it, now," Cooper said. "You know Georgia didn't have anything to do with that girl's death or Miguel's, either, for that matter."

"I don't know anything of the sort!" Todd protested.

"I thought Miguel overdosed," DeeCee said. "He wasn't murdered? Was he?"

Cooper let a little hiss of air escape through his bright straight teeth. "Ain't that a crying shame?"

"We won't know anything for a while," I said.

Daisy came into the hallway, she was smiling like usual, but upon seeing our row of serious expressions she became somber. "What's going on?" A hand fluttered to her ample chest. "Don't tell me . . . it's another . . ."

"No," Cooper said. "Nothing. We were talking about when they might let us leave and what we thought the next challenge might be."

"Oh! Well in that case I have news. We're not leaving right away, but the next challenge is supposed to start this afternoon."

"This afternoon?" I asked.

She nodded. "That's what I came out to tell you. The producer, Cheryl, said we're starting right after lunch. So she wanted everyone to report to the dining room for instructions."

Dread mixed with fear in my belly. Cheryl had just said we'd have the day off. How could they already have another challenge planned for us? Or maybe they'd been able to salvage the one from this morning. Either way, I was scared about whatever Becca and Cheryl had cooked up.

We all met in the dining room, where the large center table had already been set for lunch.

Dad was seated near where the buffet line would start. I knew his game, nothing would get in the way of his meals. He patted the chair next to him as I walked over.

"What do you know?" I asked. "Spill it."

He glanced at the others clearly within earshot. "I don't know much, Peaches."

I doubted that, but I supposed that he didn't want to say anything in front of everyone else.

The rest of the cast and crew followed me in, some from the hallway where we'd just had our heated conversation and others from the garden, where they'd taken the time to sit in sun and work on their tans.

Becca and Cheryl were in conversation with Kyle, who seemed to simultaneously be speaking with them and directing the senora of the house about our lunch.

The fragrances of garlic frying in olive oil overwhelmed me, and my mouth salivated before I even set eyes on the platters of food. Several waiters brought out trays of *jamón serrano*, roasted potatoes, *migas*, prawns in garlic sauce, and *morcilla*.

When she saw that most of us were seated, Becca cleared her throat and addressed us. "Folks, it has certainly been an unfortunate morning. While we didn't know Miguel for long, I know many of us had come to appreciate him a great deal and I know we're all going to miss him."

There was general rumble of consensus throughout the group.

"But even Miguel knew that the show must go on," Cheryl interrupted. "So, while it was a difficult decision, the line producer and I have decided that we'll go ahead and film the next challenge today and, God willing, the finale tomorrow."

There was another rumble throughout the group, this one not as friendly. One of the cameramen shouted out, "Who will take Miguel's place? Do we even have another cameraman?"

Becca indicated Kyle. "We've had a volunteer," she said.

Kyle pursed his lips, looking as sour as a blackberry out of season.

Volunteered, my foot!

More like Cheryl had given him an ultimatum.

I squeezed Dad's arm and whispered. "Seriously? Kyle is our cameraman now?"

Dad gave a curt nod. "Apparently, they're used to switching around a bit, what with a tight budget. Cheryl used to do makeup, did you know?"

I nodded. "Do you think we can convince Becca or Cheryl to assign Kyle to a different team?"

Dad quirked an eyebrow. "You want one of the locals, so you can get insider information like Miguel gave us?"

"It's not that. Kyle hates me."

"No, he doesn't."

"He does. He tried to kill me with stilettos on the last show."

Dad snorted. "He was part of the hair and makeup crew, what did you expect?"

I snarled, but said nothing. I'd have to take up the cause with Becca on my own.

The buffet was officially open and we moved through the line, piling our plates high with ham, potatoes, and prawns.

Cooper was behind me in line and I was grateful for small mercies, because he seemed to be emptying the chafing dishes onto his plate. "Man! I love these *morcillas*!" he said.

Todd, who was behind Cooper, replied with. "I'd like to try one, too, if you'd leave any."

"She'll bring out more. Just tell the senora," Cooper said. Then he flagged her down and gave her a winning smile. "Beautiful lady! Bring more food for my friend. He's hungry!"

The woman practically purred at Cooper, "*Sí, sí*," she said, scurrying back to the kitchen. Woman were putty in his hands, it didn't matter if they were eighteen or eighty-one or right in between.

Up close, I noticed Cooper's eyes were bloodshot. "How late did you stay out partying, Coop?"

"Not late." He laughed. "Two A.M. ain't late, is it? Heck, baby girl. This is a competition. I gotta stay sharp." He gave me a lopsided smile.

"Did you come back to the hotel with Miguel?" I asked.

Todd poked Cooper to move along in the line, which of course prodded me to move on, too.

Why didn't Todd want me to talk to Cooper? He was definitely hiding something; either that or he was trying to protect Cooper.

I let Cooper go ahead of me in line and waited for Todd. "How about you? What time did you get in?"

Todd frowned. "I already told it all to the *sargento*."

"Sergio? I don't think he's a sergeant."

Todd waved a hand, dismissing me and my comment. Man, sometimes I hated that guy.

I move ahead of him in line and grabbed the pair of tongs that was placed in front of the pork chops smothered in white wine sauce. I plucked the last pork chop off the chafing dish.

Todd let out a growl as if I'd shot him.

I hovered the pork chop over his plate. "If you want the last chop, tell me what time you got in last night and who you were with."

Todd pursed his lips at me and eyed the pork chop. "If you must know, pork isn't my favorite."

I motioned to slid it on my plate.

"But, I do like the way the senora cooks it."

I raised an eyebrow. "What time did you get back to the B&B?"

Todd sighed. "I never left. Cooper was with Double D. It gets boring after a while to watch everyone fawn all over him. So I stayed in. Just me and the tele. Satisfied?"

"Very," I said, dropping the chop onto my plate and turning away from him.

Home alone. He had no alibi.

Twenty

....

We'd been given limited information, but I happened to glimpse the crew loading race bikes into a nearby truck, so I gathered we were off to a bike race.

Dad and I were first on the bus, and in a hushed whisper he said to me. "Bike riding, then something to do with sheep."

"Sheep? Fortunately I didn't see them load any sheep onto the bus!" I joked. "Although I wouldn't put it past Cheryl."

"Well, you know, Spain has a lot of sheep," Dad said. "I think they're going to make us milk them or something. Should be a piece of cake."

I laughed, imagining Double D milking sheep. "The girls aren't going to like that. It'll be smelly and messy."

Dad gave me a big grin. "It's a perfect match for me."

It was true. Dad had hurt his knee about a year ago and the doctor had prescribed long bike rides for him. He loved tooling around Cottonwood on his bike and, of course, being a farmer all his life, he loved anything to do with farm animals.

"It seems like Cheryl rigged this challenge for you," I teased.

DeeCee and Daisy took the seat behind Dad and me. They were followed by Cooper and Todd. The bus seemed empty without Victoria and Parker.

I'd been so suspicious of Victoria. But she was on a flight back to the U.S. around the time Miguel died, so she obviously didn't have anything to do with his death. But what about Annalise?

If the deaths were connected, then the answer was no. And I couldn't see Sergio giving the go-ahead for Victoria to leave the country if she was a serious suspect.

But then Sergio only had one serious suspect, Scott, and Montserrat was convinced it was me.

The crew usually took another bus, but since the cast was dwindling they boarded with us along with their camera equipment and microphones. The only ones not on the bus were Cheryl, Becca, and Harris. They sped off in a yellow convertible SEAT Roadster. It must have been in Harris's contract.

The bus's engine roared to life and we left the B&B behind in a plume of exhaust.

We drove through the Pyrenees foothills, the rolling Spanish countryside taking my breath away. The golden hills were beginning to turn green under the late-spring sun and wild poppies were in bloom.

Dad leaned into me. "Spain reminds me a lot of California."

I laughed. "I thought it was just me. I feel so at home here, the people are all so nice—"

"And the food," Dad said.

"And the wine."

Dad smiled. "I could live here."

"Me, too."

Forty-five minutes later, the bus pulled into a meadow clearing, behind the yellow SEAT. We tumbled out of the bus as some of the crew began to set up the familiar blue tarp. The rest of the crew began to unload the bikes from the small truck that had followed our bus into the mountains. The cast reported to the starting line without being told what we needed to do. We all knew the drill by now.

Harris preened like a peacock, then suddenly became flustered and looked around. "Where's my stylist?"

Kyle popped out from behind a camera. "Oh! I'm over here." He shoved the camera at me and ran over to get his makeup kit.

Cheryl made exasperated noises as we all waited. Finally, she motioned over to Double D's cameraman. "You, take advantage of the scenery to get a confessional."

EXT. MOUNTAINSIDE DAY

DeeCee is looking into the camera, her face is jovial, her fire red-hair fanned around her face. She is dressed

*in a bright maroon top that shows off her cleavage.
She adjusts her hair and poses as if getting ready
for the camera to roll, not realizing that she is being
filmed.*

CAMERAMAN (O.S.)
Rolling.

DEECEE
(straightens to attention) Oh! *(waves at the
camera)* Hello, America! I'm DeeCee Duluth,
part of the Double D team. I'm here with my
darling friend Daisy competing on
Expedition Improbable. I have to say, this
has been an *amazing* trip. I've learned so
much about the culture and the music
here . . . the music . . . why, if you
don't know, America, I'm a country-western
singer.
*(She belts out a lyric from "Blue Moon of
Kentucky.")*
*(Daisy bounces into the frame and
harmonizes with her.)*

DAISY
(covering one ear) Oh, girl, you got a
little pitchy.

DEECEE
(looking offended) I did not.

DAISY
Don't get upset. I'm just sayin'.

DEECEE
(placing a hand on her hip) Well, I'm just
sayin' I didn't!

DAISY
*(placing a hand on her hip to match
DeeCee's stance)* I'm not going to have this
argument with you again! *(through gritted
teeth)* And not in front of the camera!
(Turning to the camera, she smiles widely.)
(DeeCee harrumphs and stalks off.)

We lined up in front of Harris.

"Wait a minute," Kyle said as he fumbled with
the camera. "This one's different than the one I used to
work with." He said something in a hushed tone to the
cameraman near him, who answered him back in an
equally hushed tone.

Cheryl lost her patience. "Remind me to fire you all
after the show!"

"You can fire me now if you like," I said.

Dad elbowed me, and Cheryl said, "Shut up, Georgia."

When Kyle seemed to straighten himself out he gave
Cheryl a nod and then Harris exploded into action.
"Welcome to round three of *Expedition Improbable*!
Where nothing can stop you but yourself!" He gave a

cursory recap of yesterday's events for the benefit of the viewing audience, then said, "Cooper and Todd, you've managed to finish in first place on the last two competitions, but will you keep your edge today?"

"You better believe it," Cooper said in an overly positive booming voice.

"I hope so," Todd muttered.

Harris clasped his hands in front of his chest. "Well, remember we have to expect the unexpected. There's plenty of opportunity for anyone who wants to win to make a play for it. And now, since Cooper and Todd finished the last round thirty minutes ahead, you may begin in just a few moments."

"As you can see," Harris continued. "Today's challenge involves cycling. These are the famous hills where Miguel Indurain trained for the Tour de France."

DeeCee gasped and covered her mouth at the same time that Daisy gave a childish clap.

"Poor Miguel!" DeeCee said, looking forlorn.

"We're in France!" Daisy squealed.

"Different Miguel," I said.

"I've always wanted to visit France," Daisy said, giving a little hop. "And now I'm here. I'm finally here. Can we see the Eiffel tower?"

"We're not in France," Dad said.

DeeCee and Daisy both looked confused and I couldn't help but laugh.

"Keep rolling," Cheryl said. "I'll have to splice in images of Cooper's muscular booty on that tiny bike seat to make up for these morons here."

Dad grumbled.

"Not you, Gordon," Cheryl assured him.

"Today will be a rigorous physical challenge for you all," Harris continued. "Followed by a surprise challenge. You'll all be given bikes and you have to navigate the mountain trails on your own. You'll be equipped with maps that will direct you on a treasure hunt, and the buried treasure will give you a clue for the final challenge."

As soon as Harris finished the introduction he raised his hands for Cooper and Todd to get started. They dashed off toward the bicycles followed by their cameraman.

After waiting the specified time, Double D began the challenge. DeeCee and Daisy only had a few minutes advantage over us, but it looked like they fully intended to use it. They strapped on their helmets and rushed off, ditching their cameraman.

Finally, Dad and I were allowed to begin. We rushed over to where the bikes were parked. Dad reviewed the map while I clipped on my helmet.

My ankle was throbbing just from the short jog to the bikes and I prayed it wouldn't hold us back in this competition. The sun was high in the sky, the hottest part of the day and I had already broken a sweat before I'd even mounted the bike.

Dad was in deep conversation with himself over the map. I hopped onto the bike and pedaled toward the dirt trail.

"Wait! I'm not even sure that's the right direction," Dad yelled.

"I'm following Cooper and Todd," I declared.

Dad and Kyle had a brief exchange and then I watched Dad pedal off in my direction without Kyle. Dad soon caught up with me.

"What's going on?" I asked.

"He said he'd rather film DeeCee and Daisy."

"What?" I demanded.

Dad laughed. "I'm kidding. He said they can't film and cycle at the same time. So all the cameras are going to head up the road in the bus."

"Cheryl's not letting him near that yellow convertible, is she?"

Dad chuckled. "I don't even think she'll let me near the convertible. Anyway, each cameraman will be stationed at different spots along the way. Getting us at a distance and all that. He told me to tell you to be good and to save the drama for the camera."

We rode along in silence for a while, until we caught sight of Double D.

"Let's pass them," Dad said.

We pedaled furiously up the hill, DeeCee and Daisy both had their pretty heads down, going as fast as they could muster. They looked miserable and I could sympathize completely. Biking seemed to inflame my ankle and soon after we passed them, I said, "I'm hurting, Dad."

He made a sad face. I knew it was almost unbearable for him to see me in pain, so I tried not to complain too heartily.

"I'd ride for you if I could," he said.

"I'll be okay, Dad." A few more minutes of riding yielded us a view of two cyclers. "I think that's Cooper and Todd ahead of us."

Dad laughed. "Aha! They must have made a bad turn! See, we gotta watch the map."

We joined Cooper and Todd up ahead. Todd scowled at me, but Cooper was his usual friendly self.

We pedaled together up the hill; it was a slow, steady incline, the kind that absolutely kills your thighs and calves.

Double D caught up with us, bringing up the rear. It was soon clear that Dad and Cooper were more used to biking than the rest of us as the distance between us grew. Todd overtook me, but I followed him closely. I was content to let him take the lead. It was early still and if I knew the producers, which I did, this was going to be a long bike ride full of twists and turns.

We came to a fork in the road. Two cameramen were stationed there, the crew bus parked nearby. Kyle was hidden behind the camera, although I'd recognize him anywhere with his flamboyant style of dress and fluorescent shoes.

Dad and Cooper stopped to consult the map between them, but Daisy sped past laughing. "I'm choosing the high road, y'all."

Todd and I joined Dad and Cooper.

"Where the heck do you think she's going?" Cooper asked. "It looks pretty clear to me that we need to take the low road."

"We go into the valley?" I asked.

Dad nodded. "I think so."

I glanced at Kyle for information, but only the wide camera lens greeted me. I suddenly missed Miguel. DeeCee peeked over the ridge just as we were heading past the crew bus and selecting the low road.

"Where's Daisy?" she asked. "Is she already ahead of you?"

"She's ahead of us all right," Dad said. "But she went that way."

"What?" DeeCee demanded.

Cooper shrugged. "Marches to the beat of her own drum."

"Which way are we supposed to go?" DeeCee asked.

Dad took off down the low road, kicking off with a powerful stride. Then called over his shoulder, "You have to decide on your own."

I followed Dad, then Cooper and Todd trailed me. DeeCee remained indecisive until she finally screamed loudly and took off after us. "How do I know you're telling me the truth and not trying to derail me?" DeeCee shrieked.

Todd snorted. "Okay, we're kidding, she's just up ahead here."

"I knew it!" DeeCee screamed, pedaling furiously as she passed us.

Dad and Cooper shared a guffaw, while Todd mumbled something.

"She'll figure it out soon enough," Dad said.

"I should help them though," Cooper said to Dad.

"I'd rather you and Georgia be eliminated first and keep those two hot babes in, honestly. No offense."

Todd laughed. "You got that right."

"No offense taken," Dad said. "Georgia and I feel the same about you."

The road plateaued into a valley. I could see more of the crew stationed ahead in a meadow along with a smattering of white sheep. In the middle of the meadow was our makeshift post. The flag with the show's bull's-eye emblem was billowing in the breeze.

I motioned up ahead. "I think you got the directions right, Dad."

DeeCee sighed. "Oh, well, I guess Daisy will figure it out eventually. Don't you think?"

Dad nodded. "She'll figure it out."

We all jumped off our bikes, leaving them on the dirt trail to run toward the post. As soon as I got off the bike, my knees buckled and I fell to the ground.

Dad stopped next to me. "Georgia! What is it?"

My ankle had swollen to the size of large catcher's mitt. "Go on ahead without me, Dad. I just need a minute. Get the clue."

Dad nodded and ran to join Cooper, Todd, and DeeCee. In the distance, I could see Daisy pedaling furiously down the lane. She'd finally figured out she'd gone in the wrong direction.

She collapsed next to me screaming and howling in obvious pain. Her mascara had run down her face and her hair was wild. The camera crew descended upon us like locusts.

"What is it, Daisy?" I asked.

"Georgia, Georgia," she wailed.

"Are you all right? What's happened?"

She leaned into me crying. "Georgia, I can't take it."

I patted her back. "Tell me. What's happened? Did you see something that frightened you?"

She sucked in a huge intake of breath. DeeCee barreled down the hill toward us with Dad right behind her.

"Daisy!" DeeCee cried. "What on God's green earth is going on?"

"I never wanted to ride the stupid bike," Daisy wailed. "And now I can't walk, my bottom is all bruised up and my legs have cramps."

Dad bit back his laughter.

"Oh, grow up!" DeeCee said.

"I only wanted to sing, Georgia. That's all. I never wanted to have to go on these crazy trips."

Todd and Cooper ignored our drama and headed in the opposite direction toward the sheep.

"Well, that's a fine how-do-you-do!" DeeCee said. "The show was your bright idea!"

"Look at me!" Daisy said. "I'm a mess! How am I supposed to score a Nashville contract looking like this?"

"She's really not going to like the next part," Dad said.

Daisy's eyes rounded and she looked horrified. "What's the next part?"

"We need to get some milk, before we get the next clue," DeeCee said.

"What?" Daisy wailed. "There's no stores around here! And I'm not biking anymore!"

Dad chuckled. "Not from a store, honey. From one of them." He pointed toward the sheep.

Daisy fell into a heap sobbing.

Twenty-one

....

EXT. MEADOW DAY

Gordon is looking into the camera. He is dressed in a summer plaid shirt with blue-and-yellow checks and chino pants. His hair is styled back and his face is flushed.

GORDON
(*smiles*) Hello. I'm Gordon Thornton. I'm pleased to be one of the contestants on *Expedition Improbable*. I'm competing with my daughter, Georgia, whom some of you may know from a show she appeared on called *Love or Money*. (*looks down*) I'm not sure that one ended too well . . . but . . . you know,

we're back in the saddle. Hoping for a win.
There's some pretty tough competition this
time around. *(chuckles)* We're up against a
former NFL MVP and a couple firecrackers
from Nashville. *(wiggles his finger at
camera)* But don't you count the ol' farmer
out. I might still be able to pull a rabbit
out of a hat, and you know, there's nothing
I wouldn't do for my little girl.

While Dad chased the sheep around. I elevated my
ankle. I watched as the crew set up the blue tarp
for our finish line. Each team had to fill a bucket of milk
and turn it in to Harris before we could complete the
challenge. Harris had in his possession some kind of
pass code he would give to the first two teams. The third
team would be eliminated.

Todd and Cooper seemed to be arguing more than
milking any sheep. Daisy and DeeCee, on the other
hand, had bucked up and gotten to work, although their
milking looked more like wrestling as I'd seen Daisy
take a tumble with a sheep a few times.

Once the tarp was set up, I began my hobble over to
the finish line. Dad wasn't done milking the sheep, but
I figured he wouldn't be long. Sure enough, only seconds
before I stepped on to the tarp, Dad appeared next to
me. He reeked like a sheep, but he held up the bucket
full of milk proud as a peacock.

With his free hand, he grabbed mine and we entered the circle together. Harris smiled broadly at us, all teeth. "Georgia! Gordon!" All of sudden he took a step back and said, "Whoa." He fanned his nose and I laughed.

Growing up on a farm I was used to the smells of animals, but Harris seemed mortally offended by my father's aroma.

Dad put the bucket down by Harris's feet. Harris shuddered as he got a whiff of the raw milk. He took a moment to collect himself while Cheryl and Becca giggled in the background. Finally, Harris said, "Welcome. I'm happy to say you are the first team to finish the challenge and are therefore safe from elimination." He presented Dad with a note. "You will need this to be able to complete the challenge tomorrow. Good luck."

Down the lane, Double D approached with their bucket swinging between them.

"Oh, my gosh! DeeCee and Daisy are going to finish next!" I screamed.

"Cooper and Todd are out?" Dad asked. Looking up the hill we saw Cooper and Todd fumbling around with the sheep. "He's tackling that sheep like he's a running back!" Dad said.

As they neared, DeeCee flashed a proud smile, but Daisy had a look of alarm on her face, suddenly she tripped and fell into DeeCee knocking the milk bucket out of her hand and spilling it.

DeeCee screamed out as if acid had burned her skin. "What did you just do?"

"I'm so sorry," Daisy said. "It was an accident! Look, Todd and Cooper are still out there, we have time."

They rushed out looking for any sheep that would give them the time of day, but Cooper let out a huge whoop. Todd pumped his fists in the air and then they rushed down the meadow toward the finishing circle.

This time Harris was prepared for the stench and didn't react when Cooper set the bucket at his feet, instead he beamed his over-whitened smile and said, "Cooper, Todd. I'm happy to say you are the second team to finish the challenge and are therefore safe from elimination." He presented Cooper with a note. "You will need this to be able to complete the challenge tomorrow. Good luck."

DeeCee and Daisy stood nearby, both with glum expressions on their faces. Harris clasped his hands together and arranged his features into his "sad to see you go" look. "DeeCee, Daisy, I can truly say, and I'm sure America will agree with me, it was a pleasure watching you both compete. You should be proud of yourselves and how you tackled each and every challenge. But I'm sorry to say, you didn't complete this challenge in time to continue and are therefore eliminated."

EXT. MOUNTAINSIDE DAY

Daisy is looking into the camera, her face is sun-burned, her long blond hair is matted and has blades of grass sticking out of it. She looks completely ex-hausted.

DAISY
Hello America! I'm Daisy Flowers. Yes,
that's my stage name, of course. I was one
of your fearless competitors on *Expedition
Improbable*. I would have liked to win, but
honestly, I'm glad to have it over with.
(She clamps a hand over her mouth.) Am I
allowed to say that?
(When there is no response, she shrugs.)
It's just that it was a lot of work. And
dirty stuff, too! Look at me. And what you
can't tell from looking at me on the TV is
that I stink to high heaven. Lord! Why did
we have to roll around with those sheep?
And all right, you want a confession? I'll
tell you. I rode my bike in the wrong
direction on purpose. *(sighs)* I was hoping
I could ride off to the woods where no one
would see me and take a nap. That way, by
the time I returned the whole darn thing
would be over and I could rest. But I
scared myself not knowing what was in the
woods, so I pedaled like mad just to catch
up to the group and the sheep—yuck! And
then we were about to finish before Cooper
and Todd. *(She buries her face.)* Lordie! I
just had to spill that milk.

(She glances over her shoulder.) DeeCee's
still crying about it over there, crying
over spilled milk. Ha!
Anyway, me? I'm looking forward to the next
chapter in my life. I hope Nashville will
call, but maybe first a little stop in
Paris to visit with my friend Eiffel.
(wiggling her fingers at the camera)
Georgia and Gordon, Todd and Cooper—you
big hunk of man—I wish you all the best of
luck. It really is going to be a tough one
to call and, you know *(she shoots the
camera with her finger and imitates Harris's
voice)* you have to expect the unexpected.

The ride back to the bed-and-breakfast was horrible.
We were all smelly and worn out, both from wrestling sheep and cycling in the heat.

Even though I was physically exhausted, I itched
to get back to the Jaca to speak with Sergio. Guilt
plagued me for taking the phone and I knew I'd have
to confess.

When the bus pulled into the alleyway, we all piled
out. By some miracle, we'd beat the convertible back to
the B&B. Dad patted my shoulder and said, "Honey,
I'm off to a hot shower and then bed. Before Cheryl gets
here and makes me go out dancing."

I laughed. "Yes, hide from her Dad. Hide!"

"You should do the same," he said.

"Hide from Cheryl?"

He chuckled. "No, you couldn't hide from her if you tried. I meant take a shower and get to bed. And rest that ankle." He kissed me on the check. "I'll see you in the morning."

Daisy and DeeCee were flirting with Cooper, and since the girls would likely be gone the next morning, they mutually decided to party all night.

How could they stay up after all we'd been through that day?

Todd tromped off to his room almost as quickly as Dad did. I retreated to the bar area hoping to find Sergio. Juan Jose was alone at the bar, huddled over a laptop and staring at the screen.

"Have you seen Sergio?" I asked.

Juan Jose jolted up from the laptop. I'd clearly startled him. His eyes were bloodshot and the growth of his beard heavy. "I haven't seen him in a while, why?"

"I just wanted to talk to him about something. Are you working on the logistics? They have you running around a lot, huh?"

"Yes. I need to book flights for Daisy and DeeCee."

"Have they been given the go-ahead to leave the country, then?"

Juan Jose nodded. "Yes, this afternoon. I was a given a list of the cast members allowed to leave. I hadn't been able to book a flight because I needed to plan tomorrow's event and I didn't know who would lose."

I asked. "Hey, was my name on the list?"

"What?"

"You said Sergio gave you a list of who was cleared to leave the country."

He leveled a gaze at me. "Oh, I don't think I'm supposed to say."

"I understand."

There was a manila envelope between us and I itched to grab it. Seeing that list was akin to knowing who Sergio's main suspects were. I tried to distract Juan Jose. "So, there's already an event planned for tomorrow?"

He gave me a sad smile. "Oh, yes. We know the final challenge."

I sat down next to him and propped my foot on the bar stool nearby. "Any chance you'll let slip what the event is?"

He shook his head. "I could get fired and I need the job."

"Right. Sorry," I said.

"I wasn't expecting you to be here. I thought you went to talk to Miguel's parents."

Juan Jose bit his lip. "I did. I had lunch with them this afternoon." He bowed his head as if he didn't want to say anything further.

"Did you know him very well?" I asked.

He shrugged. "We weren't good friends. It's just that Jaca is a small town and everyone knows everybody. My parents go to church with his, you know."

"Do you think he overdosed on purpose?"

"I don't know." Juan Jose closed the laptop and stood.

Señora Antonia came into the bar area holding a tray of sandwiches. The musky smell of *txistorra* sausage, a Spanish specialty seasoned with garlic and red pepper, wafting from the tray. She smiled when she saw me and pushed the tray close. "Eat! Eat!"

I happily reached for the sandwich, a slab of crusty baguette with a hunk of *txistorra* sticking out.

The senora said something to Juan Jose in Spanish.

He smiled at me. "Excuse me, the senora needs my help reaching something." He stood and followed her out of the room.

It was just me, the manila envelope, and my itchy fingers that were now smeared with sausage oil. I grabbed a napkin to wipe my hands.

Since when did I steal evidence and mess with an ongoing investigation?

Oh, heck, Scott's neck was on the line.

As I reached for the envelope I heard footsteps behind me.

Please let it be my Dad or Becca, I prayed.

I turned to see Sergio. He was dressed in white clothes, with the red sash secured around his trim waist. He had the night off.

"*Hola*, Georgia, I heard you are still in the competition, congratulations."

My hand rested on the manila folder as I pretended it was mine, but my cheeks burned and guilt seared through me. The ridiculous thought occurred to me that I wished I'd had the chance to shower, but I was grateful that at least I hadn't wrestled any sheep.

Sergio glanced down at the folder and cocked an eyebrow at me. Did nothing escape his gaze?

I removed my hand. "Have I been cleared to return to the U.S.?"

"Are you leaving? I thought you were still in the game?"

My stomach churned. I was so tired of games. "I'm still on the show. I just wondered. I figured if I've been cleared to travel, then I'm not a suspect anymore."

He shook his head. "I'm afraid not." He sat down next to me and reached for a sandwich. "Mmm *txistorra*. My favorite." He leaned into me, his shoulder bumping mine in an attempt to lift my spirits. "What do you eat in the United States? Hamburgers and french fries?"

I laughed. "That's such a cliché!"

He chuckled. "Hot dogs, too, maybe, or"—he made a face—"macaroni and cheese?"

"We have better food than that," I said.

He smiled and teased, "Kentucky Fried Chicken?" I socked his arm and he shifted away me, laughing.

We ate in silence for a moment and I hate to admit that I swallowed the sandwich practically whole and reached for another.

Sergio glanced at my ankle. "No dancing for you tonight."

"No. I have to get to bed early." A bit of sadness washed over me as I realized that Sergio was likely on his way to the fiestas and I would be at the B&B. Then I remembered the evidence I stole out of Miguel's room and shame engulfed me. I had to tell Sergio.

I took a breath and turned to him, startled to find that

his dark eyes were on me. He had a way of looking at me that made me feel completely transparent. Did he already know I'd lifted Scott's phone?

"Do you know anything about Miguel's death you can share with me?" I asked.

He reached for another sandwich. "How bad is your ankle?"

"What?"

"Maybe we can trade."

"Trade what?" I asked.

He smiled. "A dance for information."

I laughed. "I can't dance."

He bit into the sandwich. "Maybe I can think up another trade."

The senora came back into the bar and greeted Sergio warmly. They exchanged pleasantries in Spanish and I noticed that Sergio pointed at my ankle. The senora came closer to me and hugged my head to her large bosom muttering, "*¡Ay! Pobre Georgia!*"

She said something else I didn't understand, but it took all my strength not to weep in her arms. What was it about these kind people? I felt like the senora could have been my mother. She slipped behind the bar and poured us two glasses of red wine. Then she left the room again.

Sergio sipped his wine quietly, presumably waiting for me to blab on. I knew the game. Stay quiet, let the suspect confess. Even better if you can ply them with alcohol. Instead of talking, I took another bite of my *txistorra* sandwich and washed it down with red wine.

Finally, he said, "I have something to tell you. I looked into Matthew Barrett—"

"Oh, yes." I filled him in on what Cheryl had told me and he concurred that his research had uncovered the same thing. Scott wasn't sitting on millions of dollars; he just simply had worked for hire on a book for Matthew.

"I found something else though," Sergio said. "I found the woman Scott visited in Spain."

My breath caught.

"She's seventy years old. Married to one of the richest men in Jaca. The owner of the Spanish Moon. In fact, she ran the hotel for many years. Grew it into what it is now."

Relief flooded me. Scott hadn't been dating someone in Spain; he wasn't off revisiting an old fling. He'd been researching a book!

Sergio took a sip of his wine and said sadly, "She seemed as fond of him as you are."

The senora reappeared with a pill bottle and a jar of lotion in her hands. She passed the items to Sergio and left the room without another word.

He opened the small pill bottle and placed two tablets next to my wine. "For the inflammation," he said.

I looked at the pills, something nagging at me. "Do you know how Miguel died? Has the medical examiner confirmed an overdose?" I asked.

Sergio nodded. "Overdose of narcotics. It looks like he or someone else smashed the pills on the night table into a glass of water. We found the pill residue on the table."

"That almost suggests murder, doesn't it? I mean, if

he wanted to take the pills himself, wouldn't he have just swallowed them? If they were smashed on the table and then put into the water, then someone else could have done that and made him drink it, right?"

Sergio nodded. "My thoughts exactly." We were quiet for a moment. Then Sergio asked, "Did Scott do drugs, Georgia?"

"No."

Sergio looked at my swollen ankle, then reached out and lifted my foot onto his knee. "He didn't take anything for an old injury?" he asked. "Any prescription medicine?"

I shook my head, but a thought nagged at the back of my head.

Sergio unlaced my sneaker and lowered my sock.

"No, don't," I said, attempting to pull my leg away from him.

He held tight to my knee. "Do you think Spain doesn't train the police in first aid?" He winked.

I laughed. "It's not that."

"I won't let you die from a sprained ankle, Georgia," he said, in a teasing tone.

"Come on, let go," I protested. When he didn't, I said, "My feet smell. I've been riding a bike in the mountains all day—"

He ignored me. "Do you know the things I have smelled as an officer?" He wrinkled his nose and said, "Disgusting."

With his Spanish accent, I think it was the cutest delivery of the word *disgusting* I'd ever heard. I relented and let him slather the cream onto my ankle. His hands were smooth and warm as he massaged the lotion into my skin and for a moment I was mesmerized by him.

"It feels better already," I said. "Thank you."

He finished working my ankle, but kept one hand on my leg, gently stroking my calf. Electricity sparked between us and my mouth suddenly went dry. I looked into his dark eyes and his gaze was so consuming it inflamed my blood.

In a low voice, he said, "Not good enough to dance tonight, but maybe tomorrow . . ."

"Tomorrow," I murmured.

He leaned in slowly toward me and time seemed to stop. Our foreheads met. His breath was on my lips. He whispered my name.

Then from the doorway, someone else called my name.

"Georgia!" Montserrat called out.

Sergio and I both started. I overcorrected so far away from him I nearly toppled off the stool. He grabbed my elbow and steadied me.

"*Tranquila,*" he said softly. "Easy."

Montserrat smiled widely; she had a look of pure satisfaction at interrupting our encounter. "I found your *boyfriend,*" Montserrat said.

Sergio stood. "Where is he?"

Montserrat licked her lips, enjoying her triumphant moment. "Huesca hospital."

Twenty-two

······································

"The hospital!" I said. "Is he all right?"

"He's had a head injury," she said. "They have him in a medically induced coma."

"Oh, my God. Is he going to be okay?" I asked. Despair ripped through me, leaving me shaky and light-headed.

Montserrat shrugged. Clearly Scott's prognosis wasn't her top concern. "He was listed as a John Doe."

A car engine roared up the road toward the B&B and we all turned to see the yellow convertible park haphazardly on the grass. Cheryl, Becca, Kyle, and Harris flopped out of the car and burst through the doors of the B&B. It was clear that they had stopped for drinks along on the way.

Kyle and Harris immediately tracked down the senora and ordered another round while I filled Cheryl and Becca in on Scott's status.

"Let's go right now!" Cheryl slurred. "I can drive to West Gate."

"*Huesca,*" Montserrat corrected.

"That's what I said," Cheryl insisted with a snarl. She wasn't about to be out-catted by anyone.

"No, no, no," Sergio said. "You cannot drive. I will drive."

"We're going, too!" Becca said. "Where's Gordon?"

"In his room sleeping," I said.

Cheryl clapped her hands together. "Well, I'll take care of that! Give me two minutes and I'll get his little booty down here!"

Sergio and Montserrat proceeded to have a heated discussion in Spanish. I looked to Becca to see if she could make out anything. She shook her head, then whispered. "I'll get Juan Jose, see if he can eavesdrop and translate for us."

Before Becca could leave, Sergio and Montserrat came to a consensus. "I'll take Georgia in my car. Montserrat will drive the SEAT—"

Dad burst into the bar area. "No, no, no! Gordon will drive the SEAT." Dad embraced me and said, "I heard the good news."

"He's in a coma, Dad," I said, suddenly weeping.

"Now, honey, be strong. Everything is going to be fine."

I ended up riding in the SEAT smashed between Cheryl and Becca in the backseat. Dad drove and Sergio navigated. Montserrat had declined to come. She had the night off and made a rather big show of telling Sergio that she'd rather sit at the bar and drink with Harris and Kyle then come along. She said she trusted him to investigate.

Whatever that meant.

I was sure it was a dig at me, but I couldn't be bothered with that. I was too worried about Scott.

Dad drove cautiously because he didn't know the roads and I secretly wished Sergio had insisted on driving. I knew he would have gotten us to the hospital at lightning speed and right now I needed to see Scott so urgently it hurt.

The night air was warm and under any other conditions it would have been heaven to travel on the interchange in the convertible. But Cheryl and Becca were both deliriously drunk and I was sandwiched in between them. They had to scream at each other to be heard.

"That dog, Scott, better not be faking this," Cheryl yelled. "I could be out dancing right now." She snapped her fingers around as if we cared.

"I'm sure he's not faking it!" Becca said.

I chewed on my nails, trying to tune them out. Thoughts about Scott's head injury tortured me. How serious was it? Did he have brain damage? Would it be permanent? Did he remember that night? Would he remember me?

Cheryl wiggled her bottom as if dancing to a song in her head. "Well, all I can say is I'm very happy with how the filming is going. Even if our schedule was completely hosed. Today was fantastic."

Becca agreed. "Too bad about your ankle, G," Becca

said. "That really slowed you down today. How's it feel now?"

"A little better," I admitted.

"I thought Cooper's injury was going to slow him down," Cheryl said. "But the man is like a bull!"

"Cooper has an injury?" I asked.

"Old football injury," Becca said.

"The man is like a bull, I tell you," Cheryl repeated. "I'd love to have you all running with the bulls, can we arrange that?"

"I already told you we can't," Becca said. "The bull-fights are in the summer. We're too early."

"Maybe we can create some bulls with special effects or something," Cheryl insisted.

Cooper had an old football injury! That's what had been nagging at me earlier. I'd seen him take pain pills for it. I tapped Sergio on the shoulder and he turned around.

"Woo-we," Cheryl said to Sergio. "Honey, I have to tell you, you got a face that stops hearts. What's it gonna take to bring you to Hollywood?"

"Cooper takes prescription medicine," I said.

He frowned. "What kind?"

"I'm not kidding!" Cheryl said. "What's it gonna take?"

"I don't know," I admitted.

Sergio nodded. "I'll look into it."

"I'd sure appreciate that, honey. You look into it and tell me what it's going to take," Cheryl said. "I can negotiate. You tell me what you need."

Sergio frowned at her, but suddenly he looked up and said to Dad, "This exit. Take this exit!"

. . . .

We parked and walked toward the hospital's main entrance. My nerves pulsed through my body and if it weren't for Dad holding me up, I feared I'd need the wheelchair that was stationed just inside of the glass double front doors. The hospital smelled sterile and I realized with a jolt that hospitals smelled the same no matter what country you were in.

We passed by a nurses' station and Sergio inquired about Scott. He showed the nurse his badge and they had a prolonged conversation in Spanish while I chewed down my remaining nails. Thankfully, Cheryl and Becca had begun to sober up; either that, or being in a hospital had completely killed their buzz. They collapsed into the hard orange plastic chairs of the waiting room and fidgeted silently.

Finally, the nurse nodded and ducked down a narrow passageway. Sergio turned to Dad and me. "She's gone to get the doctor."

She returned with a tall, thin man. He had glasses and wore a doctor's coat. He spoke with Sergio, who translated for us. Scott had been picked up in the Pyrenees by a driver who'd brought him here, as it was the closest hospital. He'd had no ID and the hospital had classified him as a John Doe. They notified the Huesca police, but everyone had incorrectly assumed Scott was Spanish so no one had answered the Jaca Police Department requests regarding a missing American.

The emergency room doctor had immediately prescribed barbiturates because they slow the metabolic rate of the brain and with less brain activity, there would be less blood flow, which would reduce the swelling and also decrease the possibility of brain damage.

"No brain damage?" I asked.

Sergio translated my question and the doctor responded in Spanish. Sergio turned to me and said, "He says it's too early to tell. Just this afternoon, they began to decrease the medication, but it will be another twenty-four to forty-eight hours before he wakes up."

"Can I see him?"

The doctor led Dad and me down the narrow corridor. My knees were shaking as we walked. We pushed open the door to Scott's room. He lay in the bed, eyes closed, IV tube and an oxygen mask attached. Despite all the tubes stuck to him, I felt relieved to see him. I rushed to his bedside and kissed him all over his face.

I babbled like an idiot and waited for Scott to respond.

At one point, his eyelids fluttered and I wept.

I stayed with Scott for six hours and I would have stayed the entire night, but I hadn't been able to convince Cheryl to put off the show for a day. She'd argued that Scott would still be in the coma for at least another twenty-four hours and by then, she promised I'd be done with my contract and free to spend all my time with him.

So we left the hospital in the early-morning hours after I'd met the night shift nurse and knew Scott was in good hands. Sergio drove us back to Jaca. Dad was in the backseat with Cheryl and Becca, all of them asleep. I sat in front with Sergio, but neither of us spoke.

Finally, when we arrived at the B&B, everyone piled out of the car. The hotel was dark, and we crept up to our rooms quietly. Becca gave me a reassuring "Don't worry too much, G. Scott's a tough cookie. He's going to pull out of this just fine," before she fell into bed and began to snore.

I was tired but wired.

I studied the paint job on the ceiling and thought about Cooper. Could he have given his pain meds to Miguel to get him to overdose? If so, why?

There was a piece of the puzzle missing and I'd meant to stay up and figure it out, but then suddenly the sun was up and I realized it was time to report to the final competition.

Twenty-three

....

My mouth watered at the smell of freshly baked madeleines and café con leche. When I entered the dining hall I found it empty except for the senora. She welcomed me with a huge smile. "Ah, Georgia, how is your foot?" She pointed to my ankle as she prepared something behind the bar.

"Much better. Thank you."

"I heard they found your *amor*. He's in Huesca, no? At the hospital."

I nodded.

She gave me a "be brave" smile and said, "He will be fine."

"I hope so."

"Poor Sergio. He was falling in love with you."

I waved a hand, dismissing the thought. "No."

"*Sí*," she insisted. "And, I know, one more day and you

would have been in love with him, too." Before I could respond she handed me a basket. "Some madeleines and fresh fruit for you. The others are waiting outside on the bus. They wanted to wake you, but I say, 'No!'"

"Thank you," I said, rushing out.

"*De nada,*" she said.

I ran outside. The SEAT was gone, but the bus was idling on the curb. I climbed inside and the doors closed behind me with a soft hiss.

The crew was in the back of the bus chatting among themselves, and Cooper and Todd were in the front whooping it up with Dad, who in truth looked like he'd rather have slept in as well.

"Sorry I'm late," I said, sliding into the seat next to Dad's.

"Ain't no big, dollface," Cooper said.

"It's totally understandable," Todd said. "I'm glad they found your boyfriend. I hope he's all right."

"Thank you," I said, hiding my shock. That was the first time I'd heard Todd say anything nice.

The bus rolled along the city streets of Jaca, until we ended up on the outskirts in front of the citadel.

"Cool!" Todd said.

In front of us was a fortress that had been built in the Middle Ages. It had a huge rock wall that ran the length of at least five city blocks.

We got off the bus and walked into the citadel. Inside,

we had to cross a moat to get over to where we saw the blue tarp in front of a Baroque-style military chapel.

Cooper clapped his hands together. "Oh, yeah. The fun is about to start!"

Cheryl and Becca were standing around with Harris and they snapped to attention when they saw us approach. After the cameras set up, Harris launched into his welcome speech.

"Cooper, Todd, Georgia, Gordon. Congratulations on making it to the final round of *Expedition Improbable*! Where nothing can stop you but yourself!" He gave the customary recap of yesterday's events, then said, "Cooper and Todd, you managed to finish in first place on the first two competitions, but yesterday, you were edged out by Georgia and Gordon. Are you nervous?"

Cooper chuckled. "My momma taught me only fools don't get nervous."

"Smart woman," Harris said. "Now, remember. Even though this is the last competition, there's still plenty of time for anything to happen. Today we're at the world famous Citadel of Jaca. As you may have noticed, the buildings are guarded by walls of cypresses and a moat." He moved his hands in a dramatic gesture toward the military chapel that we stood in front of, and I knew that in the final show, Cheryl and Becca would have the team splice in images of everything Harris had just mentioned.

"In today's challenge," Harris continued, "you will have to find your way around this pentagonal maze to a hidden clue. The clue will lead to you another destination, where you'll retrieve an item that, when brought to the medieval Bridge of San Miguel, will unleash the fireworks celebration. The team to do this will win our generous cash prize of a quarter of a million dollars!"

Cooper and Todd high-fived each other.

I turned to Dad, and caught him stifling a yawn.

Poor man! I'd kept him up until the late hours of the night and now as his reward for sticking with me, he got to walk around lost in a maze.

Harris said, "Georgia, Gordon, because you came in first place yesterday, you may now begin the challenge."

Dad and I rushed out toward the moat, with Kyle filming us. "What are we looking for?" I asked.

"A clue," Dad said.

"I've been looking for a clue my whole life."

Dad laughed.

We reached the moat and looked out at the water. "No seriously. I mean, how are we supposed to find the clue?"

He shrugged.

"Were you listening?" I asked.

Dad looked guilty. "Uh. Yeah."

"Right. Me, too. But I don't think he gave us any direction, just sort of said we had to find the clue to get the next clue."

We crossed the small trestle bridge over the moat and then glanced back at the bastion where there was a cannon at each corner.

Staring at the cannon, Dad said, "Maybe if we don't find the clue in time, Cheryl will have us shot."

We ducked under a covered walkway that led to the parade ground. "Maybe the clue is around there," I said and motioned toward the parade ground. It was an open space.

"Nah, too easy," Dad said. "I'm sure we have to make a few more twists and turns before we'll find anything."

Cooper and Todd suddenly came into view, obviously following our lead.

"They think this is the right direction," I said.

Dad stopped in his tracks and watched them. "Whatever they do, let's do the opposite."

"Why?"

"I think this place is too big for us to wander around all day. If they find the clue first, we'll know because likely we'll see them leave. But if we find the clue first, then we found the clue first."

I shrugged. "Sure. That almost makes sense and I'm too tired to argue."

Dad put his arm around me as we stared off toward Cooper and Todd. They stood at a distance, probably going over much of the same logic Dad and I had just run through. Finally they broke left, so Dad and I went right.

We jogged around the external perimeter looking for anything resembling a clue. The day was starting to heat up and I'd already broken a sweat. Kyle began to complain about the distance we were hiking along with the weight of the camera. At one point, we stopped and sat on the grass to take a breather, but after a few minutes Dad hiked up to one of the stone walls and scaled it.

"Hey, I got a view from here," he said.

"Yeah, see anything interesting?" I asked.

"I think I see the barracks and maybe a storage office. Lots of old munitions stacked about, too."

I motioned for him to come down.

He ignored me, shading his eyes with one hand as he squinted. "Wait! I see something. Next to the munitions. A flag!" He scuttled off the wall and raced down the hill. We had to get around the moat again to close in on the barracks.

I sprinted after him, my ankle protesting the faster pace. I slowed a bit and heard Kyle mutter, "Thank God!"

We rounded the nearest wall of cypresses and raced toward the little bridge that crossed the moat. Every so often, when the breeze blew, we could just make out the tip of the bull's-eye flag that peeked over the crest of a grassy mound.

When we reached the top of the hill, we found the now familiar makeshift pole with the clear plastic box mounted to it. Dad ripped the note out of the box.

It read: *At the bodega find your bullring and enjoy a* calimocho *with Carmen.*

"What?" asked Dad, as he reread the note. "What's a *calimocho*?"

"You've had *calimocho*s before, you just don't remember. Bullring!" I shouted. "We have to go to the Plaza de Toros!"

Dad nodded. "Uh . . . okay. Who's Carmen?"

"They probably hired someone to give us the next clue," I said.

Kyle began to giggle and we stared at him, but he collected himself and stopped laughing.

Dad and I barreled down the hill, with Kyle in hot

pursuit. As we exited the citadel, Todd and Cooper spotted us and began to frantically run in the direction we'd come from, figuring we'd located the clue.

On the street, we ran to the nearest corner and looked for a cab.

"At least we won't get run off the road this time," Dad said.

Soon enough a cab pulled into view and we waved it down. We didn't have the luxury of Miguel along this time to translate, so I had to mutter, "Plaza de Toros," on my own, only to have the driver correct my pronunciation.

Kyle began to giggle again, but I ignored him.

On the interchange, I saw the sign with the red cross on it and the little bed, the Spanish symbol for hospital. My heart felt heavy as I thought about Scott. *Had he woken up yet?*

EXT. CITADEL DAY

Todd is standing in front of an eight-foot wall of cypress. He chews on his lip as he looks away. He is dressed in a green jersey that does little for his coloring. In fact, he looks nauseous.

TODD
(*Licks his lips*) I'm Todd Nelson. One of the contestants on *Expedition Improbable*. I'm competing with my buddy, Cooper Bowman. Big NFL guy. (*He waves his hand around as*

if dismissing Cooper.) Everybody knows
Coop. Everybody loves Coop.
Anyway, I figured we were probably a shoe-in
from the start. Cooper's just so competitive.
Man, he's not going to let anyone get
between us and the prize money. But, hey,
I'll say this. That little girl, Georgia, and
her dad. They are tough competition. They
are in it to win it. But so are we.

CAMERAMAN (O.S.)
Are you enjoying yourself?

TODD
Oh, heck yeah. *(waves his hands around)*
This is some beautiful country, lots of
partying, too. But maybe it got a little
too wild the other night. Well, shoot, who
am I kidding? The partying has been out of
control since we got here. Ever since the
first night when Cooper hooked up with that
Spanish woman in the mountains. *(He pulls
on his ear.)* Well, I probably shouldn't talk
about that on camera. Coop's done a pretty
good job keeping it under wraps. I don't
think anyone knew except for me and
Victoria. And he kept her quiet by keeping
her happy. And he can keep me quiet by
doing his all to win this prize money. *(His
face flushes and he turns red with anger.)*

Because I'll tell you, I'm tired of keeping
secrets and getting no thank-you in return.
*(He looks off in the distance, chewing on
the inside of his mouth.)*
But anyway, I know he feels bad about
hooking up with the woman. Well, not
exactly bad about hooking up with her, but
bad about what happened to her later and
he wonders if it's his fault. *(He sighs.)* I
suppose there's things we all regret.
Things we wonder if we caused . . . *(He
pauses and buries his face in his hands.
After a moment, he suddenly jolts upright.)*
Can you guys edit this last section out?
I'm exhausted and just talking nonsense.
Ignore me.

Twenty-four

······································

The Plaza de Toros was at the end of a long street lined with pubs and restaurants. The cab dropped us off in front, but the aroma of calamari and potatoes frying that came from a nearby bodega nearly detoured Dad.

I pulled on his shirtsleeve and directed him toward the main door of the plaza. The entrance was large enough for horses and carriages to enter and above the door was a central balcony decorated with wrought-iron metalwork. On either side of the balcony were two tall Tuscan columns with the royal shield of Spain in the center, bordered by Baroque edging that depicted images of bullfights.

"Wow," Dad said as we entered the ring. "This is amazing!"

There was a matador in the center of the ring, dressed in a white shirt, gold close-fitting tights, and a short red jacket that had rich embroidery and sequins. The matador waved a red cape, and Dad looked around nervously.

"Are we sure a bull's not going to pop out of nowhere and charge at us?" he asked.

As we rushed toward the matador, Kyle snickered. He ran ahead of us and positioned himself for the next shot.

When we approached the matador, I realized it was a woman. She must be Carmen, but she had a rather surprised expression on her face.

"Hello! We're here for the clue!" I said.

Her expression turned from surprised to confused. "Clue?" she asked, with a heavy Spanish accent. "I'm sorry?"

"The clue," Dad said.

She blinked thick black eyelashes at us. She was breathtakingly beautiful and I knew instantly why Cheryl had hired her. "Are you Carmen?" I asked.

"Carmen? No. I am Monica."

Dad frowned. "We're looking for a clue. We're on the show *Expedition Improbable*."

A moment of recognition crossed her face as she looked from Dad and me over to the camera Kyle had fixed on her. "The show? The American show that everyone in Jaca is talking about?"

Out of the corner of my eye, I saw Kyle smirking and I knew something was wrong.

"Have you come to film me?" Monica asked. She raised a coquettish shoulder at the camera. "Because I am a woman matador. There are few of us. Will you put me on American TV?"

"No, no, no." I turned to Dad.

"Is it because we are reopening the ring for the first time this summer after the ETA attack? Have you come to do a story on that?"

"This is a mistake," I said. "We made a mistake. Let me see the clue again."

At this, Kyle laughed outright.

I glared at him. "Shut up! If you're not going to help you can just—"

"Georgia!" Dad admonished me. "It's not his fault. Let's just take a look." He dug around his pocket for the clue.

"Maybe I can help," Monica said. "What are you looking for?"

Dad pulled the clue of his pocket. "At the bodega find your bullring and enjoy a *calimocho* with Carmen," Dad read.

Monica laughed. "Ah! It's like a scavenger hunt, no? I know because my cousin's, cousin's, second cousin's, brother-in-law is working on the show."

"What?" Dad asked.

Monica smiled. "My cousin Maria Fernada's cousin, Maria Juliana, has a second cousin, Juan Gabriel, who is married to Harrieta—"

"You had to ask," I said to Dad.

"And Harrieta is Juan Jose's sister. Juan Jose works on your show, no?"

Dad looked at me, confused. "I didn't hear a Carmen in there, did you?"

Monica laughed. "Carmen owns the bodega across the street. Come, I will show you."

Dad and I nearly flew out of the bullring, although we were slowed down because of my ankle. As we crossed through the main gate, Monica pointed to one of the Tuscan columns. She indicated new plaster at the base. "This is what we had to reconstruct last year after the bomb."

We exited the plaza and in front of us was the bodega with the aromatic frying foods. Dad smiled, despite himself. "My nose knows!" he said, happily.

Monica ignored him and continued. "It's terrible what ETA does. I told Juan Jose not to get involved with that woman Annabelle . . . or AnnaLuisa? Anna, whatever, it doesn't matter now."

I froze.

Annalise?

Suddenly we saw Cooper and Todd dart out of the bodega. They were startled to see us and Cooper waved madly, a large gold bull ring in his hand.

"See ya later, suckers!" Todd yelled, as they dashed to the corner to hail a cab.

Dad grabbed my arm, but I shook him off. "Wait, wait. What did you just say?" I asked Monica.

She frowned. "About what?"

"Juan Jose and Annalise? Was it a woman named Annalise?"

"*¡Sí!* He was in love with that woman from ETA. Somebody killed her and I can't say that I'm sorry."

Dad wanted to rush into the bodega, have a *calimocho* with Carmen, and get the bullring, but I remained frozen in place.

Juan Jose?

Could it be that he'd killed Annalise?

If he had been in love with her, it didn't seem likely, but what did he know that he hadn't told us?

"Come on," Dad said, pulling me forward.

"I need to talk to Juan Jose," I said.

"Later!" Dad insisted. "Come on, Cooper and Todd aren't that far ahead of us, we can still win this thing."

Inside the bodega, there was a transgenerational mix of an old crowd playing cards along with young families eating tapas. The bar was so dark in contrast to the bright daylight that Kyle had to boost the light on his camera. The light didn't seem to bother the people at the bar much, as Cooper and Todd's cameraman had probably done the same.

There was a musky smell in the bar that made me want to root myself to a bar stool and hibernate.

The woman behind the counter smiled expectantly and quirked a finely shaped eyebrow at us. "*¿Calimocho?*"

"Carmen?" Dad asked.

"*Sí*," she said, filling two glasses with ice and mixed red wine and cola together.

"Do you have a bull ring for us?" I asked.

"*Sí,*" she said, "but first enjoy!" She pushed the *cali-mochos* in front of us and suddenly someone with a guitar began to strum and sing a folk song.

Dad downed his drink. "That hit the spot! Do we have to stay for the show in order to get the ring?"

"I think so. It must be someone's cousin's, cousin's, somebody that cut a deal with Cheryl when she was out drinking yesterday with Becca, Kyle, and Harris."

Dad laughed. "Well, do you think I can at least have some fried potatoes?"

"Don't order food. I'll kill you if we lose the competition because you were sitting here stuffing your face instead of having your head in the game."

Dad looked longingly at the card game going on near us and eyed their plate of *jamón serrano*. "Drink your *cali*-whatever. It's not bad," he said.

I pushed it toward him. "You can have it. Let's wrap this up, I want to find Juan Jose and talk to him."

Dad polished off my *calimocho*, just as the singer finished his solo.

We applauded, then looked at Carmen. She smiled and handed us the gold ring.

INT. BODEGA DAY

Cooper is smiling good-naturedly at the camera. He is dressed in a white shirt and chinos. He sits in the chair with his back to the wood paneled wall.

He is holding a tall tumbler filled with dark liquid. In the background faint Spanish guitar music plays.

COOPER
(*Sips the drink*) I'm Cooper Bowman.
One of the contestants on *Expedition
Improbable*. I'm competing with my
buddy Todd Nelson. He's a strange cat,
I know, but I put up with him and he
puts up with me. Not that he hasn't
pissed me off this trip, but . . .
(*shrugs*) Winning this game is important
for me. I have some bills . . . well,
the wife and I . . . ex-wife? (*shrugs
again in a repeated fashion*) I don't
know what to call her anymore. Expect
that it's over and she's taken
everything! Not that she doesn't
deserve it, cuz she does, but
then . . . (*He sips his drink.*) I gotta
earn some money for me. That's all. And
I can do it. This here race is going to
put us over the top.
(*He switches positions in the chair and
grimaces.*)

CAMERAMAN (O.S.)
You okay, Cooper?

COOPER
Oh, yeah, yeah. It's only the old football
injury; sometimes it rears its ugly head. I
just wish I had my pain med . . . *(He
stops suddenly as if he recalled something
disturbing.)* Uh, never mind. I'm fine.

Twenty-five

....

After we left the bodega, the bright daylight stung my eyes. We said our good-byes and caught a cab on the corner. We asked him to speed toward the Bridge of San Miguel.

Kyle arranged himself in the front of the cab, switched off the camera and then swiveled around to face us.

"Boy, I thought you guys were really going to lose the contest when you went to the Plaza de Toros instead of the bodega, but I got some fantastic shots of that lady matador. Cheryl's really going to be pleased."

"I knew something was up when you kept laughing like a hyena," Dad said.

Kyle took offense to the hyena comment and flipped back around to feign interest in the road.

"What about Juan Jose?" I asked Dad. "The matador lady said he was in love with Annalise."

Dad shrugged. "Yeah, so?"

"I have a really bad feeling. Sergio told me Annalise had been with a man the night she was killed. He said that Montserrat thought I might have come upon Scott and Annalise together. And Scott killed her."

"That's ridiculous!" Dad said.

"I know, but the theory works the other way around, too, right? What if Juan Jose was in love with the girl and he found she'd just been with someone else?"

"Like who?"

The cab driver exited the interchange, leaving the town behind. We were once again headed into a more rural area of northern Spain. Ahead of us another cab lumbered in the same direction we were heading, toward the medieval bridge.

"As much as I hate to say it, Cooper. He'd been skulking around camp that night . . . Actually, come to think of it, what about his leg injury? He takes meds for the pain sometimes. Miguel died of an overdose . . . What if he figured out that Cooper was with Annalise that night?"

"You think Cooper killed Annalise and Miguel?"

"Cooper's not a killer!" Kyle piped up from the front seat.

We were now directly behind the other cab. Both Cooper and Todd turned in the backseat to look at us. Cooper was all smiles and waving, while Todd had a mean look on his face. There was no oncoming traffic, except the little yellow SEAT, which crossed our path like a shot. I wondered where Cheryl might be running off to. Had she forgotten something for the finale?

Ahead the Bridge of San Miguel came into view. It was long with an asymmetrical profile. One side rested directly on the right hand bank of the *Río Aragón*, which was higher, while on the left-hand bank, the bridge rose above from the river's floodplain.

The bridge had a central arch and a double-sloped profile. On our side of the road, the bridge was barricaded. There was a temporary rock-climbing wall affixed to the south side entrance. On the other side of the bridge, I could see Cheryl and Becca standing off to the side chatting with Harris. Our blue tarp was visible and some crew members were huddled near it. Presumably, we were meant to scale the rock wall in order to reach the finish line.

The cabbie pulled to the side of the road. "I cannot go any further," he said.

We piled out of the cab, just as Cooper and Todd tumbled out of the cab ahead of us.

I darted toward Cooper. "I have to talk to you!"

He grinned widely. "Sure darling, in a minute. I'm kinda busy winning right now."

Todd rushed the wall, scaling the bottom piece in no time. Below, the Rio Aragon raged by and for a moment I feared he'd fall off the makeshift rock wall and into the river.

Dad sprinted to the wall, yelling over his shoulder. "Come on, Georgia! You can talk to him later."

I grabbed Cooper's arm. "It's important! That night at camp—"

"You can't talk about that on film!" Kyle shouted,

suddenly angling the camera away from us toward the river. "Cheryl will kill us."

"I don't care what Cheryl thinks," I screamed. "That night at camp. The girl, Cooper, did you hook up with her? What happened? Tell me!"

Todd turned back, looking down at us from the wall. "Cooper! Come on! We need the cash, buddy. Let's go."

Todd and Cooper's cameraman had already found an alternate route to the other side of the rock wall and was capturing us from a different angle.

Cooper chuckled. "Don't worry now, darling. I didn't hurt that pretty lady. Everything I ever do is consensual. You hear what I'm saying?" He jogged over to the rock wall. I noticed he limped as he ran.

"What's up with your leg? Why are you limping?" I chased after him. "Where's your medicine?"

"Shut up!" Todd screamed at me from the wall. "Leave him alone!"

Dad was already at the top of the wall, just beginning his descent. "Georgia! Come on!"

"Did you kill her, Cooper? What about Miguel? Was he asking questions? He figured you out and you overdosed him with your meds, right?"

"No!" Cooper said. "You got it all wrong. I never hurt no one!"

"Get away from her! Cooper," Todd yelled. "Leave her! We can win this thing."

Cooper scrambled up the wall, it seemed a ridiculously easy effort for him. Dad jumped off on the other side and sprinted toward the finish line. Todd scaled down the wall in hot pursuit after Dad. The one cameraman jogged after them.

I climbed the wall, while Kyle found his way around it in order to keep filming. Cooper got to the top and stayed in place, one leg dangling on each side of the wall.

He reached out and helped me to the top. "Georgia, you have to believe me. I didn't hurt that woman. I would never kill anyone."

We sat on top of the wall, looking down at that mighty river as it rushed past us.

"Someone did, Cooper. Do you have your pain meds?"

He closed his eyes and sighed. "They're gone." When he opened his eyes, he looked in Todd's direction with a sad expression on his face.

I recalled their argument in the halls of the B&B that morning I'd found Miguel.

"Todd?" I asked. "Did he kill Miguel in order to protect you?"

"Hell no! Girl, are you kidding me? Todd ain't no killer! Just a little bit of an addict, you know?"

We looked at the finish line, both Todd and Dad had made it to the blue tarp and each one was watching us expectantly.

I hitched my legs over the wall and started the descent. "I guess we need to finish this thing, so I can talk to Todd."

Cooper stayed in place on top of the wall. "Go on ahead."

"What? No, come on, Cooper."

"My leg hurts, you go on."

"No! You've got to run, fair and square. Suck it up. Walk it off, or whatever else they tell you in the NFL."

He chuckled. "I wouldn't be here if it weren't for you, girl. You gave me that chalice and got us a two-hour advantage."

"Well, if you look at it that way, Cooper, I wouldn't be here if it weren't for you, either. I'd be dead." I turned to run the length of the bridge and shouted over my shoulder. "Now, come on down off that wall and beat me to the finish if you can!"

He perked up and slide down the wall in no time. I ran as fast as I could, ignoring the pain that shot through my ankle with each step. Cooper must have been in similar pain, because he yelled out with each stride.

I heard him, right behind me and willed my legs to churn faster.

"Georgia, run!" Dad yelled.

"Cooper, get the lead out!" Todd screamed.

The tarp was in sight, directly ahead of me. Perhaps ten more strides and I was there! Cooper was upon me, the bullring in his hand. He laughed that locomotive laugh, making me chant in my head: *I think I can, I think I can, I think I can.*

Five strides left. I stretched my legs to the limit, my hamstrings burning.

I know I can, I know I can, I know I can.

Two strides left!

Suddenly Cooper overtook me and flew into the blue tarp, leaping through the air as if he were tackling a Super Bowl opponent in the final play of the game.

Everyone let out a roar, even Harris in an uncharacteristic moment of emotion screamed, "And the winners are Cooper and Todd!" Fireworks erupted from a metal canister near the tarp and Cooper and Todd jumped toward each other, bumping their chests together and dancing in a typical end zone celebration.

Harris arranged his expression back into his usually blank Botoxed face and said, "Georgia, Gordon. You found the hidden clue in the citadel, had a drink with the beautiful Carmen at the bodega, and recovered the last item to complete the challenge. But, I'm sorry to say, you were not the first team to arrive and are therefore eliminated."

Dad hugged me.

"I'm sorry, Dad."

"It's not your fault, honey. We were a long shot. I'm so happy I got to be your partner and spend this time with you."

"Cooper, Todd!" Harris said. "Congratulations." He extended his hand to receive the bullring from Cooper and held it up ceremoniously. "You are the official winners of *Expedition Improbable* and I'm happy to award you with the generous cash price of a quarter of a million dollars!"

Cooper and Todd began to dance around again, and it took all my effort not to pull them apart and demand answers from Todd.

While they celebrated, I took Becca aside and recounted quickly what I'd found out about Todd and Cooper.

She frowned. "We better call Sergio, don't you think?"

Around us the crew began to pack up the tarp and load up the cameras.

"Yes, he'll want to talk to Todd, I'm sure." Todd and Cooper grew silent as if they realized we were discussing them.

Todd approached me. "Cooper said you wanted to talk to me?"

"I know you gave the meds to Miguel, I just want to know why—"

"I didn't give the meds to Miguel!" he said.

"Look, you can tell it to the police—"

"I will! I didn't give anything to Miguel! It's not my fault. I know it was a bad decision to steal the bottle from Cooper, but I didn't know if we'd win the contest and I needed the money. Juan Jose told me he really needed them and—"

"What? Juan Jose?" I looked around for him.

"Yeah," Todd said. "I sold the bottle to Juan Jose. I'm sure he and Miguel were partying late and overdid it. It's not pleasant, and I'm really sorry about it, but it was an accidental overdose."

I looked around the set. "Where is Juan Jose?" I asked Becca.

"Oh, he went to Huesca," Becca said.

I froze. "What? Huesca for what?"

Becca shrugged. "I don't know. Cheryl and I were talking about Scott and how great it was that Monse found him. And I mentioned that Scott was at the hospital in Huesca, then Juan Jose said that reminded him he had some unfinished business in Huesca. So he asked Cheryl if he could take the afternoon off. She even let him borrow the SEAT. Can you believe it? I wish she'd give me an afternoon off and let me drive the car." She shook her head at the injustice. "Anyway, he left right before you guys got here."

My blood drained to my toes and I felt light-headed. "Oh, my God. He's after Scott! Scott can ID him." I ran toward the crew bus. "I need a driver!" I screamed.

Cheryl, Dad, and the others piled onto the bus, not wanting to be left behind.

"What's going on?" Dad asked.

"We have to get to the Huesca hospital before Juan Jose. He's going to try for a second chance at murder!"

Twenty-six

······························

The driver didn't take kindly to my telling him to crash through the rock wall on the other side of the bridge, but when Cheryl got in his face, he did it without question.

Becca dialed Sergio and Montserrat, explaining the situation and asking them to meet us at the Huesca hospital.

I grabbed the phone from her. "Sergio, can you call the hospital and ask them to place a security guard at Scott's door?"

He was silent a moment.

"Sergio?"

"I can try, Georgia, but it's not likely I'll be able to reach anyone at the hospital, and if I do, they probably won't be able to spare the staff to guard the door."

I groaned.

"I'll do my best," Sergio said.

"Thank you!"

When I hung up Cooper said, "I didn't think it was him."

"What?" I asked.

"All this time. I didn't know it was him. I hooked up with that woman. You were right about that and she told me after that she had a boyfriend. I thought it was Scott. I thought he killed her and took off. That's why I didn't tell you anything. I figured soon enough you'd figure out that the guy had been two-timing you, but I didn't want to be the one to break your heart."

Becca's mobile phone rang and she passed it to me. "Looks like it's Sergio."

I picked up and Sergio's voice filled the line. "Georgia! I finally got through to the hospital. They agreed. They won't allow visitors. They're waiting for me, okay? I'm ten minutes away."

We hung up just as Cheryl screamed at the driver, "Get that pedal to the metal!"

After a few more minutes of speeding down the interchange a yellow car came into view.

"That's him!" Dad shouted.

"Run him off the road!" Cheryl said.

The driver gave a terrified, "*¿Que?*" while the crew shouted out their protests.

"Let's not get carried away," Cooper said. "Todd and I got reasons to live now!"

The bus lumbered toward the yellow car. My heart raced as we all scrambled to the right side of bus to get a better view of the car. Cooper yanked down a window and began shouting inaudible jeers at the vehicle.

The car had the top up and a huge scratch on the side and it somehow looked different.

"*No es, no es,*" the driver said.

"It's not him!" Becca screamed.

The yellow car was an older version of the flashy convertible SEAT Cheryl had rented. Behind the wheel of the little yellow car was an older woman. Suddenly, the air came out of us, as we collapsed back into our seats dejected.

The hospital was still a few kilometers down the road and I took solace in the fact that Sergio had gotten through to them and they had promised no visitors.

As soon as we pulled into the main parking lot, I sprinted off the bus while it circled looking for parking. Dad and Becca were right behind me, but my legs had new energy and I was unstoppable.

I heard Dad joke to Becca, "Man, if only she could have run like that an hour ago, I'd be a quarter of a millions dollars richer."

I barreled through the front doors of the hospital, smashing directly into an orderly. He grabbed me and said, "*¡Tranquila!*" followed by a rush of Spanish I didn't understand.

I shook my head, indicating I didn't speak Spanish. "It's an emergency," I said. "I have to see Scott Tailor."

The orderly looked alarmed and held his arms out blocking further entry into the hospital. "*No, no, no! No se permiten visitantes.*"

267

I didn't have to speak Spanish to know he'd just put the kibosh on my visiting Scott. "No! That's not meant for me! I'm okay! It's—"

Dad and Becca trailed me into the hospital shouting, "The SEAT's here! Parked in the lot. He's here."

I pushed past the orderly and sprinted down the hall to Scott's room. The orderly dove for me, tackling me and knocking the wind out of me. I fell forward, breaking my fall with my hands but twisting my bad ankle awkwardly.

Dad grabbed the orderly, and suddenly a rush of staff was in the hall, everyone screaming and shouting at each other. Cooper and Todd joined us in the crowded hallway and I scrambled to my feet.

Cooper caught up with me. "What room's he in?"

"This way!" I said, darting past the nurses' station where Sergio had asked about Scott the night before. Thankfully, it was now abandoned with the commotion we'd just caused down the hallway. Cooper and I ducked down a narrow passageway, both of us limping and in pain, hobbling as fast as our battered bodies would allow.

Down the hallway, I could see someone in scrubs leaving Scott's room. "That's him!" I yelled.

Juan Jose turned to see us, his eyes wide. He jolted as if electrocuted and rushed away from us. Cooper and I shuffled after him.

A voice from behind us called out, echoing off the walls. "Hey, hey! Stop!" It was another hospital staff member, he looked imposing and ready to stop us at all costs.

"I have to get to Scott," I said to Cooper.

Cooper, now trotting awkwardly, said, "You go. I got Juan Jose. He ain't getting away from me!"

I reached Scott's door just as the staffer grabbed me.

Another pair turned down the corridor, screaming in rapid Spanish. Montserrat and Sergio.

"Juan Jose went that way," I said to Sergio. He nodded and took off after Cooper and Juan Jose. "Let me go!" I said to the staffer.

Montserrat showed her badge to the man and while she explained something in Spanish to him, he released me.

I pushed open the door to Scott's room. It was dark and deathly silent.

"Scott!" I yelled out.

He lay stiff and unmoving under the stark hospital sheet. Tears sprang to my eyes.

"Scott!" I repeated.

All the tubes that been in place the night before were still in place. The IV, the respirator, the catheter, but something was wrong. The room was too quiet and dark.

I realized with a jolt a box was at the foot of the bed. The backup battery to the respirator had been removed and discarded, the respirator unplugged from the wall.

I screamed and rushed to plug the machine back into the wall. It let out an angry beep and a flash of red lights, but nothing else happened. I scrambled to the door, opened it and shouted for help. Dad and Becca were already making their way down the long corridor. "Get a doctor! Stat!" I yelled.

Becca heard me first and turned and ran back away

from me. Dad ran toward me. "What's happened? What is it?"

Dad joined me in the room, where I was huddled over Scott, feeling helpless. The same doctor from the night before rushed into room, instructing us to stand back.

I wept into Dad's shoulder. More staff crowded the room, and Dad pulled me out into the hallway. Becca and Cheryl joined us.

"Sergio and Cooper got him," Cheryl said.

It was little consolation to me now. I only wanted Scott to breathe. Dad explained to them what had happened, while I paced the hallway. After a moment, a staffer emerged from Scott's room and ushered us toward the waiting room.

I collapsed into the hard plastic chair and prayed.

Becca eyed the vending machine nearby and squeaked out, "Anyone want a Coke?"

I ignored her, but she squeezed my hand. "You probably haven't eaten anything all day."

"I'm not hungry."

Dad stood and bought us all Cokes.

The doctor appeared in the waiting room. I stood and walked to him, but he glanced around nervously.

My stomach dropped.

"*¿Dónde está la policía?*" the doctor asked.

I realized he needed someone to translate. "Get Sergio or Monse," I said to Becca.

She sprang to her feet and left the room.

The doctor held my hand, smiling and patting it reassuringly. "*Está vivo.*"

I knew enough Spanish to understand what the doctor had said.

Scott was alive!

Thank God, he was alive!

Becca returned with Sergio in tow. He had a long conversation with the doctor and finally turned to us. "Scott seems to be recovering nicely. Luckily, the coma-inducing medication had already been reduced. And while he's not completely breathing on his own, when Juan Jose disconnected the respirator, Scott still had enough lung capacity to take some shallow breaths. It was lucky Georgia got here in time. Anymore of a delay and we would have been too late."

My knees felt weak and I leaned into Dad for support.

"It's okay, honey. It's okay," Dad said, rubbing my back.

"Is he going to be all right?" I asked.

"The doctor said it's still too early to tell, but all the signs look really good," Sergio said. "He'd like to keep the respirator on overnight as the medication is still in his system. In the morning, Scott will be more awake and he'll be able to answer some questions."

"Can I see him?" I asked.

Sergio turned to the doctor and translated my question, but he shook his head saying, *"Mañana."*

Sergio had to leave us to help Montserrat with Juan Jose. He squeezed my hand and leaned in close to me. "I will come later to the B&B."

"What about my car?" Cheryl called after him.

He turned on a heel and smiled at her. "I'm sorry, you will have to go back on the bus. The police are confiscating the SEAT."

"What?"

Sergio winked. "There could be evidence in there. I have to test it on the interchange and see what flies out!"

Cheryl snarled at him, but he only chuckled as he left the waiting room.

Dad, Cheryl, Becca, and I piled into the bus. Cooper was entertaining the crew with his version of Juan Jose's capture. He acted out an overly dramatic slow-motion rendition of his dive to stop the killer in his tracks. The crew was riveted. Especially Kyle, who screamed out with laughter at everything Cooper said and like a small child kept saying, "Again! Tell the story again."

Harris was silently sulking at not being the center of attention and taking great interest in the state of his cuticles.

Dad and Cheryl sat together and I took the seat behind them. Becca was ready to slide in next to me, when Cooper reached out with one of his big frying pan hands and blocked her.

"Are you trying to steal my best friend?" Becca asked.

"Nah, sweetness," Cooper said. "Georgia has room in her heart for all of us."

He scrunched in next to me, leaving Becca to sit with Todd.

"It didn't really happen like I said," Cooper admitted.

"Your cop friend tackled him. But I got a reputation to uphold."

I laughed. "It's okay, Coop. They got him, that's the important thing. And you're still my MVP, no matter what."

He shrugged. "I feel bad I didn't let you win. I was thinking after this show airs, with that bit at the monastery, I think I can land an insurance sponsor. You know? You're in good hands with Cooper, or something like that."

I chuckled. "I'm sure that will happen anyway. I mean if Cheryl doesn't leave that bit on the cutting room floor."

Cheryl's head flung around so fast, I thought we'd have to go back into the hospital for whiplash. "Leave that bit on the cutting room floor! Are you kidding me? Boy, we are going to top the charts!"

"Where's our bus driver?" Becca asked.

"I think he went to play cards over there," Kyle said, pointing to a small cantina across the street.

"Oh, for goodness sake!" Cheryl said. "Can't these Spaniards go a few hours without tapas?"

"I want to live here," Dad said wistfully.

A white van with a gray satellite dish on top and the Aragón Televisión logo emblazoned on the side of it pulled up next to our bus. From the passenger side, a dark-haired woman with a microphone in her hand rushed out.

"Oh! It's the press!" Cheryl said, jumping to her feet. "Give me a moment. We're not only going to the top the charts. We're going to be an international sensation!"

After a moment, our driver left the cantina; the remnants of a chorizo sandwich still in his hand. He boarded the bus, popping the rest of the sandwich in his mouth, and then patted his ample belly with his free hand and gave us a happy smile.

Cheryl followed him onto the bus after chatting with the reporter. The bus started up and we tore off in the direction of the B&B.

Twenty-seven

....

Once at the B&B, I phoned Scott's mother, Bernice, and filled her in on the latest developments. She was overjoyed that we'd found Scott, but understandably concerned about his head injury. I reassured her that I'd phone her back after I visited with him in the morning.

Downstairs in the bar area, the remaining cast and crew were all gathered around, dressed in white clothes and already enjoying pitchers of *sangría*.

Cooper had his leg elevated and I limped over to join him.

The senora appeared with a bag of ice for each of us and the same ointment from the other night.

"This stuff is magic," I said to Cooper slathering it on my ankle.

Cooper was happy to apply some on his knee, but said he thought whiskey would help more.

At that point the door to the bar swung open and Sergio stepped in. Cooper excused himself and Sergio sat next to me.

"We got a confession from him," Sergio said. "It was as you thought. Juan Jose was in love with Annalise. She had snuck out to camp to visit him, but was more charmed by Cooper than Juan Jose."

He swiveled in his chair to look at Cooper, who was downing a whiskey and singing off-key with Dad.

"It's easy to see why, isn't it?" I joked.

Sergio laughed. "Well, Juan Jose figured it out, had a fight with Annalise, then Scott came upon them. He tried to stop Juan Jose, but it didn't work out. Juan Jose stole his phone and passport. Thought he left them both for dead. He was surprised in the morning to realize that Scott wasn't dead alongside Annalise. He figured the only way to get us to stop searching for him was to send you a message pretending he was Scott and telling you it was over."

"It might have worked, but he sent the message to my dad," I said.

Sergio shrugged. "He didn't know that. He actually blamed me. Said if I was a better Casanova I could have distracted you from Scott and you would have let go of the investigation."

I laughed. Sergio laughed, too, putting a hand on his heart as if part of him were wounded.

I sipped my *sangría*. "I wouldn't worry about it. I think you're a pretty damn fine Casanova."

He waved a hand around to dismiss the thought, but I persisted. "Monse thinks so, too."

He stood. "*Ay, Monse.* She's real trouble. Not like you."

"Me? What? I'm fake trouble?"

He leaned in close. "No. You are very real. How's your ankle? Better?"

I shrugged. "It's healing, I think."

"It better be, tonight is our last night together and I still need to teach you how to dance the Jota."

"What about Miguel?" I asked.

"He saw a picture of Annalise that Juan Jose had on his phone. He confronted him. It was just a matter of time, so Juan Jose had to get rid of him."

"There something I haven't told you," I said. "Scott's phone was in Miguel's room. I figured it was a setup of some sort so I took it. I'm sorry." Shame burned at my cheeks and I lowered my head.

Sergio sighed. "I'm going to pretend I didn't hear that. Stealing evidence is illegal and I think if I arrest you now your father or his lady friend Cheryl might kill me. He smiled and then ambled up to the bar, between Cheryl and Dad. He requested his own drink. Becca came to sit with me. "Cheryl's going to work on him. Try to soften him up," she said.

"Try to soften who up?" I asked.

"Sergio."

"About what?" I asked.

"About featuring him in a show."

I laughed so hard, I choked. Several people turned to look at me. When they'd turned away, I said, "Come on. He's not going to do a show. He's a cop."

Becca gave me a look. "So were you!"

"It's different. She can't be serious."

"Oh, she's serious all right. And it's too bad you and Gordon didn't win. I know you need the money. Maybe we can come up with an all-star show or something."

"Bite your tongue!" I said.

Just then, Dad, Cheryl, and Sergio joined us at my table. Followed by Cooper, Todd, Kyle, and Harris. The senora began to play some cheerful music on the stereo and then joined us, too.

"We've finally been given clearance to leave Spain," Cheryl said to Becca.

"Not yet," Sergio said, grabbing my hand. "This is *La Jota Aragonesa*. No one can leave Spain, until you all learn it!"

The senora grabbed Dad and the others followed suit, grabbing the closest available partner. Sergio put his arms up and led us in the joyful bouncing dance. And for the first time in what seemed like a long time, I *was* joyful. I knew Scott would be all right and I was filled with appreciation for the new friends I'd made and so very happy to be surrounded by the people I loved.

Read on to see how it all began
in Diana Orgain's first Love or Money Mystery,

A First Date with Death

Available now.

One

· · · · · · · · · · · · · · · ·

The bungee-jumping harness bit into my shoulders and legs as I looked over the railing of the Golden Gate Bridge. To say the water looked frigid was an understatement. The whitecaps of the bay screamed out glacier and hypothermia.

"You're not in position," Cheryl, the producer, yelled.

I felt the camera zoom in on me. They needed an extreme close-up of my every facial expression so they could broadcast my terror to the world. Magnify my embarrassment and mortification.

One of the techs said something to Cheryl and she shouted, "Cut!"

The cameraman lost interest in me.

"Why am I doing this?" I asked Becca, my best friend and the assistant producer on this god-awful reality TV show, *Love or Money.*

"To find your dream man," Becca answered.

"I found him already, remember? Then he left me at the altar."

A makeup artist appeared at my elbow and applied powder to my nose.

"Dream men do not leave their brides at the altar," Becca said. "Clearly, he was not the one."

I studied the woman brushing powder on my face. She had beautiful chocolate-colored skin, a straight nose, and eyes so dark and intense they looked like pools of india ink. She looked familiar, but before I could place her, she turned and walked away.

"I thought you always liked Paul," I said to Becca.

"I did until he left me at the altar," Becca replied.

"He left *me*."

"Me, too. I was standing right next to you in a stupid tulle and taffeta dress. Anyway, enough about your horrible fashion sense—"

I laughed.

"Even if you don't find your dream man here," Becca continued, "focus on the cash prize. You need it."

She was kind enough not to add "since you were fired," but I felt the sting anyway. If anyone had told me, six months before, that I'd be on a reality TV show looking for love and/or money, I'd have called them 5150, a.k.a. clinically insane. But here I was, ex-cop, ex-bride-to-be—with a broken heart and broken career—looking to start over.

Ty, one of my "dates," sauntered over. He was wearing jeans and boots and his trademark cowboy hat. A bungee harness crisscrossed through his legs. Despite the harness, or perhaps because of it, he looked hot. Although I was hard-pressed to think of any outfit that he wouldn't look hot in.

"Are you nervous, Miss Georgia?" he asked.

I found myself absently wondering if he'd wear his hat while bungee jumping.

He reached out tentatively and touched the back of my hand with a single finger. "Miss Georgia?" he repeated.

I suddenly became aware of the camera rolling again and snapped to attention. "Yes. I'm nervous. I thought I'd get to pick the dates, but I didn't. I would have never picked this. Only a lunatic—"

I heard the producer, Cheryl, grumble.

I wasn't supposed to say anything negative about the dates, of course. They were supposed to look authentic, so that the audience wouldn't know that I had absolutely zero control over anything. The crew would have to edit out my last comment.

Ty seemed to notice the same thing because he replied smoothly, "I've always wanted to bungee jump." His lips quirked up in an irresistible manner. "And now we get to do it off this beautiful bridge."

Cheryl, who was standing behind him, smiled. He'd just saved the scene. She liked him.

Well, in those tight jeans and boots, and with the cute southern drawl—who could blame her?

I glanced around at the others. They seemed ready to go and had started heading my way. It was inevitable, once someone started showing interest in me, that the others would follow—like a pack of dogs fighting over a lone piece of meat.

Bungee jumping off the bridge was my first date, and I'd selected five of the ten eligible bachelors—or not so eligible. The gist of the show was for me to pick a guy who was emotionally available for a relationship, someone who was on the show for love.

During casting, each guy had given a heart-to-heart interview with the producer, Cheryl Dennison. They'd confessed whether they were ready to be in a relationship. Five guys were searching for love; five guys weren't. Because I'd worked for SFPD, somehow Hollywood thought I'd be able to figure out everyone's motives.

I had my doubts.

If I picked the right guy, we'd split $250,000. If I picked a guy who was emotionally unavailable he'd walk off with the cash prize on his own and, maybe worse, a piece of my heart.

America would be privy to the interviews. I'm sure those clips would expose me as a fool along the way.

I pictured Cheryl's editing staff. As soon as I said someone was cute or hot or sweet, she'd revel in playing a clip of the heart-to-heart where he told America all the reasons he couldn't fall in love. That kind of thing would be great for ratings.

The guys I'd asked on this date were the ones I suspected might be on the show for the cash. Best to eliminate the fakes ASAP.

I'd selected Ty, the cowboy, because at the first night's

cocktail party I couldn't actually get him to tell me what he did for a living.

Edward, the hot doctor—tall, with dark hair, a great smile, and a wonderful gentleness about him—had to have student loans from med school up the wazoo.

Scott, the brooding writer, wrote horror stories—I'd been meaning to read some to get an idea about him. He was mysterious and supersexy, with a tight body and a bit of a swagger, and he had a shaved head and dark, piercing eyes.

But who made any money as a writer?

Aaron, the investment banker, looked like the boy next door. Clean-cut, respectable, and polite.

I wouldn't typically peg investment bankers as needing money, but something about Aaron was unsettling, as though he had some desperation vibe wafting off him.

And then there was Pietro, the Italian hunk with an accent that drove me wild.

I'd invited him because I had a weakness for accents, and weakness must be sought out and destroyed at any cost.

Everyone was suited up and ready to go. My harness felt so tight I thought I might explode out of it. It was cutting into my shoulders and crotch—certainly not a woman-friendly look. But I didn't complain for fear they would make it too loose and I'd slip out of it at exactly the wrong moment.

Was there no happy medium for me?

The crew was urging us toward the edge of the bridge. We didn't have time to dillydally, as the show had been granted special access for the shoot. Bungee jumping was not ordinarily allowed off the Golden Gate Bridge due to boat traffic, but the producers had been able to close down the shipping lanes for one hour. Everything is for sale in San Francisco.

Car traffic, on the other hand, was still open on the bridge. Everything may be for sale, but even Hollywood has a budget. It was nerve-wracking and noisy to have the cars whizzing by.

"If you're nervous, maybe someone else can go first," Ty offered.

Cheryl said, "Someone needs to go, for God's sake. We need to get the show on the road. Aaron, want to go?"

Aaron looked surprised and Ty seemed relieved.

"Uh, yeah, certainly. Love to," Aaron said, although he looked unsure.

Cheryl turned to me and shouted, "You, get over here and watch him jump. We need the shot."

I don't know what I'd imagined when I thought about possibly finding love on this show, but it certainly hadn't included this six-foot-tall blond woman yelling at me constantly. In fact, she'd never even entered my mind and now she seemed never to leave.

Aaron took his place near the edge of the bridge and I stood next to him. The crew maneuvered around us, although one camera remained trained on my face, my every expression being recorded for posterity.

I hoped I didn't look nauseous. I certainly felt it.

Despite the tech people assuring me it was safe, jumping off the bridge was the last thing I wanted to do.

Down below I could see the Coast Guard boat hovering, one of the conditions the City of San Francisco had put on our use of the bridge.

Cheryl hadn't cared about the condition. In fact, she'd used it in negotiations for the show, requesting two cameramen be allowed to board and film our jumps.

"Are you ready, Aaron?" I asked, remembering to smile for the camera, but fearing it came off more as a grimace.

Aaron returned my smile, only his seemed genuine. "Oh, yeah. I've been jumping before. It's really a hoot. Feels like you're flying." He grabbed my hand and said, "Georgia, will you jump with me?"

Before I could reply, he turned to the tech. "Is her line ready?"

I heard the tech say, "She's—"

The din of traffic seemed to grow, a car honking at precisely that moment.

Then someone touched the small of my back and Cheryl yelled, "Action!"

Aaron let out a war cry and leapt, still squeezing my hand and pulling me forward. Someone pushed sharply on my back. I was off balance, trying to stay on the bridge.

Aaron didn't release me and his momentum propelled me forward. I slipped off the railing, falling with him, our hands finally disentangling.

The wind howled furiously at me. I howled back. My face tight, completely stretched with the force of gravity, my own saliva streaming across my checks as I screamed.

Aaron was screaming, too, only his yells were ones of sheer delight.

His arms were flung out from his sides and he held them horizontally, imitating a plane.

We were soaring through the air like birds—only birds on a sharp descent, toward water that looked like a sheet of solid glass.

Adrenaline surged through my system, everything happening in slow motion: Aaron's expression of pure joy, the sunlight reflecting off the water and blinding me, the sound of the boat nearby.

The Coast Guard.

We were speeding, rushing closer and closer to the water. My breath caught in my throat, gagging me. I fought the impulse to retch.

How close to the water were we supposed to get?

When would the cord tighten?

What had the tech said?

All my mind could process was the water seemingly racing toward me.

And then, suddenly, my cord pulled taut and my descent stopped. I bounced up, the water receding rapidly. The negative g-force playing havoc with my stomach.

Out of nowhere a horrific crashing, splashing, screeching sound pierced my ears.

Water shot upward.

I pressed both hands over my mouth and tried to keep the bloodcurdling scream inside, but failed.

Aaron had hit the water.

His bungee cord finally tightened and snapped to position, but he was already underwater.

I continued flying upward, the distance between Aaron and me an eternity.

It felt as if I would crash right through the bottom of the bridge.

And then my descent began again, water rushing toward me.

Dear God, would I crash into the water, too?

I was paralyzed with fear as the cord tightened and then the water raced away. Then I was falling again, zooming toward the water, now my nemesis beckoning me, luring and tempting me to give up the fight.

The cord tightened one last time and I came to an abrupt stop, suspended above the bay—so close I could feel the salt spray on my skin.

I filled my lungs with air and screamed. I kicked and thrashed about, trying to break the harness that had just saved my life. Aaron was so close to me, I needed to grab him and pull him out of the water. I was vaguely aware of the Coast Guard boat nearby, the sound of the engine revving, the fumes of the diesel gagging me.

I heard the crackle of the Coast Guard's radio and then Cheryl's voice frantically shouting, "Hoist him up! Holy Christ! Hoist him up!"

I raised my head and was surprised to see the Coast Guard boat so close. Without words the entire crew had sprung into action. But one camera was still trained on me. The other camera zoomed in on Aaron.

I felt a jolt and realized I was being raised back toward the bridge.

"No, no, stop! Let me go—I can reach him!" I yelled.

Then the hoist on Aaron's harness began to crank and he was lifted out of the water.

His dripping, lifeless form hung like a rag doll from the bungee.

FROM *USA TODAY* BESTSELLING AUTHOR
DIANA ORGAIN

A First Date with Death

· **A LOVE OR MONEY MYSTERY** ·

Reality TV meets murder in the first in a new mystery
series from the author of the Maternal Instincts Mysteries
and coauthor of *Gilt Trip* from *New York Times* bestselling author Laura Childs's Scrapbooking Mysteries.

*When brokenhearted Georgia Thornton goes looking for
romance on reality TV, she has nothing to lose—apart
from a good man, a cash prize, and maybe her life...*

dianaorgain.com
penguin.com

M1731T0915